MW00465636

ALSO BY LUDMILA ULITSKAYA

*Medea and Her Children*

*The Funeral Party*

# *Sonechka*

# Sonechka

## A NOVELLA AND STORIES

# Ludmila Ulitskaya

*Translated from the Russian by Arch Tait*

Schocken Books New York 2005

Copyright © 2005 by Schocken Books, a division of Random House, Inc.

All rights reserved under International and Pan-American
Copyright Conventions. Published in the United States
by Schocken Books, a division of Random House, Inc.,
New York, and simultaneously in Canada by Random House
of Canada Limited, Toronto. Distributed by Pantheon Books,
a division of Random House, Inc., New York.

Schocken and colophon are registered trademarks of Random House, Inc.

The novella "Sonechka" was originally published in Russian in *Novyi Mir*,
(Na7) Moscow, in 1992. An earlier version of the translation of "Sonechka"
by Arch Tait appeared in *"Sonechka and Other Stories," Glas New Russian Writing*,
no. 17, Moscow, in 1998. All of the remaining stories in this collection
were originally published in Russia as *Pervye i poslednie*, by Izdatel'stvo
"Eksmo," Moscow, in 2002. Copyright © 2002 by L. Ulitskaia.

Library of Congress Cataloging-in-Publication Data
Ulitskaia, Liudmila.
[Short stories. English. Selections]
Sonechka : a novella and stories / Ludmila Ulitskaya ;
translated from the Russian by Arch Tait.
p. cm.
ISBN 0-8052-4195-7
I. Tait, A. L. II. Title.
PG3489.2.L58A28 2005
891.73'5—dc22        2004059154

www.schocken.com

Printed in the United States of America

First Edition

2   4   6   8   9   7   5   3   1

# CONTENTS

# Sonechka

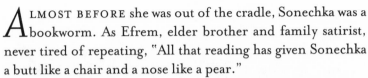

ALMOST BEFORE she was out of the cradle, Sonechka was a
bookworm. As Efrem, elder brother and family satirist,
never tired of repeating, "All that reading has given Sonechka
a butt like a chair and a nose like a pear."

Unfortunately, his formulation was not too far off the
mark. Her nose really was pear-shaped, and lanky broad-
shouldered Sonechka, with her skinny legs and flat unmemo-
rable rear end, had only one indisputable physical asset: large
womanly breasts, which ballooned at an early age but seemed
out of proportion with the rest of her thin body. She slouched
round-shouldered and favored shapeless loose-fitting dresses,
daunted by her uncalled-for endowment in front and dis-
mayed by her flatness behind.

Her concerned and caring elder sister, herself safely married, remarked charitably on her lovely eyes, but they were
run-of-the-mill, rather beady, if anything, and hazelnut
brown. To be sure, she had eyelashes of a rare luxuriance that
sprouted three rows deep and weighed down the puffy edge of
her eyelids, but what was fetching about that? Indeed, they
were a hindrance, since Sonechka was also shortsighted and
obliged to wear spectacles from an early age.

For a full twenty years, from seven until twenty-seven,

Sonechka read almost incessantly. She went off into her books as if going into a trance and came back out only when she reached the last page. She had a rare talent, perhaps even a genius, for reading. Her receptiveness to the printed word was so great that fictional characters seemed no less real than the sentient beings around her, and she found the luminous suffering of Tolstoy's Natasha Rostova at the bedside of the dying Prince Andrey at least as convincing as the grief and torment of her sister, who carelessly lost her four-year-old child. Deep in conversation with the next-door neighbor, she failed to notice when her fat, ungainly, slow-witted daughter fell into the well.

What are we looking at here, total inability to recognize the element of play that is the premise of all art? The mind-boggling naive trust of a child who has failed to grow up? A lack of imagination leading to inability to distinguish between the real and the imaginary? Or was it a surrender to the realm of imagination so complete that everything outside its bounds lacked meaning and substance?

Sonechka's reading mania did not relinquish its hold on her even when she was asleep. She seemed indeed to read her dreams, imagining breathtaking historical romances. She was able to visualize, from the nature of the plot, which font the story must be printed in and had a strange background awareness of paragraphs and punctuation. The sense of spiritual displacement that her obsession produced was if anything more pronounced when she was dreaming, because she then existed as a fully fledged heroine (or hero) walking a tightrope between the will of the author, of which she was fully aware, and her own autonomous urge to movement, deeds, and action.

It was the late 1920s, and Lenin's laissez-faire New Economic Policy was on its last legs. Sonechka's father, the son and heir of a blacksmith in a little Jewish shtetl in Belorussia, was a born engineer with a practical streak. Sensing a threatening change in the political climate, he prudently closed down his clockmaking business and, suppressing an innate aversion for all forms of mass production, signed on at a watch factory, salving his conscience in the evenings by repairing unique mechanisms created by the ingenious hands of predecessors of various races.

Her mother, who until her dying day wore a silly little wig under a clean polka-dot headscarf, illegally stitched away on her Singer sewing machine, making for her neighbors the straightforward cotton frocks that were suited to those strident years of poverty, whose terrors were personified for her solely by the dread figure of the tax inspector.

Sonechka for her part, just about managing to struggle through the official school curriculum, did her utmost every minute of every day to wriggle out of having to live in the shrill pathos of the 1930s and let her soul graze the expanses of the great literature of nineteenth-century Russia, descending into the disconcerting abysses of politically suspect Dostoyevsky and emerging into the shady avenues of Turgenev and the little provincial estates warmed by the generous and socially incorrect love of Leskov, who for some reason was said to be a second-rate writer.

She graduated from a college of librarianship, began working in the store in the basement of an old library, and was one of a fortunate few who left her dusty, muggy cellar at the end of the working day with the gentle ache of a pleasure curtailed, never quite having had her fill of either the succession of catalog cards and off-white reader's request slips that came down to her daily from the reading room above or of the living weightiness of the tomes lowered into her thin arms.

For many years she regarded the act of writing as a religious practice. She assumed St. Gregory Palamas, Pausanias, and Pavlov to be writers of equal merit, since each qualified for a place on the same page of the encyclopedia. With the passing years she learned to distinguish for herself between the great breakers in the vast ocean of books and the minor ripples, and between the ripples and the shoreline scum that almost entirely clogged the ascetic shelves of the contemporary Soviet fiction section.

Having served several years like a devoted nun in the library basement, Sonechka gave in to the urgings of her superior, a reader no less obsessive than herself, and decided to read Russian language and literature at university. She started plowing through the vast ridiculous preliminary syllabus, with all its ideological baggage, and was just ready to sit her entrance exams when everything collapsed. In an instant all was changed with the outbreak of war.

This was possibly the first event in all her young life to jolt her out of the hazy world of incessant reading that she inhabited. Together with her father, who in those years was working as a toolmaker, she was evacuated to Sverdlovsk, where she very soon found herself in the only safe place to be: the library basement.

Was this a continuation of the long-standing Russian tradition of hiding away the precious fruits of the spirit, like the fruits of the earth, in dank underground places? Or was it an inoculation for the next decade of Sonechka's life, which she would spend with an underground figure, the husband who appeared for her in this desperately difficult first year of evacuation?

On the day Robert Victorovich came to the library, just before closing time, Sonechka was at the circulation desk, standing in for her senior colleague, who was off sick. He was short, thin, and angular, his face gray and his hair graying, and he would not have caught Sonechka's attention but for asking where the catalog of books in French was kept. The library did have books in French, but the catalog had been mislaid long before, due to lack of demand. As there were no other visitors at this hour of the evening, Sonechka took this unusual reader down to her basement to the remote West European corner.

He stood, dazed, before the shelves for a long time, his head to one side, with the incredulous expression of a hungry child confronting a plateful of cakes. Sonechka stood behind, taller than him by half a head, and was herself rooted to the spot by his excitement.

He turned round to her, unexpectedly kissed the long fingers of her hand, and in a low voice that trembled like the flickering light from a blue lamp remembered from the endless colds of her childhood, said, "How miraculous! What riches! Montaigne, Pascal . . ." And, without letting go of her hand, added with a sigh, "And in the Elsevier edition!"

"We have nine Elseviers," Sonechka said, nodding proudly, pleased to be so conversant with the arcana of librarianship. He looked up at her in a strange way that felt as if he were looking down, smiled with his thin lips, disclosing several missing teeth, and paused as if preparing to say something important—but evidently thought better of it and said, instead, "Please issue me a reader's card, or whatever you call it here."

Sonechka extricated her hand, which had been overlooked between his own, and they went back up the cold vampire stairs, which drew the least warmth from any foot coming into contact with them. Here in the cramped reception room of what had been a merchant's villa, she wrote out his surname in her own hand for the first time, a name of which until then she had known nothing, but which in just two weeks' time would become her own. All the time she was writing the clumsy letters with an indelible pencil that kept turning in her much-darned woolly gloves, he was looking at her pure forehead and smiling inwardly at her marvelous resemblance to a patient, gentle young camel, and thinking, *She even has the coloring: that swarthy, sad umber tint, and the pinkishness, the warmth. . . .*

She finished writing, raised her forefinger, and pushed back her spectacles, which had slipped down. She looked at him benignly, without interest but expectantly. He had not given her his address.

He, however, was completely thrown by something that had befallen him as unexpectedly as a cloudburst from the heights of a clear tranquil sky: an overwhelming sense that his destiny was being accomplished. He had recognized that the person before him was to be his wife.

He had turned forty-seven the previous day. He was a living legend, but because he had suddenly and, in the opinion of his friends, inexplicably returned from France to his native land in the early 1930s, the legend had become separated from him and was now living a life of its own, by word of mouth, in the threatened art galleries of Nazi-occupied Paris. His strange pictures too were threatened with extinction, although having suffered obloquy and neglect they would know resurrection and posthumous acclaim. But of this he knew nothing. In his arch black quilted jacket, wearing a gray towel draped around his neck (which sported an unusually prominent Adam's apple), he was the luckiest of life's losers, having been imprisoned for a paltry five years. Now he was working on probation as an industrial artist in the offices of a factory, and he stood before this gangly girl and smiled, fully aware that at this very moment he was about to commit one of those betrayals of which his volatile life had been so full. He had betrayed the faith of his forefathers, the hopes of his parents, and the love of his teacher; he had betrayed science and abruptly and harshly ruptured the bonds of friendship just as soon as he began to sense a fettering of his freedom. . . . This time he was betraying a solemn vow never to marry, which, assuredly, had never been remotely similar to a vow of celibacy, and which he had taken in the years of his early deceptive success.

He was a committed ladies' man and obtained a great deal of sustenance from the seemingly inexhaustible supply of women, but he guarded himself vigilantly against addiction, fearful of becoming fodder for that feminine allure which is so paradoxically generous to those who take from it and so destructively cruel to those who give.

Sonechka, meanwhile, placid soul that she was—cocooned by the thousand volumes of her reading, lulled by the hazy murmurings of the Greek myths, the hypnotically shrill recorder fluting of the Middle Ages, the misty windswept yearning of Ibsen, the minutely detailed tedium of Balzac, the astral music of Dante, the siren song of the piercing voices of Rilke and Novalis, seduced by the moralistic despair of the great Russian writers calling out to the heart of heaven itself—this placid soul had no awareness that her great moment was at hand, preoccupied as she was by the question of whether she was taking rather a risk in allowing a reader to borrow books that she was only allowed to issue for use in the reading room.

"Your address?" she asked meekly.

"Well, you see, I am here on a temporary assignment. I am living at the factory offices," her strange reader explained.

"Let me have your passport and residence permit then, please," Sonechka requested.

He delved into a deep pocket and pulled out a crumpled document. She looked at it through her spectacles for a long time before shaking her head.

"No, I'm sorry. You live outside the city limits."

Capricious Cybele stuck out her pink tongue at him. All, it seemed, was lost. He pushed the document back down into the depths of his pocket.

"What I can do is take the books out on my own account, and you can bring them back to me before you leave," Sonechka said apologetically.

And then he knew that all was going to be well.

"Only I would ask you to be very sure not to forget," she added, in a kindly voice, and wrapped the three small volumes up in dog-eared newspaper.

He thanked her tersely and left.

While Robert Victorovich was musing with distaste on techniques for striking up an acquaintance and the rigors of courtship, Sonechka unhurriedly concluded her long working day and prepared to go home. She was no longer in the least concerned about the return of the three valuable books she had so insouciantly issued to a complete stranger. All her thoughts now focused on her passage home through the cold dark town.


THOSE SPECIAL feminine eyes that, like the mystical third eye, open at an improbably early age for a girl, were in Sonechka's case not so much shut as screwed up tight.

In early adolescence, around the age of fourteen, as if in obedience to some ancient programming of her Jewish heredity, which for millennia had given virgins in marriage at a tender age, she fell in love with a comely classmate, snub-nosed Vitya Starostin. Her infatuation manifested itself only in an uncontrollable desire to gaze upon him, and her searching eye was soon noticed not only by the pretty boy but by all her other classmates, who spotted this entertaining phenomenon even before Sonechka herself.

She tried to control herself, she kept trying to find something else to look at—the rectangle of the blackboard, her exercise book, the dusty window—but with the stubbornness of a compass needle her gaze kept swinging willfully back to that head of yellow hair and seeking contact with the cold attractive blue eyes. . . . Her understanding friend Zoya had whispered a warning to her to stop ogling so, but there was nothing

Sonechka could do. Her greedy eyes continued to feast on the fair-haired boy.

The upshot was dreadful and never to be forgotten. Wearying under the burden of her infatuated goggling, her brutal young Onegin arranged a rendezvous with his silent admirer on a side avenue of the park and slapped her a couple of times, inflicting not pain but deadly humiliation, as guffaws of approbation proceeded from the bushes where four of their classmates were hidden. One might chide their insensitivity, were it not that every one of the young peeping Toms was to perish in the first winter of the impending war.

The lesson in manners administered by our chivalrous thirteen-year-old was so compelling that the lady fell ill and lay for two weeks in an ague, the fires of infatuation evidently abating in this time-honored manner. When she recovered and returned to school in the full expectation of new humiliation, her escapade had been totally eclipsed by the suicide of Nina Borisova, the prettiest girl in the school, who had hanged herself in a classroom after the end of the evening's classes.

As for our hard-hearted hero, Vitya Starostin, to Sonechka's great good fortune he and his parents had already moved to a different town, leaving Sonechka with the bitter certainty that her sex life was over before it had begun, and for the rest of her life she was freed from any inclination to try to be liked, beguiling, or attractive. Toward more fortunate friends she felt neither soul-destroying jealousy nor ruinous resentment but reverted to her intoxicating and overweening passion for reading.

ROBERT VICTOROVICH came back two days later, when Sonechka was no longer at the circulation desk. He had her called. She came up from the basement, emerging in three short stages out of a dark hole, shortsightedly taking a long time to recognize him and then nodding as if he were someone she knew well.

"Sit down, please," he said, offering her a chair.

There were several warmly dressed visitors sitting in the small reading room; it was cold and the heating was barely on.

Sonechka perched on the edge of the chair. A floppy fur hat lay by the edge of the table, next to a package that the man was unhurriedly and very carefully unwrapping.

"It quite slipped my mind the other day to ask," he said, in his glowing voice, and Sonechka smiled at his pleasingly old-fashioned phrasing, long gone from common speech, "I quite forgot to ask your name. Do please forgive me."

"Sonya," she replied briefly, her eyes all the time on his undoing of the package.

"Sonechka. . . . Yes," he said, as if consenting.

When the wrappings were finally peeled away, Sonya saw before her the portrait of a woman, painted on loose coarse-fibered paper in a warm sepia brown. It was a wonderful portrait; the woman's face was genteel and refined and belonged to a bygone age. And it was her, Sonechka's, face. She breathed in, a little, and smelled the tang of the cold ocean.

"It is my wedding present to you," he said. "Actually, I have come to make you a proposal of marriage." He looked at her expectantly.

At this point Sonechka took a proper look at him for the first time: straight eyebrows, a finely ridged nose, a thin mouth with straight lips, deep vertical wrinkles on his cheeks, and faded eyes, clever and brooding. . . .

Her lips trembled. She was silent, her eyes lowered. She wanted very much to look one more time into his face, so grave and attractive, but the shade of Vitya Starostin gibbered behind her back and she stared fixedly at the light flowing lines of the picture, which had suddenly ceased to represent anything feminine, let alone her own face, and she said in a voice barely audible, but chilly and discouraging, "Is this some kind of joke?"

Then he was suddenly frightened. He had long since given up making plans for the future. Fate had brought him to this dismal place, truly the gates of hell. His animal sense of self-preservation was almost exhausted, and the twilight shadowy existence that was life in this world no longer held him. Now he had found a woman radiant with an inner light and had a presentiment that she was the wife whose frail hands would be the saving of his failing life, which still clung to earthly existence. He had seen her also as a sweet burden for him to bear, unencumbered as he was by a family, a burden for his cowardly virility, which had jibbed at the arduousness of fatherhood and the obligations of the family man. But how could he have thought . . . how had it not occurred to him before . . . perhaps she already belonged to another man, some young lieutenant or engineer in a mended sweater?

Cybele again stuck out her pointed pink tongue at him, and a merry cohort of dreadful unsuitable women, all of whom he had known, cavorted in flickering scarlet reflections. He gave a hoarse, strained laugh, pushed the portrait over toward her, and said, "I was not joking. It simply had not occurred to me that you might already be married." He rose to his feet and picked up his unspeakable fur hat. "Forgive me."

In the manner of a czarist officer he bowed abruptly, jerking his cropped head downward, and made for the door. At that Sonechka shouted after him, "Stop! No! No! I am not married!"

An old man sitting at a readers' table with a file of newspapers looked over disapprovingly. Robert Victorovich turned, smiled a smile with his straight lips, and from his recent state of distraction at the thought that this woman was slipping away from him, graduated to a state of even greater distraction. He had absolutely no idea of what he ought now to say or do.

WHERE DID emaciated Robert and naturally frail Sonechka find the strength to carve out their new life in the desolate circumstances of evacuation, amid poverty and depression and the shrill sloganeering that barely managed to conceal the underlying horrors of the first winter of the war? Where did they find the strength to create a new, hermetically isolated life in an ivory tower with room to accommodate fully every aspect of their separate pasts? Robert's fractured life, like the flight of a blinded moth, with its quick, exuberant, lightning turns from Judaism to mathematics and then on to his life's work, senseless but addictive paint-daubing, as he himself defined his craft. And the life of Sonechka, feeding off the bookish imaginings of other people, untrue but captivating.

Sonechka brought a sublime and sacrosanct lack of experience to their life together, an unlimited receptiveness to all the important, lofty, and not wholly comprehensible things with which Robert deluged her. He for his part never ceased to be amazed by how much their long nightly talks revealed his past to him in a quite new and different light. These nocturnal conversations with his wife transmuted the past as magically as the touch of the philosopher's stone.

Of the five years he had spent in the labor camps, Robert recalled the first two as having been the harshest. After that, things settled down somehow. He began painting portraits of the camp authorities' wives and copying art reproductions to order. The originals of these were sad examples of Russian art at its worst, and as he churned them out Robert usually amused himself with technical trickery of some sort, like painting left-handed. In the process he discovered that his temporary left-handedness affected his perception of color.

In the management of his personal affairs, Robert inclined toward asceticism and had always managed to get by with little, but having for many years been deprived of what even he regarded as the bare essentials—toothpaste, a sharp razor blade and hot water for shaving, a handkerchief, and toilet paper— he rejoiced now in every little thing, in every new day lit up by the presence of his wife, Sonya, and in the relative freedom of a man miraculously let out of the camps and obliged to register his presence with the local police a mere once a week.

They had an easier life than many. The factory's industrial artist was allocated a windowless room next to the boiler house in the basement of the office building. It was warm. The electricity supply hardly ever got cut off. The boilerman boiled potatoes for them that Sonechka's father brought, the old man's unfailing craftsmanship providing essential extra rations.

One time when Sonechka murmured dreamily, with a touch of really quite uncharacteristic sentimentality, "When the war is over and we have won, our life will just be so happy—" Her husband interrupted crisply.

"Don't delude yourself. We are living very nicely right now. As regards winning, you and I will always be losers, whichever of those cannibals wins the war." He concluded darkly with an enigmatic phrase: "To my teacher I owe having become neither a green nor a blue, neither *parmularius* nor *scutarius*. . . ."

"What are you talking about?" Sonechka asked, startled.

"Not I: Marcus Aurelius. Blue and green were the colors of the parties in the hippodrome. I meant that I have never been interested by whose horse comes in first. It is of no importance for us. In either case the human being is destroyed, private life is forfeit. Go to sleep, Sonya."

He wound a towel round his head, a strange habit acquired in the camps, and fell asleep instantly. Sonechka lay awake for a long time in the darkness, tormented by a sense of things left

unsaid and trying to drive away the even more frightening suspicion that her husband possessed knowledge so dangerous it
was better not even to approach it. She diverted her unquiet
mind to another place, to the aching delicate explorations
going on beneath her stomach, and tried to imagine little fingers a quarter the size of a matchstick in just the same darkness
as now surrounded her, lightly running over the soft wall of
their first dwelling, and she smiled.

Meanwhile, Sonechka's talent for vivid and realistic perception of life in fiction seemed to atrophy, to become opaque
and clumsy, and she suddenly discovered that even the most
ordinary event on this side of the pages of a book—catching a
mouse in a homemade trap, the burgeoning of a gnarled,
withered twig in a glass of water, a handful of China tea that
Robert acquired quite by chance—was more significant than
the first love or the death of a fictional character, more important than his or her descent into Hades itself.

Only a week after their breathtakingly swift marriage,
Sonechka learned a horrifying fact from her husband: He was
completely indifferent to Russian literature, finding it bare,
tendentious, and unbearably moralistic. He excepted only
Pushkin, reluctantly. In the debate that followed this revela-
tion, Robert parried Sonechka's spirited defense with cold and
rigorous argumentation that she did not wholly understand,
and their domestic seminar ended in bitter tears and sweet
embraces.

Pigheaded Robert always had to have the last word and, in
the bleak hour before dawn, found a moment to say to his
wife just as she was falling asleep, "They're a curse! They're a
curse, all these authorities from Gamaliel to Marx. As for
those writers of yours, Gorky is all hot air, Ehrenburg is scared
witless . . . and Apollinaire is all hot air too."

At the mention of Apollinaire, Sonechka was jolted back to
wakefulness. "I suppose you knew Apollinaire as well?"

"Well, yes," he admitted reluctantly. "During the Great War we shared the same quarters for a couple of months. Then I was transferred to Belgium, near Ypres. Have you heard of Ypres?"

"Yes, veteran of Ypres, I have," Sonechka murmured, enchanted by the inexhaustible richness of his biography.

"Well, I'm glad of that. . . . I arrived just in time for the famous gas attack, but as I was up on a hill, to windward, I wasn't gassed myself. One stroke of good luck after another, really. I must be a winner." To confirm to himself once more just how amazingly and uniquely lucky he was, he slid his arm in under Sonechka's shoulders.

They abandoned the topic of Russian literature.

ONE MONTH before their baby was due to be born, the term of Robert's rather vague assignment, which he had been extending by every means at his disposal, ended. He was instructed to return without delay to the Bashkir village of Davlekanovo, where he was to live in exile in the hope of better things to come, in a future that Sonechka still imagined would be beautiful, despite his grave reservations.

Both Sonechka's father and her mother, whose lungs were by now very bad, did their best to persuade her to stay in Sverdlovsk, at least until after the baby was born, but Sonechka was firmly resolved to go with her husband, and Robert indeed had no wish to be parted from his wife. This was the only area in which a shadow of dissatisfaction crept into the old clock-maker's relations with his son-in-law. Sonechka's father had by this time lost both his son and his other son-in-law in the war, and he and Robert took to each other warmly without a word being spoken. The difference in their social status was now, in a world turned upside down, not so much of no significance as tending to show up the uselessness of the supposed advantages of an intellectual over a proletarian. As for the rest, the underwater part of the cultural iceberg, their Jewish heritage, was something they had in common.

Sonechka's family packed her things in just twenty-four hours, that being the time allowed for Robert to ready himself for departure. Her mother, shedding yellow tears, purposefully hemmed diapers and, with a fine needle, lovingly stitched tiny jackets out of an old nightdress of her own. Sonechka's elder sister, recently widowed by the front, knitted little booties out of red wool while staring straight ahead with unseeing eyes. Her father, who had managed to acquire a twenty-eight-pound sack of millet, measured it out into little bags and kept glancing doubtfully at Sonechka who, even though in her ninth month, had lately become so thin that she hadn't even had to move the buttons on her skirt: her pregnancy was evident less from any change in her figure than from a puffiness of her face and swollen lips.

"It's going to be a girl," her mother would say quietly. "Daughters always steal away their mother's good looks."

Sonechka's sister nodded noncommittally, while Sonechka herself smiled absently and kept repeating to herself, "Lord, grant that it be a girl, a little fair-skinned girl. . . ."

THAT NIGHT a railwayman they knew got them onto a small three-carriage train that was standing a mile outside the station, into a coach that still retained traces of its noble origins in the form of good solid wood paneling, although its soft seats and folding tables had long since been ripped out and the Pullman luxury replaced by slatted benches.

It took them over a day and a half to get from Sverdlovsk to Ufa in the packed train, and for the whole of the journey Robert kept for some reason remembering a maverick trip to Barcelona in his youth. He couldn't wait to get there after receiving his first big fee in 1923 or 1924 because he wanted to meet Gaudi.

Sonechka slept trustingly for almost the whole of the journey, with her feet pressed into a great tangle of blankets and her shoulder resting on her husband's thin chest. He meanwhile was remembering the twisting street in which his hotel stood and which crept uphill, the naive little round fountain in front of his window, and the swarthy face and chiseled nostrils of the exceptionally beautiful prostitute with whom he had caroused like a merchant for the whole of his week in Barcelona. He rummaged through his memory and readily found small vivid details, like the totally owlish face of a waiter in the hotel restaurant and the marvelous shoes plaited from ocher calf leather, bought in a shop with an enormous dark blue sign that said HOMER; he even recalled the Barcelona girl's name: Concetta! She had been born in the Abruzzi mountains in Italy but had come to Barcelona. He didn't hit it off with the great architect, though. Now, a quarter of a century later, he could visualize Gaudi's odd constructions down to the last detail, completely vegetative, and every one of them contrived and unconvincing.

Sonechka sneezed, half woke, and murmured something. He pressed her sleepy hand to himself and came back to the outskirts of Ufa, to the wilds of Bashkiria. He smiled, shaking his gray head in bewilderment. "Was that really me in Barcelona? Am I here now? No, truly, there is no such thing as reality. . . ."

AFTER HER period of gestation, at the first sign that the birth was imminent, Robert took Sonechka to a maternity hospital in a trampled, muddy, treeless area on the outskirts of a big flat-roofed village. The building itself was of clay bricks mixed with straw, a wretched place with small opaque windows.

The only doctor was a blond man of middle years with fine white skin who blushed easily. This was Pan Szuwalski, a refugee from Poland and until recently a fashionable Warsaw physician, a cultivated man and a connoisseur of fine wines. He had his back to the new arrivals, his dazzling blue-tinged white coat incongruous here but reassuring, and he was nibbling the ends of his blond mustache and wiping the lenses of his large spectacles with a piece of chamois leather. He came over to the window several times a day, to look out at this amorphous land with its grubby tufts of grass—instead of elegant Jerusalem Avenue, onto which the windows of his Warsaw clinic had looked—and to dab at his watering eyes with a red-and-green checked English handkerchief. The last one he had left.

He had just examined an aging Bashkir woman who had come twenty-five miles on horseback, shouted, "Give the lady a wash!" to the nurse, and was standing now, trying to control an involuntary tremor of resentment in his breast as he remembered longingly his satin-skinned lady patients, and the sweet milky smell of their costly pampered genitals.

He turned, sensing somebody behind his back, to discover a large young woman sitting on his bench in a light-colored, very worn coat and a sharp-featured gray-haired man in a patched double-breasted jacket.

"I am making so bold as to trouble you, doctor," the man began, and Pan Szuwalski, identifying someone from his own caste of the downtrodden European intelligentsia the moment he heard the voice, advanced on him with a smile of recognition.

"You are most welcome, please. . . . You have brought your wife," Pan Szuwalski said half interrogatively, taking in the large difference in their ages, which invited conjecture as to a different relationship between this seemingly rather ill-suited couple. He gestured toward a curtain, behind which a tiny office was partitioned off for him.

Fifteen minutes later he had inspected Sonechka, confirmed the imminence of parturition, but advised that she might need to be patient for as much as ten hours, even if everything went smoothly and according to plan.

Sonechka was laid on a bed covered with stiff cold oilcloth. Pan Szuwalski patted her belly with a gesture more befitting a vet than a doctor and retired to attend to his Bashkir patient, who, they heard, had had a stillborn baby three days ago. Everything had been all right, but now it was all wrong.

Two and a half hours later the doctor, with big tears on his clean-shaven cheeks, came out to the veranda where a morose Robert was doggedly sitting it out and confessed to him in a tragical stage whisper, "I ought to be shot. I have no business operating under conditions like these. I have nothing, literally nothing. But I cannot not operate. In twenty-four hours from now she will die from sepsis!"

"What's wrong with her?" Robert asked numbly, picturing to himself the death of Sonechka.

"Oh, goodness me! Forgive me! With your wife everything is in order; the contractions have begun. I meant that unfortunate Bashkir woman."

Robert ground his teeth and swore under his breath; he could not stand neurotic men who felt compelled to blurt their feelings out to all and sundry. He chewed his lips and looked away.

The little four-and-a-half-pound girl Sonechka gave birth to in the fifteen minutes Pan Szuwalski was making conversation on the veranda was as fair-skinned as could be and had a narrow little face, exactly as Sonechka had hoped.

EVERYTHING CHANGED for Sonechka as completely and radically as if her old life had turned away from her and taken with it all the bookishness she had so loved, leaving her in return unimaginable travails from the disruption and poverty and cold and from her daily anxieties over little Tanya and Robert, who took turns in being ill.

Their family would not have survived but for constant help from her father, who managed somehow to procure and send them the essential supplies on which they lived. To all her parents' attempts to persuade her to move to Sverdlovsk with the baby while things were at their most difficult, Sonechka's invariable reply was, "I have to be with Robert."

After a wet summer that was more like an interminable autumn, a severe winter suddenly set in without any season of transition. Living in a shaky little house built of damp adobe brick, they remembered their room in the factory basement as a tropical Garden of Eden.

The main worry was fuel. The school for combine operatives where Robert worked as a bookkeeper sometimes gave him the use of a horse, and already in the autumn he would quite frequently ride out to the steppe to cut quantities of tall reedlike dead grasses, the names of which he never did learn. With the cart piled high, there was fuel enough to heat the house for two days, as he knew from his experience of the winter spent in the village before he had gone to Sverdlovsk.

He compressed the grass and crammed their lean-to full of homemade briquettes. He took up part of the floor, which he himself had laid earlier without thinking he would need somewhere to keep potatoes, and dug a storage pit, dried it out, and lined it with stolen planks. He built a lavatory, which made old Rahim, his neighbor, shake his head and smile wryly. In these parts a wooden plank with a hole in it was considered a needless luxury; since the beginning of time people had simply used a place not too far from the house, which they called "out in the wind."

Robert was wiry and sturdy, and physical fatigue was a balm for his soul, which was strongly averse to the absurd adding up of sham statistics, the compiling of false reports and fictitious documents for writing off fuel that had been stolen, spare parts that had been filched, and vegetables that had been sold on the side at the local bazaar. These were diverted from the small college farm, whose manager was a wily nursery-man, a cheery Ukrainian with a maimed right hand and no conscience.

But by way of recompense, each evening Robert would open his front door and see Sonechka in the living fire-breathing light of the oil lamp, wreathed in an uneven flick-ering nimbus, sitting in their only chair, which he had refashioned into an armchair. Firmly attached to the pointed end of her pillowlike breast was the little grayish head, soft and shaggy as a tennis ball, of his baby. In the mildest way imagina-ble, the whole picture would shimmer and pulsate, with waves of uneven light, with waves of the unseen warm milk, and with other invisible currents that left him unable to move or close the door. "The door!" Sonechka would urge in a trailing whis-per, all smiles at the return of her husband, and, laying their daughter down across the one and only bed, would produce a saucepan from beneath a cushion and place it in the middle of the bare table. On good days this contained thick soup made from horsemeat, potatoes from the college fields, and millet sent by her father.

Sonechka would be wakened at daybreak by the little scuf-fling movements of her daughter and would press the baby to her tummy, feeling with a sleepy back the nearness of her hus-band. Without opening her eyes, she would unbutton her nightdress, draw out her breasts, which hardened toward morning, press the nipples, and two long jets would spurt onto a bright-colored cloth with which she would wipe her nipple. The little girl would start to twist and turn, puckering her lips, slurping and trying to catch the nipple like a little fish trying to latch on to a large piece of bait. Sonechka's milk was plentiful and flowed easily, and feeding her baby—the little tugs at the nipple and the nibbles at her breast of toothless gums—gave her a pleasure that mysteriously communicated itself to her husband, who unerringly woke at this early hour of the morning. He would embrace her broad back, possessively squeezing her to himself, and she would be overwhelmed with pleasure at this double load of unendurable happiness. She would smile in the first light of morning, her body wordlessly and joyously satisfying the appetites of these two precious beings who were inseparable from her.

This morning feeling illuminated the whole of the day. Her housework seemed to take care of itself easily and adroitly, and every God-given hour remained in Sonechka's memory, not blurring into those on either side of it but in all its special separateness: one day with its lazy rain at noon; one with the large rust-colored bird with bandy legs that flew in and perched on the fence; one with that first ribbed stripe of a new tooth in her little daughter's swollen gum. What is the need for this minutely detailed and senseless working of memory? For the rest of her life, Sonechka retained the pattern of each day, its smells and nuances and, particularly, in a grave and exaggerated manner, every word her husband uttered, along with all its attendant circumstances.

Many years later Robert was more than once to be amazed at his wife's capacity for indiscriminate memorizing, which tucked away in some recess of her brain that whole great heap of numbers, hours, and details. Sonechka would even remember every last one of the toys that Robert made in great numbers for his growing daughter, with a creative delight he had long forgotten. She later took all sorts of bits and bobs with them to Moscow: carved wooden animals, birds in flight made from twisted string, wooden dolls with scary faces. Nor did she forget the toys that were left behind for Rahim's children and grandchildren: a cheery flock of identical thin little sparrows; a fortress for a puppet king, with a Gothic tower and drawbridge that opened; a Roman circus with matchstick figures of slaves and wild beasts; and a rather large contraption with a handle to turn and a great many little colored slats that moved, clattered, and produced weird, droll music.

His projects were well beyond a small child's capacity for play. His daughter had a good memory, which, like her mother's, retained a host of memories from this time, but it did not register these toys, perhaps partly because, when the family went from the Urals to Alexandrovo in 1946, Robert was to build her entire fantastical towns out of wood chips and colored paper, great strides in the direction of what was later to be called paper architecture. These fragile toys were lost in the course of the family's many moves in the late 1940s and early 1950s.

The first half of Robert's life had passed in huge unpredictable geographical leaps, from Russia to France, then to America, the Balkans, Algiers, and again to France, and finally back once more to Russia. The second half, however, cut off from the first by his time in labor camps and exile, passed in little moves, from Alexandrovo to Kalinin, Pushkino to Lianozovo. In this way he spent an entire decade gradually moving back toward Moscow, a city he was far from seeing as a new Athens or Jerusalem.

During those first postwar years the breadwinner was Sonechka, who had inherited her mother's sewing machine and the innocent recklessness of a self-taught seamstress who knew how to stitch a sleeve into an armhole. Her customers were undemanding, and the seamstress conscientious and not given to overcharging.

Robert worked at jobs more appropriate to a semi-invalid: one time as a school watchman and another as the bookkeeper of a cooperative that produced monstrous iron brackets of unknown purpose. Brought up under the free skies of Paris, he never entertained the thought of working as an artist in the service of the dull and dismal state he lived in, even if he could have reconciled himself to its imbecility, bloodthirsty stupidity, and shameless mendacity.

He realized his artistic imaginings on snow-white boards on which he built a third generation of the paper-and-wood-chip structures with which he had earlier amused his daughter. In passing he revealed a special ability to visualize evolvents and a precise knack for getting spatio-planar relations right; it was impossible to tear your eyes away from the whimsical figures he would cut from a single sheet of paper. Squeezing something through here, twisting something there, and turning the whole thing inside out, he would have composed an object that had never before existed in nature and for which there was no name. He began to play the game for himself.

Sonechka's womanly certainty of her husband knew no bounds. Having already taken his talent on trust, she now looked in awed delight at everything that proceeded from his hands. She had no understanding of the complex spatial problems he set himself, and even less of the elegant solutions he found, but in his strange toys she sensed a reflection of his personality, a moving of mysterious forces. She happily murmured to herself her cherished catchphrase, "Lord, Lord, what have I done to deserve such happiness?"

Robert abandoned painting. From his earlier attempts to amuse little Tanya he developed a whole new craft. As always, fortune smiled on him: In the local train he bumped into Timler, now a famous artist, whom he had known back in Paris and who had bravely stayed in touch with Robert after he returned to Moscow right up to the time of his arrest.

Timler had been branded a *formalist*. Who is going to explain to us, and when, what the talentless upstarts canonized by officialdom had in mind when they came up with that label? At the time, Timler had gone to ground in the theater. Now he came to visit Robert. He stood for an hour and a half in his insubstantial clapboard shed looking at several of the structures captioned with series of Arabic numerals and Hebrew letters and, while appreciating their exceptional quality, was too embarrassed—as the son of a carpenter in a little Jewish shtetl who had studied two years in the *heder*—to ask their creator the meaning of these strange ciphers. As for Robert, it never occurred to him that there could be any need to explain what for him was the obvious connection between the kabbalistic alphabet—a dry relic of his adolescent enthusiasm for all things Jewish—and his bold games that took space apart and turned it inside out.

For a long time Timler drank his tea in silence and, just before taking leave, said with a frown, "It is very damp here, Robert. You can move your works to my studio."

This offer was tantamount to unqualified recognition and was extremely decent on Timler's part, but Robert did not take it up. His nameless items, called into existence by chance, returned to nonexistence when they rotted away in one or another of his later sheds and failed to survive the many house moves.

However, it was in that shed that the celebrated Timler gave Robert his first commission to design a theater set. Before long, his models of settings were the talk of theatrical circles in Moscow, and new commissions rained down on him. On a stage eighteen inches across he could re-create Gorky's night shelter for the denizens of the lower depths, the ownerless study of Tolstoy's intestate living corpse, or cram onto it the ever-popular shops of Ostrovsky's grain merchants.

AMONG THE woodsheds, dovecotes, and creaking swings stalked odd Tanya. She liked wearing her mother's old dresses. The tall scrawny girl was swamped in Sonechka's loose shifts, girt with a faded cashmere scarf. Around a narrow face, like a mature dandelion head as yet unblown by the wind, her wavy, wiry hair stood proud, untamable by comb, unbraidable into pigtails. She would scuttle about in the dense air—heavy with the aromas of old barrels, moldering garden furniture, and the solid, oh-too-solid shadows that surround decrepit and unneeded things—and suddenly, chameleonlike, vanish into them. She would remain immobile for a long time and start if somebody called her. Sonechka was worried and complained to her husband about their daughter's brooding and edginess. He put his arm on Sonechka's shoulder and said, "Leave her be. You wouldn't want her marching in step with the rest, would you?"

Sonechka tried to instill a love of books in Tanya, but as Tanya listened to her mother's deeply expressive reading her eyes would glaze over, and she would sail away to places beyond Sonechka's imagining.

Over the years of her marriage, Sonechka herself changed from a highbrow spinster into quite a practical housewife. She longed for a perfectly ordinary house, with water from a tap in the kitchen, a separate room for her daughter and a studio for her husband, with meat and stewed fruit for dinner and starched white sheets that were not sewn together from three different-sized pieces. In pursuit of this grand vision, Sonechka took on a second job, sitting at night over her sewing machine and, without letting on to her husband, saving up. She also dearly wanted her widowed father to be able to move in with them. He was almost blind, now, and very frail.

Subjected to the vagaries of suburban buses and ramshackle suburban trains, Sonechka rapidly grew old and ugly. The soft down on her upper lip turned into a sprouting, unfeminine growth; her eyelids sagged, giving her a doglike expression; and the shadow of fatigue in the bags under her eyes no longer disappeared after her day of rest or, for that matter, after her two weeks' holiday.

But the bitter cup of aging did not by any means poison Sonechka's life, as it does the life of proud beauties; her husband was immutably much older, and this gave her an unfailing sense of her own unfading youthfulness. Robert's matrimonial vigor, which showed no sign of abating, confirmed as much. Her every morning was colored by undeserved feminine delight so brilliant it could never become a matter of routine. Deep in her heart she harbored a secret readiness to be deprived of this happiness at any moment, as something wholly adventitious, something that had come her way by mistake or through an oversight of some kind. Her sweet little daughter Tanya also seemed to her a chance gift, and this, in the fullness of time, was indeed confirmed by the gynecologist: Sonechka had what the medics called an infantile uterus, immature and ill-adapted to childbearing. After Tanya's birth she never became pregnant again, which grieved her to the point of tears. She constantly felt she must be unworthy of her husband's love if she could not bear him any more children.

IN THE early 1950s, Sonechka's Herculean labors were rewarded when the family half exchanged, half bought a new place to live and moved into a whole quarter of a two-story wooden house, one of the few buildings still standing in the by then almost completely demolished Petrovsky Park, near Moscow's Dynamo metro station. It was a delightful house and had been the dacha of a famous prerevolutionary lawyer. One quarter of the garden adjoining the house went with the apartment.

All Sonechka's dreams had come true. Tanya had a sunny room of her own on the second floor. Sonechka's father, living out the last year of his life, had the little corner room, and Robert set up his studio on the heated glazed terrace. They had space to breathe. They even had some money.

By the luck of the apartment-exchange draw, Robert found himself on the fringe of Moscow's answer to Montmartre, ten minutes' walk from a whole colony of artists. To his complete surprise he found, in what he had supposed to be a despoiled and trampled place, people who, if not exactly kindred spirits, were at least colleagues he could talk to: Alexander Ivanovich, a Russian Barbizonian, benefactor of stray cats and injured birds, who painted his wild pictures while sitting on the damp earth and claimed that his posterior's Antaean contact was a source of creative energy; Gregory, a bald Ukrainian Zen Buddhist who achieved an effect of translucent porcelain and silk by covering layers of watercolor dozens of times alternately with tea and milk; the poet Gavrilin, with his variously colored hair, broken nose, and inborn gift of draftsmanship, who drew his palindrome poems among intellectually testing configurations on large, unevenly cut sheets of wrapping paper—Robert delighted in his calligraphic and verbal encryptions.

All these odd people, revealing themselves in the early years of what was to prove a deceptive political thaw, gravitated toward Robert, and his once very private home became a kind of club, with the proprietor himself assuming the role of honorary chairman.

He was, as always, laconic, but a single skeptical comment from him, a single jibe, was sufficient to put back on course a discussion that was in danger of losing its way or move the conversation in a new direction. Russia, burdened for many years with silence, found its tongue again, but these freewheeling conversations took place behind closed doors, and fear was still at their elbow.

Sonechka would be mending one of Tanya's stockings, pulling it over the smooth wood of the darning egg while she listened to the men. The things they talked about—sparrows in winter, the visions of Meister Eckhart, techniques for infusing tea, Goethe's theory of color—bore precious little relation to the concerns of the times outside the door, but Sonechka basked reverently in the warmth and light of their universally relevant conversation and kept repeating to herself, "Lord, Lord, what have I done to deserve all this?"

FLAT-NOSED Gavrilin, devotee of all the arts, was in the habit of delving into every conceivable journal. In the library he happened one day upon a long article about Robert in an American art history journal. A brief biographical sketch concluded with an exaggerated report of his death in Stalin's labor camps in the late 1930s. The critical section of the article was written in language beyond Gavrilin's linguistic capacity, but from what he did manage to translate it was evident that Robert was regarded as virtually a classic painter and, at the very least, as the pioneer of an artistic movement currently all the rage in Europe. Four reproductions in full color were appended.

The very next day Robert, accompanied by his Barbizonian friend, descended on the library of the Artists' Union, unearthed the article, and flew into an indescribable rage upon finding that one of the four paintings reproduced had absolutely no bearing on his work since it belonged to Morandi, while another had been printed upside down. When he read the article he became even more furious.

"Back in the 1920s America gave me the impression that it was a country full of complete idiots. They don't seem to have got any brighter," he snorted.

Gavrilin, however, bruited the article abroad to all and sundry. Robert's theater-set models were remembered even by the bright-eyed, quickfire theater designers, and soon they were again beating a path to his door.

One unexpected consequence of all this commotion was his being accepted into membership of the Artists' Union and allocated a place to work. It was a good studio looking out onto the Dynamo football stadium, and not a whit worse than his last studio in Paris, in an attic on rue Gay-Lussac with a view of the Jardin du Luxembourg.

BY NOW Sonechka was nearing forty. Her hair had turned gray and she had filled out markedly. Robert, as light and wizened as a locust, changed little, and the difference in their ages seemed somehow gradually to even out. For Tanya the great age of her parents was slightly embarrassing, as were also her own large stature, feet, and breasts. It all seemed out of scale, disproportionate in a decade when accelerated development had yet to be heard of in Russia. But Tanya had the advantage over Sonechka in that there was no elder brother to mock her, and from all the walls wonderful portraits of her at every stage of childhood looked beneficently down, mitigating her dissatisfaction with herself. By the time she was in seventh grade she was beginning to receive convincing evidence of her attractiveness from pubescent classmates and older boys.

From infancy onward, all Tanya's wishes were readily satisfied. Her loving parents were only too eager, and usually anticipated her desires. Goldfish, a puppy, and a piano would appear, almost on the same day the little girl began talking about them.

From the day she was born she had been surrounded by marvelous toys, and playing on her own, without needing anyone else to join in, was the most important thing in her life. So it came about that, emerging from the diversions of an extended childhood, she had a couple of years of dormancy during which she underwent the transition of puberty, before coming to an early recognition of which game exactly was preferred by grown-ups, and throwing herself into it with a confident awareness of her right to pleasure and the uninhibitedness of a personality that had never been repressed.

Tanya endured nothing remotely comparable to Sonechka's humiliating love for Vitya Starostin. Although she was no beauty in a conventional sense, and not even pretty by most people's standards, her elongated face with its fine ridged nose and light vitreous eyes, framed by springy, curly hair, was in fact very alluring. Other young people of her age were attracted also by the way she was constantly playing with a book, a pencil, her own hat. A little performance was always in progress in her hands that only her immediate neighbor could see.

On one occasion she got rather carried away in playing with the fingers and lips of her friend Boris, whom she went round to see in order to copy her math homework from him. She discovered that he had something that she did not, which intrigued her very much indeed. At that hour of the evening the door to Boris's parents' room was partly open, and the broad chink of light with two large shadows in front of the television set seemed all to be part of a game whose rules they observed to perfection, exchanging lines of dialogue with each other that bore absolutely no relation to what was going on between them. And although the session began with inno-cent childish questions like "Haven't you ever done it?" and "How about you?"—followed by a proposal from Tanya, who never stinted herself, to "Let's try it!"—it concluded with the brief introduction, both figurative and literal, of some-thing new.

At the very moment they were catching fire, an untimely invitation to supper came from the next room, and further trials had to be postponed to a more propitious moment.

Their subsequent liaisons took place without the presence of Boris's parents. For Tanya the most interesting thing was a new awareness of her body. She discovered that every part of it, her fingers, her breasts, her stomach, her back, responded differently to touch and had the ability to allow all manner of

delightful sensations to be elicited, and the shared experimen-
tation gave both of them no end of pleasure.

The puny freckled boy with the buck teeth and the mouth
inflamed at the corners also displayed exceptional talent, and
for the next two months the young experimenters, laboring
inventively and tirelessly from three in the afternoon till half
past six, when Boris's parents came home, mastered every
aspect of the physical side of love without in the process experiencing the least emotion beyond the bounds of a friendly
and practical partnership.

But then they fell out over a business matter: Tanya bor-
rowed Boris's geometry notes and lost them. To make matters
worse, she reported the fact to him in a completely unserious
manner without even apologizing. Boris, an orderly and even
pedantic boy, was outraged, not so much by the loss of his
notes as by Tanya's complete failure to appreciate the impro-
priety of her behavior. Tanya told him to stop whining, and he
called her a slob. They were no longer together.

In the time now free between three in the afternoon and
half past six, Boris settled down to study mathematics inten-
sively, establishing beyond doubt that his vocation lay in the
exact sciences. Tanya, however, was in no hurry to sort her life
out and played a flute rather woodenly and badly in her sunny
room, bit her nails, and read. . . . Alas for Sonechka and her
blissful youth passed on the sublime uplands of world literature! Her daughter, unschooled in the humanities, read only
sci-fi and more sci-fi, Western and Russian alike.

Meanwhile, the faltering sounds of Tanya's flute were
attracting droves of admirers. The very air around her was
charged, her curls rising up electrified and sparking with tiny
discharges if a hand so much as approached them. Sonechka
barely had time to open and close the door for all the young
men in zoological sweaters with angular deer and the dove-
gray military jackets and tunics that were the anachronistic

school uniform of the late 1950s, dreamed up by some senescent minister of education in an access of feebleminded nostalgia.

One Vladimir, an outstanding musician whose defection to Europe caused an immense scandal at a time when such a thing was accounted a political crime on the Soviet side of the Iron Curtain, would later describe in his memoirs, published in the late 1990s and revealing a redoubtable literary talent, the musical soirées in Tanya's room with the upright piano with the marvelous tone that had to be retuned every day. He would tenderly recall how this ancient instrument revealed the secret individuality of a piece of music to a musician at the beginning of his career. He would speak of it as one might of an elderly lady relative, long since deceased, who had baked unforgettable cherry pies for the author in his childhood.

Vladimir further testified that it was in Tanya's room, with its intricate little window looking out onto the garden and an old apple tree with a double trunk, while accompanying Tanya's uncertain flute-playing, that he first experienced the tumult of mutual creative understanding and joyously accepted a measure of musical self-abnegation to afford greater prominence to the tremulous flute.

At that time Vladimir was a short, dumpy boy who looked like a tapir and was in love with Tanya. She left an indelible trace in his life and in his heart, and both his wives, the first one in Moscow and the second in London, were unmistakably of the same type.

Tanya's second musical soul mate was Alyosha Petersburg, as the young Leningrader styled himself while in Moscow. In contrast to Vladimir's classical training, he offered improvisation on the guitar and mastery of any item capable of producing sound, from a mouth organ to a pair of tin cans. He was, moreover, a poet, and in a raucous fairground voice he delivered the first songs of the new culture of dissidence.

There were a few other boys, more spectators than partici-
pants, but they too played an essential part in providing the
admiring audience so necessary to both budding celebrities.

IN THE years of his youth, Robert too had been the center of
invisible swirling currents, but these had been currents of a
different, more intellectual quality. They too, like Tanya's tin
whistle, had drawn together a crowd of young people. Perhaps
surprisingly, this circle of precocious Jewish boys, teenagers as
they would be called nowadays, was studying, in the fraught
years before the First World War, not the Marxism that was
modish at the time but *Sefer ha-Zohar,* the Book of Splendor,
the ground-laying treatise of the Kabbala. These boys from
the Jewish Podol suburb of Kiev gathered at the house of
Avigdor-Melnik, Robert's father, whose house abutted the
house of Shvartsman, father of the future philosopher Lev
Shestov, whose friendship, twenty years later when he was
already in Paris, Robert was to enjoy.

Not one of those boys whose lot it was to live through the
years of war and revolutions was to become either a traditional
Jewish philosopher or a teacher of doctrine. They all grew up
to be *apikorsim,* freethinkers. One went on to become a brilliant
theoretician—and slightly less successful practitioner—of the
nascent art of cinematography, another became a famous
musician, a third was a surgeon with life-giving hands, and all
of them had been nourished by the same milk and invigorated
by the youthful electricity that accumulated under the roof of
the house of Avigdor-Melnik.

What Tanya had going on around her was, as Robert
guessed, the same thing as had electrified his own younger
years, but the charge was quite different, a female polarity
wholly inimical to him and further modified by the quirks of a
beggarly decadent generation.

It was Robert who first noticed that Tanya's late-night visitors sometimes stayed over until the following morning. An early riser throughout his life, he emerged sometime after five in the morning from the house's living quarters to go through to his studio on the terrace, where he specially enjoyed passing these first hours. To his sensibility they were the purest of the day. In the freshly fallen snow he noticed footprints leading from the veranda to the side gate. He noticed them again a few days later and tentatively asked his wife whether her sister had stayed the night with them. Sonechka, surprised, said no, Anya had not been staying.

Robert did not need to investigate further, since the following morning he saw a tall young man in a very thin anorak going out through the yard. He said not a word to Sonechka about his discovery, and Sonechka laid a head heavy with sleep on her husband's shoulder and complained. "She is not studying properly. . . . She is not doing anything. . . . She is getting into trouble at school. . . . That Raisa Semyonovna keeps dropping disgusting hints. . . ."

Robert comforted her. "Just forget all about it, Sonechka. All that is dead and stinks to high heaven. What does it matter if she walks out of that pathetic school? What's the use of it?"

"Robert, what are you saying?" Sonechka exclaimed in horror. "She can't get by without an education—"

"Calm yourself," her husband interrupted. "Leave the girl in peace. If she does not want to go to school, what matter? Let her toot away on that flute of hers; she'll learn just as much that way."

"But Robert, those boys. I am so afraid." Sonechka went timidly on the offensive. "I think one stayed in there with her the whole night. She did not go to school the next day."

Robert did not share his morning observation with Sonechka. He made no reply.

After Tanya had given Boris his marching orders, she had attracted admirers like a bitch in heat. Boys throbbing with testosterone swarmed obdurately around her, insistent and relentless. She tried out her new amusement with a few: Boris beat the lot of them hands down.

In the spring it became evident that she was not going to be allowed to progress to the ninth grade. The hassle at school became completely intolerable, and, without a word to Sonechka, Robert transferred Tanya to evening school. His initiative was to have far-reaching consequences for the whole family, and primarily for Robert himself.

THE SAME potent capricious fate that had determined that Sonechka should become the wife of Robert now singled out Tanya. The object of her passionate infatuation was the school cleaning lady, who doubled as her classmate, a little eighteen-year-old Polish girl called Jasia, with a face as smooth as a new-laid egg. Their friendship blossomed slowly in the second to last row of desks. Large, expansive Tanya gazed adoringly at Jasia, transparent as an apothecary's gleaming flask, and was overcome with bashfulness. Jasia said little, responding mono-syllabically to the infrequent questions Tanya addressed to her, and appeared reticent and aloof. She was the daughter of Pol-ish communists who had fled the Nazi invasion: as luck would have it, in opposite directions. Her father went west; her mother, her baby in her arms, headed east, to Russia. She failed to dissolve without trace among the country's millions but was leniently only exiled to Kazakhstan, where she had a hard time, clung tenaciously for ten years to her exalted and crazy ideals, and then died.

Jasia was put in an orphanage, where she displayed extraor-dinary determination to cling to life under conditions that appeared specially devised to ensure the slow death of body and soul, and wrenched herself free through her knack of exploiting to her best advantage whatever circumstances she found herself in.

Her eyebrows, arching high above gray eyes, and her delicate little catlike mouth seemed to be begging for protection, and protection was duly forthcoming. She had protectors and she had protectresses, but a natural independence of spirit led her to prefer men, having at an early age mastered an inexpensive technique for settling her debts to them.

One of her most recent protectors, who materialized after she had been sent to a particularly monstrous skills training center for orphans and devised an ingenious plan of escape, was a fat forty-year-old Tatar called Rafil, a railway carriage steward who conveyed her all the way to the Kazan station in the city of Moscow, chosen as the starting point for her meteoric rise. In the side pocket of a checkered shopping bag she had a passport, made out in her name a short time previously, which she had stolen from the principal's study, and a very modest twenty-three pre-reform rubles pinched from the somnolent Rafil as the train was approaching Orenburg. She had no problem with this stolen money for two good reasons: first, she really had peeled off very little from a very thick wad; and second, she felt she had earned every kopek of it in her four days on the train.

Rafil did not notice the theft and was keenly disappointed when, twenty-four hours later, his young protégée failed to return to carriage number seven to make the return journey to Kazakhstan with him as she had promised.

With a slight self-deprecating smile for having so recently been such a naive little fool, Jasia related to Tanya how she had dampened a gray railway towel in one of the washbasins in the Kazan station public toilets, dumbfounded the Asian women thronging that malodorous place by stripping herself stark naked in front of them, and washed herself from head to toe. She then drew from the checkered bag a white blouse with a frilly collar, double-wrapped in newspaper, that she had long been keeping for just this moment, changed into it, and, tossing the towel into the rusty wire basket for toilet paper, went out to conquer Moscow, her bridgehead being the immediately adjacent and justly notorious Kazan Square, abutting three railway terminuses.

The checkered bag further contained two pairs of knickers, a blue blouse in need of washing, a notebook with some poems she had copied down, and a set of postcards of famous actors. She was hard, she was streetwise, and she was, in all honesty, naive beyond belief: She wanted to be a film star.

Everything pointed toward Jasia's becoming a full-time prostitute, but that is not what happened.

During her first two years in Moscow she scored some notable successes, obtaining a temporary residence permit and temporary accommodation in a storeroom at the school where she had a cleaning job. From time to time Malinin, the local policeman, would drop by, for it was through the good offices of this florid-faced middle-aged protector that all these temporary blessings came her way. Malinin's visits were perfunctory, not unduly burdensome for Jasia, and indeed no big deal for Malinin himself; but he was an officer deeply committed to bribe-taking and extortion, and since Jasia had nothing else for him to extort, he had to rest content with what she offered.

It was in that very storeroom and on that very sports mat, which doubled so satisfactorily as a bed, that Jasia told Tanya her story. Tanya took it all to heart, experiencing in the process a powerful emotion compounded of pity, envy, and shame at being so irredeemably well off herself. Jasia, having wryly related everything she could remember about herself in merciless detail, unexpectedly gained an outsider's perspective on all she had been through and was filled with such loathing for it that she never told the truth to another living soul. She invented herself a new past, complete with aristocratic grandmother, a family estate in Poland, and relatives living in France (who will indeed be appearing like a deus ex machina at just the right moment).

Apart from Jasia's storeroom, the school had a unit of accommodation occupied by Taisia Sergeevna, a war widow who taught Russian language and literature. She disapproved of Malinin's visits, but this did not prevent her from delegating Jasia to babysit with her young children and do her laundry. In return for these neighborly services, Jasia was given access to her bookcase and excused attendance at literature classes, which Taisia Sergeevna preferred her to spend babysitting.

The gamut of her duties performed, Jasia would lie down on the mat with its smell of sweaty bodies and set about memorizing Krylov's fables, which in every age has been a prerequisite for admission to any Russian drama school. Or she would recite Shakespeare, from the first volume of his collected works to the last, acting out all the female roles in a tragic whisper, from Prospero's daughter, Miranda, to Marina, daughter of Pericles.

The teachers of the evening school were worn out well before dinnertime from teaching the younger daytime brothers and sisters of their evening pupils. These consequently were let off lightly with their lessons. In any case, half the class were the occupants of a nearby police dormitory, and the weary young men dozed peacefully in the ill-lit classroom, achieved grades of *satisfactory,* and went on to continue their studies successfully before becoming lawyers or something in the Communist Party. Jasia was the only person in the class whose desk fitted her; the others got stuck in the wooden frameworks designed for the torture of small children.

Tanya, abrupt, expansive, moved about noisily with the untrained willfulness of a young colt. When she sat down at her desk, she shifted it in a way that made Jasia with her light little head jump. Jasia got up from her desk by raising the lid soundlessly and making a slinky movement with her hips. As she advanced up the narrow aisle toward the blackboard, the lower part of her body seemed to lag slightly behind the upper part; the foot that was behind dragged slightly, the toe motionless for a moment, and the movement of her knees suggested they were pushing against the heavy fabric of a long evening dress rather than her tatty frock. There was something special about the curve of her loins, and every part of her moved separately, yet all of them taken together, from the slight thrusting of her breasts to the sinuousness of her hips and a particular rolling movement of her ankles, were, in concert, not the practiced techniques of a flirt but the feminine music of a body that demanded attention and admiration. Police Constable Churilin, a mature thirty years of age with dark pockmarks on his jowly face, shook his head at her retreating form and muttered, "Get a load of that! I don't believe it!"

There was no telling whether his muttering denoted disgust or delight, but Jasia's demeanor was in any case so aloof that Churilin's muttering went as far as any of the policemen attempted to take it.

On her way home, Tanya would try to imitate Jasia's walk in the darkness of the nighttime park, to play that music with her own knees, hips, and shoulders. She craned her neck, dragged her feet, and rolled her hips. She thought perhaps it was her height that kept her from being as pleasingly sinuous as Jasia, and tried slouching. She is elfin, Tanya thought and, wearying of her balletic ambulatory exercises, marched off back home, striding out with her long legs, swinging her arms unevenly to the right and left, raising her head high, and tossing back her hair, to which the evening mist attempted to cling. Robert, who often came out to the park at this hour of the evening to see her home, recognized her gait in the distance, her whole personality so fully expressed in the gawky movements, and smiled at the strength and ungainliness of his daughter, who was already half a head taller than her father.

They both loved the park at evening and cherished their laconic mutual understanding, a secret affirmation of a tacit conspiracy against Sonechka. Robert from an inborn sense of his own superiority, and Tanya from her youth and heredity, both laid claim to an agreeable intellectual elitism, leaving Sonechka her humble round of cleaning and cooking.

It never entered Sonechka's head to feel ill-used or to envy her Olympians. She washed the dishes and scoured the saucepans, cooking their meals with passionate commitment, checking against the recipes she had copied in blotchy violet ink from her sister's prerevolutionary cookbook. She boiled up vats of laundry, blued, and starched, while Robert would sometimes peer attentively round her broad back at the soap flakes or the semolina, the bluing or the kidney beans, and with characteristic perspicacity take in the truly aesthetic quality, the sublime meaningfulness and beauty of Sonechka's domestic creativity. *Go to the ant, thou sluggard,* he thought in passing and, closing the door of his heated terrace behind him, returned to the realm of his austere paper, white lead paint, and the few other elements he allowed in his severe études.

Tanya took no interest whatsoever in her mother's culinary activities, since she was now floating in a cloudland of infatuation. Waking of a morn, she would lie long with her eyes closed, imagining Jasia, or herself and Jasia, in some agreeable fantasy: galloping on white horses over a young green meadow or sailing in a yacht in, perhaps, the Mediterranean.

Her uninhibited and even slightly peremptory treatment of her sacred reproductive apparatus led her instincts to stray a little and, while she shared lots of fun with well-built boys, her heart cried out for some higher communion, a conjoining, a fusion, a reciprocity beyond all bounds. Her heart chose Jasia, and she strained all her mental resources to give her choice a rational foundation, an explanation in logic.

"Oh, Mother, she looks weak and as if she might blow away in the wind, but actually she is incredibly strong!" Tanya enthused, telling her mother about her new friend, the cruel life in the orphanage, the times she had run away, the times she had been beaten, the victories she had gained. Jasia's natural caution had led her to omit a number of things from what she told Tanya: her mother's exile, the cheap trading of her body in childhood, her ingrained penchant for petty thieving.

Sonechka, however, heard enough even before meeting her to respond to the suffering of a child and to be able to guess at what remained hidden from Tanya. *That poor, poor little girl,* she thought. *She could just as easily have been our Tanya.* The things that went on!

She thought back over the many occasions when God had saved them from an early death: the time Robert had been thrown out of the local train in Alexandrovo; the time a beam gave way at her workplace and half the room that she had left only a moment before became a pile of dark old-brick rubble; the time she nearly died of peritonitis on a hospital operating table. "Poor little girl," Sonechka sighed, and the little girl she had yet to meet took on the features of Tanya.

RIGHT UP until the New Year, Tanya was unable to persuade Jasia to visit her home. She just shrugged her shoulders and kept declining the invitation without volunteering any reason for her persistent refusal.

The reason was, however, that Jasia had long had a generalized but keen sense of anticipation of a new and highly promising territory and, like a commander before a crucial battle, she was meticulously making secret preparations for a visit on which she pinned great, if indefinite, hopes.

In the drapery shop at Nikitsky Gate she bought a piece of taffeta that was cold to the touch but fiery to the eye, a scalded color, and late at night she hand-sewed with tiny stitches a very fine dress. She sewed alone, silently, mindfully, prayerfully, like an expectant mother half afraid of attracting the evil eye and endangering her baby's birth by being too hasty in sewing clothes for it.

She came in the hour before midnight on the thirty-first of December to a set table at which there sat the Barbizonian, the poet, and a film director with a beaky nose and froglike mouth. Even before she had time to take a proper look at their imposing faces she was exultant, conscious of having hit the bull's-eye of her long-anticipated target. These grown-up men of means were just who she needed if she was to take off, to fly, to achieve full and final victory.

She threw Tanya a glance both loving and grateful, and rouged Tanya glowed back at her, pink and happy. She had been on tenterhooks, wondering whether Jasia would come, and now she was as proud of Jasia's beauty as if she had imagined and painted it herself.

Jasia's dress rustled loudly and silkily, and her light brown hair lay heavy, as if molded from light-colored resin, and clung prostrate to her shoulders just like Marina Vlady's in *The Sorceress,* a film much in vogue that year. Her neckline plunged and her little nanny-goat breasts, squeezed together, created an inviting cleavage pointing downward. Her waist was naturally narrow and further constrained into the shape of an hourglass. Her ankles were slim beneath firm calves, while the slenderness of her wrists was brought out by a slight chubbiness of the forearm. Hers was not the vulgar figure of some guitar-shaped broad; she had the petite glassy charm of a wineglass, as Robert fleetingly noted.

Only Sonechka was a little disappointed. Her heart having already gone out to Tanya's friend for all she had suffered, she was not expecting to see, in place of a woebegone Cinderella, this tastefully attired beauty with eyeliner, radiating all the sweetness of a fair-skinned Slav maiden.

Jasia responded to questions monosyllabically, her eyes lowered until she fluttered eyelashes heavy with mascara to implore—just that, to implore—in the resigned and regal tones of her late mother, "Thank you, but no"; "You are very kind; yes, please." In her brief responses a sensitive ear could detect the Polish accent, a blurring of the boundaries between *l* and *w*.

Sonechka, touched, kept putting more food on Jasia's plate. Jasia would sigh and decline it, but then nonetheless manage to put away a leg of duck, another serving of galantine, some crab salad.

"I really can't eat any more, you are too kind," she simpered, almost piteously, and still Sonechka's heart was brimming with sympathy for the waif, the poor little girl from the orphanage. Lord, how could such things have been possible?

Alexander Ivanovich, the Barbizonian, was by this time singing Italian arias in a languid churchy voice. Gavrilin, well oiled, performed a killingly funny imitation of a dog looking for a flea. Rolling his eyes, he was snarling one moment, growling blissfully the next, shoving his head under his armpit, and making everyone laugh until the tears rolled down their cheeks. Robert smiled, his eyes and his newly crowned teeth gleaming simultaneously.

Sometime after two in the morning, Tanya's zealous admirer Alyosha Petersburg, of a future celebrity he was already trying on for size, turned up bearing a little packet of gray herbal matter: he was one of the first devotees of Central Asian grass in the city on the Neva. Without ado, Alyosha peeled the case from his guitar and sang a few songs, wittily knowing or comic, while furiously grimacing and contorting his mouth like a clown at the fairground.

Alyosha was in love with Tanya, Tanya was in love with Jasia, and Jasia on this New Year's Day fell in love with Tanya's home. Toward morning, when the guests had left and the girls had helped to clear the table, Sonechka gave Jasia the empty corner room to sleep in, where she was found later that day by Robert who came in looking for a roll of gray paper.

All was quiet in the house. Having tidied up after her guests, Sonechka had gone off to visit her sister. Tanya was asleep in her room, while Jasia, awakened by the creaking of the door, opened her eyes and for a time observed Robert rummaging around behind the cupboard, cursing softly. She stared at his back, trying to remember which Western film star it was he reminded her of. She had seen a face just like that, and the same silvery crew-cut in *Przeglad Artystyczny,* a Polish magazine she had studied from cover to cover. She could not for the life of her remember his name, but she was fairly sure he had even worn the same shirt, with a simple large checked pattern.

She sat up in bed. The bed creaked. Robert turned round. Out of Sonechka's enormous nightdress there peeped a little fair-haired head on a short neck. The girl ran her tongue over her lips, smiled, and tugged at the sleeves of the nightdress, which slipped down easily. With a movement of her leg she pushed the blanket onto the floor and stood up to her full height; the huge shirt slid off easily. With little childish steps she ran over the cold stained floor to Robert, took from him the roll of paper he had finally managed to locate, and, as if replacing it with herself, was in his arms.

"Okay, just a quickie," the businesslike nymph said, without the least flirtatiousness, in the tone of voice she customarily used to her protector, Police Constable Malinin. But with him she knew exactly why she had to do what she had to do, while here there was no self-interest or calculation. She could not have explained it. Out of gratitude to this house, perhaps . . . and then, he really did look like that film star. . . . Peter O'Toole, was it?

The possibility that a man could refuse a proffered favor, this token of attention and gratitude, was something of which she simply had no knowledge. Petite, her body looking as if it had been turned on a lathe from warm light-colored wood, she stretched her inviting little face up toward him.

Robert retreated slightly in the direction of the cupboard, said sternly, "Back under that blanket straight away, you'll catch cold!" and left the room without his roll of paper. Never before had he seen a body with such a lunar metallic gleam.

Jasia pulled the still-warm blanket over herself and was asleep again in a trice. She slept luxuriously, aware even in sleep of the sweetness of this family dream in a family home; Sonechka's nightdress, which she did not put back on, rested beneath her cheek and smelt heavenly.

Meanwhile the stricken Robert was pacing around in the next room, hunched and twisting his head from side to side. The early twilight of a year that had only just begun peeped in at the window, and there was no sign of Sonechka, and still Tanya did not come down the creaking staircase. He cautiously opened the door of the spare room and went quietly over to the bed. The girl was almost completely covered; only the light brown hair of the back of her head was showing. He pushed his dry hands under the warm snowdrift of the blanket. Their intrusion did not disturb Jasia's sleep or spoil a thing. She opened up toward his arms, and yet another final life began for Robert.

A GOOD, honest, New Year's frost strengthened toward evening. On the table the despoiled leftovers of last year's banquet were going stale. Robert had lost his appetite. Yesterday's food turned his stomach, and he thought how wise his forebears had been to burn the food left over from the Passover supper and not allow it to be thus degraded.

Sonechka was pointlessly stirring her tea (there was no sugar in it), and had it on the tip of her tongue to say something important to her husband, but was unable to find the right words.

Robert was looking thoughtful, listening to the muffled reverberations of a joyous hubbub in the marrow of his now-old bones and trying to remember when it was he had felt it before. Where had he felt this strange sensation? Perhaps there had been something of the kind in his boyhood, when he had capered to the point of exhaustion in the heavy waters of the Dnieper before climbing out onto the crunching, unbelievably hot sand, burrowing into it, and basking in a sandy Turkish bath until he was warmed right through to his bones.

And there was about it something akin to a moment of illumination when he had gone out for a pee one night. Avigdor's little Rubim—who, with the passing of the years, had been transformed into Robert Victorovich—had thrown back his head and seen all the stars in the universe looking down at him from the sky with live inquisitive eyes, and a quiet pealing of bells filled the firmament like the folds of a cloak, and he, a small boy, seemed to hold in his hands all the bellpulls of the world, each with a little bell at the end of it which rang piercingly, and he himself was the heart of this gigantic musical box, with the whole world obedient to the beating of his heart, to his every sigh, to the pounding of his blood and the coursing of his warm pee. He lowered the hem of his nightshirt again, raised his hands slowly upward as if conducting the celestial concert, and the music flooded through him, a wave of sweetness permeating his very bones. . . .

How completely he had forgotten that music, and it was only the memory of it that had survived all these years.

"Robert, we should let that girl live here with us in our home. The corner room is empty," Sonechka said quietly, the teaspoon motionless in her glass of tea.

Robert glanced at his wife in astonishment and said what he always did say when the matter in hand concerned him little. "If you think that is the right thing to do, Sonechka. Do as you think right."

He got up and went to his room.

JASIA MOVED into Sonechka's home. She had a pleasant appearance, said little, and Sonechka enjoyed having her there, as well as being secretly proud of having taken in an orphan. It was a mitzvah, a good deed, and for Sonechka, who was becoming ever more aware as the years went by of her Jewish identity, her good deed was both a joy and a pleasurable fulfillment of her duty.

She had again become mindful of the need to observe the Sabbath and felt drawn to the ritually ordered life of her ancestors with its unshakable foundation, the solid heavy-legged table covered by the stiff ceremonial tablecloth, with candles and homemade bread, and the family sacrament celebrated on the eve of the Sabbath in every Jewish home. Uprooted from the old ways, she put all her unrecognized religious fervor into fussing over the cooking of the meat with onions and carrots, into the crisp white napkins and the setting of the table, where the condiment set, the stands for the knives, and the side plates were correctly placed to the right or left as decreed by a quite different, more recent, middle-class canon. But Sonechka did not think about all that.

These last few relatively prosperous years, she had suddenly begun to feel that her family was too small and was secretly grieved that it had not been her lot to give birth to many children, as was the custom of her race. She bought more and more nonmatching Kuznetsov sauce boats and English bone china plates at bargain prices from the antique shop on Lower Maslovka, as if making preparations for the large family that her daughter Tanya would have.

Sonechka's religion, like the Old Testament itself, had three components, only instead of the Torah, Nevi'im, and Ketuvim hers were the first, second, and third courses of dinner.

Jasia's presence at mealtimes gave Sonechka the illusion that her family had increased, and she did grace the table. She comported herself so naturally and sweetly, seeming to eat little but with an insatiable appetite until she was comically exhausted, because there was no rooting out the memory of the hunger endemic in her childhood. Leaning back in her chair she would groan quietly,

"Oh, Aunt Sonya! That was so good. . . . I've made a pig of myself again. . . ."

And Sonechka would smile blissfully and bring out the shallow glass dishes of stewed fruit.

TWO MONTHS went by, and Jasia's catlike adaptability and innate tact enabled her to establish herself not merely as the lodger in the corner room but almost as a member of the family.

Early in the morning she would rush off to swab the uneven school corridors and slushy toilets; and in the evenings she would go back, together with Tanya, to the same school as a pupil. They did not always make it to school, playing truant from the uninspired lessons of teachers who could hardly keep awake themselves. The relationship between her and Tanya resolved itself into sisterliness. Moreover, with Jasia's moving in, Tanya, although younger in years, imperceptibly took on the role of elder sister, and her love for Jasia became less rapturous and intense.

The girls would often take themselves off up to Tanya's chamber. Tanya, adopting the lotus posture, would play her flute badly while Jasia, curled up at her feet, would whisper Alexander Ostrovsky's now sadly dated dramas of the merchant class with a slight lisp in preparation for drama school.

Sonechka was touched by Jasia's enthusiasm for reading and also supposed that Tanya was thereby becoming conversant with high culture. She was mistaken.

When the girls talked at all, Jasia mainly contented herself with polite listening. She listened to Tanya relating her amorous escapades without great interest or empathy. Her friend's enthusiasm left her cold, though Tanya mistakenly put Jasia's indifference down to the insignificance of her own experience when compared with the extravagant sexual adventures of her friend. It never entered her head that, for the first time since the age of twelve, Jasia was at last free from having to allow "their revolting thingies" into her wholly unresponsive body.

FOR ROBERT, Jasia's presence was a torment. The episode in the corner room in the early twilight of the first day of the year had the quality of a recurring hallucination, as if he had accidentally happened in on someone else's dream. Now he allowed Jasia only into his peripheral vision, his eye lingering stealthily on her tranquil whiteness while he melted into jelly on the fires of youthful lust. He never allowed himself to make even the slightest pass, but not because he was held back by small-minded moral considerations. His lust belonged to him but this woman did not; moreover, now placed through Sonechka's exertions in a taboo situation alongside his daughter, she never would.

He gazed for hours at the snow outside the window, its whiteness subtly changing with the light and humidity. He stared at the almost vitreous white side of a porcelain jug, at the scraps of flocked drawing paper on the table, and the matte white plaster casts of ancient reliefs with the barely discernible physical presence of the letters of an ancient script in them.

As the second month drew to its close he started painting again, twenty years after his prison camp exercises, when he had whimsically copied utterly boring kitsch.

Now these were totally white still lifes, in which Robert gave order to complex thinking on the nature of whiteness, its shape and texture, and this subjugated the purely painterly aspects. The syllables and words of his meditations were porcelain sugar bowls, white tea towels, milk in a glass jar, and all the other things which, to a practical person, seem merely white, but which to Robert seemed a tortuous path in the search for the ideal and the occult.

One day when winter was already on the wane and the snowy splendors of Petrovsky Park had faded and shrunk, the two of them came out in the early morning onto the veranda at the same time: Robert with two canvas stretching frames and a roll of kraft paper, and Jasia with a red tote bag with two of her bulky evening-school books.

"Hold this a moment, please," he said, shoving the roll of paper into her arms with a vague sense that something of the kind had occurred somewhere before.

Jasia hurriedly clutched the roll to herself while he got a better grip on the frames.

"Perhaps I can carry something for you," the girl offered, without looking up.

He made no reply, she raised her head, and for the first time since they had been living together under the same roof his keen gaze plunged deep into her unresisting eyes. He nodded and she accordingly lowered her head in its downy white headscarf and followed him, stepping magically with her childish rubber boots in his footprints.

He did not once turn round on the way, which was not far.

Thus, one behind the other, they arrived at the entrance to a block of flats in whose long corridors, behind door after door, rather well-paid socialist art was being created in a diligent and workmanlike fashion, cumbersome by-products of the bald intellectual Titan, and were periodically brought out into the dreary corridors.

His back pressed against the granite pedestal of the inevitable statue of the Founder of the World's First Socialist State, he awkwardly held the door open with one foot to let Jasia go in. The instant the door slammed shut he felt the powerful beating of his heart reverberating, only not in his chest but from the pit of his stomach. The pounding of his heart rose in him like the sun rising from the horizon, the roar of the sea filled his head, his temples, extended even to the tips of his fingers. He put down the frames and took the roll of paper from Jasia's arms, recollecting as he did so where that last time had been.

He put his hand on the by now very damp nap of her headscarf and smiled; Jasia, never slow on the uptake, was already undoing the huge buttons on her homemade overcoat, tailored in the course of many evenings by her and Sonechka from an old tartan blanket. That year large buttons were much in vogue. Both Jasia's skirt and her blouse were sewn with swarms of brown and white buttons and, having cast the coat aside, she set solemnly and thoughtfully about the task of pulling them one after the other from their neatly finished buttonholes.

The pounding of his heart, like a tocsin pealing from a belfry, drove the blood into every nook of every last capillary but then abruptly ceased, and in a dazzling silence she sat down in the broken armchair and tucked her firm little legs under herself. Then she set loose her hair, which had been gathered up on her head with a band, and sat waiting for him to emerge from his state of paralysis and help himself to the slight thing she did not begrudge him.

FROM THAT day on, Jasia ran over to the studio almost daily. Their affair was ardent and strangely wordless. Usually she would come, sit in the now-traditional armchair, and let her hair down. He would put the kettle on the gas ring, brew up some strong tea, dissolve five lumps of sugar in a white enamel mug—her years in the orphanage meant that even now she could not get enough of sweet things—and set the white porcelain sugar bowl before her, because she liked not only to dissolve sugar in her tea but also to crunch sugar lumps in her mouth as she was sipping it.

For a long, long time he watched her slowly sipping her syrup, and he analyzed the whiteness of her all the while, which shone more vividly before him than the colors of the rainbow against the matte whitewashed background of a blank wall. The gleaming enamel of the kitchen mug in her pink but ultimately white hand, the chunks of loaf sugar with their crystalline sections, and the watery white sky outside the window: All this could be meaningfully derived, like a chromatic scale, from her little face, which was the color of egg white, a miracle of whiteness, warmth, and vitality. That face was the keynote from which everything else developed and grew, playing and singing the secret of the whiteness of dead things and the whiteness of things alive.

He delighted in the look of her, and she could sense that and was elevated by his gaze and melted with a glow of feminine pride, reveling in her unequivocal power, knowing that she had only to say to him that shamelessly childish "Fancy a quickie?" for him to nod and take her to the couch; and if she did not say it, there he would be, goggling at her, the poor sad idiot, so weird, so special, and so madly in love with her.

"Madly in love" she repeated to herself, a proud smile barely playing on her lips, and he was aware of her slightly foolish sense of triumph, but carried right on gazing at her until she said, "That's enough . . . I have to go."

He never asked her any questions, and she never volunteered any information about herself. There was no need. That he was attracted to her beyond all reason, and that she unfalteringly desired to be near him, needed no confirmation in words. When she was with him she felt she had already achieved all her ambitions and was rich, beautiful, and free—without any need for drama school.

In mid-April he started painting her portrait. First one, with a teapot and white flowers, then another. A whole succession of white faces began to form, one overshadowed by the next, only to reemerge later; and by some curious optical illusion each face was associated with all the others.

Robert painted rapidly, and although she was beside him, and that was important, he was not painting from life. It was as if he had absorbed her into himself and had now only to look inside the secret place where she was stored. He worked all the hours of daylight, spending ever more time in the studio. He had always loved slipping away to the studio very early in the morning, and now he often stayed there overnight.

At just this moment, when the gravitational pull of his home had weakened and the center of Robert's life was increasingly shifting toward his studio, which gently and bawdishly admitted his taciturn lover, thunderclouds gathered over his home.

The whole of their little suburb was designated for "slum clearance." Rumors, which had been persistently circulating for many years without being taken seriously, resolved themselves one fine day into a mean little slip of paper with a smudged rubber stamp ordering the demolition of their house and the resettlement of its occupants. The letter was not delivered by hand, as it should have been, but sent by mail. It was the middle of the day, after she had finished the morning's housework, before Sonechka noticed the document of ill omen in the letterbox.

Clutching it in her hand, Sonechka ran to the studio to tell her husband. She did not usually go there, observing an unspoken prohibition. Robert was alone, working. She sat down in the armchair, which protested beneath her. Her husband sat opposite in silence. Sonechka looked long at the canvases, with their pallid white-eyed women, and recognized the identity of the original snow queen. And Robert knew she knew. They said nothing to each other.

Sonechka sat there in silence for a time, then put the sad notification on the table and left. As she came out of the building she stopped in amazement. It seemed to her that the ground should be covered in snow, but all around the young shoots of May were billowing and curling in many shades of green, and even the long trilling of the trams seemed tinged with green.

She walked back toward her home, her beloved, happy home which for some reason was to be reduced to a pile of logs, and the tears flowed down her flabby, wrinkled cheeks, and she whispered with suddenly parched lips, "This was all supposed to happen long, long ago. . . . I always knew it was too much to hope for. . . . It was all an impossibility. . . ."

In the ten minutes it took her to walk home, she recognized that her seventeen years of happy marriage were over and that nothing belonged to her: not Robert (when had he ever belonged to anyone?); not Tanya, who was quite, quite different from her, perhaps taking after her father or her grandfather, but at all events not of her shy breed; and not the house, whose sighing and groaning she identified with in the night, as the old become aware of their bodies growing ever more alien with the passing years. How right it is that he will have someone so young and beautiful at his side, so soft and clever, and as exceptional and outstanding as he is himself; and how well it has all turned out that life should bring about a miracle in his old age that has made him turn again to the most important thing about him, his painting, thought Sonechka.

Completely devastated, weightless, and with a transparent ringing in her ears, she entered her home, went to the bookcase, took down the first book that came to hand, and, lying down, opened it in the middle. It was Pushkin's *The Peasant Mistress.* Liza had just come down for dinner, powdered white to the eyeballs, her eyelashes and eyebrows even more raven black than those of Miss Jackson. Alexey Berestov was being absent-minded and lost in thought, and from those pages there shone out onto Sonechka the quiet joy of literary perfection, the embodiment of true nobility of spirit.

THE RITES of departure took many days. Sonechka tied up bundles, forced saucepans and clothing into cardboard boxes intended for cigarettes, and went around in a curious state of exaltation: She felt she was burying her past life, that each of the boxes had packed in it the minutes, days, nights, and years of her greatest happiness. She stroked the cardboard coffins tenderly.

Tanya wandered abstractedly about the house without bothering to get herself dressed, bumping into furniture that had been shifted from where it usually stood and appeared to be endowed with mobility. Cupboard doors would unexpectedly open of their own accord, and chairs tripped her up. She did not help her mother. Focused only on her own sensations, she was completely overcome by distaste for what was going on in her house.

One further circumstance was greatly depressing her. An inward-looking girl, Tanya was still at that time relatively inarticulate. She had emptied out for Jasia's benefit all the complexities of her disorderly heart, and Jasia with her talent for intelligent listening had proved a unique confidante, receiving her extremely superficial experiences with a benign neutrality. This was so propitious for Tanya that in the course of their tête-à-têtes, which were to all intents and purposes monologues, she learned to formulate her thoughts and conjure up imagery as she went along, which gave her a great sense of satisfaction.

Her other friends, laugh-a-minute Alyosha, with his talent for turning everything upside down, and Vladimir, with his cosmic talent, omnivorous memory, and information on every topic in the world neatly filed away with its assistance, forced her to enter their own seductive worlds. Only Jasia gave her a chance to think for herself, to reason out loud, tentatively picking the little things from which a person arbitrarily pieces together that first outline from which the whole subsequent pattern of a life will follow. This was the source of Tanya's feeling of real intimacy with Jasia and of her vague sense of gratitude.

During one of Tanya's rare moments of respite from her habitual self-absorption, she noticed that Jasia did appear to have a life of her own. However, all her efforts to probe the mysterious daytime period when Jasia was neither at school nor at home foundered on affectionate but evasive silence or bland replies. The first explanation to occur to her, a secret love affair, faced Tanya with the crucial question of whom it could be with.

The question was answered in the most casual way imaginable. Tanya happened upon Jasia and her father by the metro station and was the unseen witness of a quite improbable scene: They were walking along, eating ice cream and laughing. The ice cream was dripping, and Robert wiped a gooey white splodge from Jasia's cheek with a movement of his fingers that made Tanya, a considerable expert on touches, shudder with a previously unknown sensation: jealousy.

Neither her mother's interests as a woman nor any moral considerations gave Tanya a moment's pause. The one thing that really got her goat was that the romance had been kept from her in such an unprincipled manner. Otherwise, it was of no concern to her whatsoever.

Tanya made a scene. Jasia, long ago inured to the prospect of eventual discovery, packed her bags and slipped out via the carved veranda, leaving Tanya bereft and uncomprehending, for she had supposed her friendship with Jasia far more important than any affair. Robert was in the process of dismantling a bookcase he had once put up and did not even register Jasia's absence right away.

THE DAY finally arrived for their belongings to be carried out. In the bright light of a summer's day, the scuffed furniture, so comfortable and familiar, bought in a feverish spate of bargain-hunting at Preobrazhensky Market, suddenly seemed positively beggarly. Everything was loaded into a covered truck and driven off to the dismal suburb of Likhobory, to an out-of-the-way three-room flat where everything was humiliatingly cut-price, from the wretchedly thin walls and tiny kitchen, in which Sonechka had barely room to turn, to the bathroom, which hadn't been properly finished.

With help from Gavrilin, Robert arranged the furniture. Each item resisted obstinately, reluctant to fit the space allotted it: invariably some corner stuck out, invariably a few extra centimeters were needed. Robert had to rip the pediment from a single wardrobe which was really no size at all in order to squeeze it into its wall space. Tanya was almost in tears over the metal-bound trunk with its bowed lid, which promised to end up completely homeless.

Sonechka decided Tanya's divan and Jasia's bed should go in the room at the end of the corridor and named it the girls' room.

Jasia, invited by Sonechka to help with the move, was on her guard. She really could not work out what was going on, and to tell the truth she was not all that bothered. This was not the house she had coveted, and in any case she was fairly sure she had a firm grip on what really mattered.

Sonechka produced a large brown carryall from somewhere and drew out of it a magic tablecloth, which spread itself with napkins, rissoles, and ice-cold summer soup in a vacuum flask.

As if nothing had changed, Sonechka continued to serve Jasia nicely at table, and Jasia smiled back gratefully. She found Sonechka amazing. "Or perhaps she's just very cunning," she told herself, not entirely spontaneously, knowing in her heart that this was not the case.

In the middle of the meal, Tanya suddenly threw up her arms and, with her hair flying everywhere and her breasts heaving, started sobbing before bursting out in guffaws of hysterical laughter. When the fit abruptly ceased she announced, still wet with tears and the water that had been thrown over her, that she was leaving for Petersburg without delay.

Jasia took her to the newly designated girls' room, although both its girls were now well into unambiguous womanhood. They climbed into Jasia's bed. Jasia took the hairband from the abundant mane crowning her head, and they were reconciled completely, stroking each other's hair.

Tanya did not, however, change her mind and returned that very evening to her skunked bard.

Robert went back to the Maslovka studio with Gavrilin and Jasia, and, having seen off her nearest and dearest, Sonechka was left to spend her first evening in Likhobory alone. She reflected sorrowfully on the way her life had come apart at the seams, on how suddenly loneliness had befallen her, and then lay down on the unmade divan in the communicating room. At random she took a volume of Schiller from a parcel tied with string and read until morning. Not many people could have read *Wallenstein* without falling asleep, but Sonechka voluntarily abandoned herself to the literary trance in which her youth had passed.

SONECHKA WAS wrong. Robert had no intention of abandoning her. He came out to Likhobory every Saturday without fail, and once or twice during the week as well. He would bring quiet little Jasia with him, and while she busied herself in the girls' room to the accompaniment of silken rustling, sorting through her own and Tanya's frocks and papers, Robert replaced the narrow windowsills with wider ones, strengthened weak shelving, cut his old bookcase up to make two, and hung the apartment with Tanya's portraits.

They had supper in the middle room, which devolved to Sonechka. They talked a bit about Tanya, who had been in Petersburg for a month and kept putting off her return to grisly Likhobory.

It was not late when they went to their rooms to sleep: Jasia to the girls' room, Robert to the separate room allocated to him by the front door, while Sonechka flopped down heavily on the divan and, drifting off to sleep, rejoiced at the thought that Robert was there, on the other side of the thin partition wall, and that clever pretty little Jasia was to her left. It was just a shame that Tanechka was not home. . . .

In the morning Sonechka put yesterday's salad, the leftover rissoles, and buckwheat porridge into jars, covered the tops and tied them tightly, put everything in the brown carryall, and handed it over to Jasia.

"Thank you, Aunt Sonya," Jasia said, looking down as she thanked her.

When Alexander Ivanovich had a birthday party, Robert

told Sonechka to come round to the studio so they could go together. It was their first joint family outing. Alexander Ivanovich, as celibate as a monk since the day he was born, had never in his life been observed in dalliance with the opposite sex and was, on that basis, suspected by a well-intentioned society of sins considerably more interesting; he was the only person in the entire assembly who accepted their ménage à trois as entirely a matter of course.

The other guests, especially the artistic ladies, salaciously discussed the love triangle in the corners of the room, getting themselves as high as dough in a loaf tin. Ginger-haired Magdalena, slightly dotty at the best of times, was so overcome with anguish and sympathy for Sonechka that she suffered a migraine attack. They need not have bothered: Sonechka was happy that Robert had brought her. She was proud that he was, as she saw it, such a faithful husband to his ugly old wife, and she was openly admiring of Jasia's beauty.

At Alexander Ivanovich's request she acted as hostess for a time, taking the brought-in food round to the guests. Mindful of Jasia's ever delicate stomach, she whispered in her ear, "My dear, I think the stuffed cabbage is a bit—you know. You'd better go easy on it."

Some of the grand ladies were inclined to condemn Sonechka for hypocrisy—she really did seem to be coming much too well out of what should have been a thoroughly disadvantageous situation. Others would have liked to condole with her and to censure Robert, but this was completely impossible for they seemed to be a family unit, a perfectly well-adjusted matrimonial triangle sitting there at the table with Robert in the middle, Sonechka rising half a head taller than him to the right, and Jasia to his left, her whiteness gleaming and a sharp little diamond sparkling on her finger.

It was preposterous to imagine Robert going into a jeweler's shop to buy a diamond ring for his bit on the side, although in fairness it has to be said that Jasia really was just the kind of vulnerable little waif onto whose tiny finger one might well wish to slide a ring and to drape a fashionable cloak over her chilled little shoulders.

Robert gave outsiders—that is to say, friends—no opportunity of siding with one or the other of his spouses or of expressing condolence, censure, or indignation concerning them.

The party started to swing. Gavrilin got a bit the worse for wear and did his impression of a dying swan, then of Lenin, and then for an encore the already familiar dog-looking-for-a-flea. Then they played charades, featuring a specter that did not so much haunt as flounder over Europe in the shape of a kind of six-legged cow comprising three fat ladies with a linen curtain draped over them.

At this point in the festivities everybody remembered Tanya, most ingenious deviser of charades, and the more alert ladies exchanged glances as if thinking, Poor girl!

The poor girl was, however, at this time agreeably installed in a crash pad on Vasilievsky Island with her pal Alyosha. It was the season of midsummer white nights in Petersburg, and Tanya was fearless and inquisitive, ready at the drop of a hat to take any new game seriously. They had no wish at all to split up. In a world of their own they looked about them, and Alyosha found to his surprise that having her on board not only did not cramp his unpredictable lifestyle, it seemed rather to open up additional opportunities for dropping out of the *sovbourgeois system,* as he contemptuously referred to conventional existence.

A few days after Alexander Ivanovich's celebration, Sonechka went to Leningrad to visit her daughter, waited half a day in the little courtyard for her to come home, then sat forty minutes with Tanya and Alyosha at a table piled high with books, records, leftovers, and empty bottles, drank a cup of tea, and returned to Moscow on the evening train after urging her daughter to ring her aunt a bit more often and leaving her some money.

Sonechka did not sleep in the train. She thought on and on about what a lovely life Tanya and her boyfriend were having, how much all the young people around her seemed to be enjoying themselves, and what a pity it was that it was all over for her. But what a joy it was that it had all happened. . . . Her head nodded like an old woman's, in time to the rhythms of the railroad car and in anticipation of the tremor she would develop two decades later.

THEN IT was winter again. The girls should have been in their last year at school but both had dropped out. Tanya spent the whole winter traveling to and fro. She was forever quarreling with Alyosha and going home to Mother, but then she would find Likhobory so utterly depressing that she hastened back again to her beloved Petersburg.

Robert spent the entire winter painting. He lost a lot of weight, but in this new incarnation his expression became less clouded and he treated everybody more kindly. His little concubine lived quietly by his side, rustling her candy wrappers or cheap silks (she was forever making herself dresses of different colors but to the same pattern, stitching busily away with her glinting needle), or looking through Polish magazines.

At that moment, in the Soviet Union under Brezhnev, Poland was all the rage, with its breath of Western freedoms, slightly less heady after their turgid passage through Eastern Europe.

By now Jasia had ceased to conceal her Polish origins and proved to have remembered admirably the language she had spoken with her mother as a child. Robert, along with the more common European languages, also spoke Polish, and this bewitching, lisping, caressing language got them talking together. As once he had to Sonechka, he now told little stories to Jasia, comical, improbable, or frightening incidents that had really happened in his life, although because of a kind of verbal chasteness it was a rather different, bowdlerized version of his life from what Sonechka knew from his tales.

Jasia laughed and cried and exclaimed, "Jesus Maria!" and was proud and delighted, so pleased that she even learned to experience certain agreeable sensations during their lovemaking of whose existence she had previously had no inkling, despite her precocious and protracted commerce with the male sex.

He could not stop gazing at her unblemished neck, her fresh young face, the white down beneath the slender eyebrows, and thought how precious young physical being was, and about that form of perfection which Russia's only genius had said should be "a little silly."

Robert's subjection bore fruit. He had to have a new mezzanine built in his studio to house his canvases. His various white series were completed, but it seemed to him that the big discovery had eluded him. He had turned over the ground he had been allotted and that was no mean achievement, but the actual secret he had seemed so close to revealing had slipped through his fingers, leaving behind a sweet ache at having come so near, and leaving to him also its vicarious representative, whose charms were so devastatingly potent that they vanquished his weariness and old age and the decrepit lassitude of his flesh. Old Robert found his immoderate labors of love no burden at all.

At the end of April, in the middle of a raw nocturnal thaw, Robert squeezed Jasia's shoulders hard and sank his jerking head heavily into the hard pillow.

It was some time before Jasia realized he was dying. With a shriek she leaped out into the corridor, onto which the doors of seven other studios opened. The artists did not live there permanently and few stayed overnight. She tugged desperately at the two nearest door handles before rushing down from the third floor to the telephone in the lodge.

The old woman with her scrawny pigtail let down for the night gave a little squeal when she saw Jasia naked but was pushed aside. "An ambulance, quick, we need an ambulance!" Jasia dialed the number with a shaking hand.

When the medics arrived, Robert was not breathing. He was lying on his stomach, his dark face buried in the pillow. Jasia had been unable to turn him over.

The circumstances of death were obvious. "Cerebral hemorrhage," barked a fat unpleasant doctor who smelled of alcohol and cheap food. He wrote down the telephone number of the mortuary.

The ambulance men went back down the stairs, rattling the now redundant stretcher. "Bit old to die on the job. Quite young she is too," one said.

"So? Better than rotting in hospital," the other responded.

THE LIKHOBORY apartment did not have a telephone. Jasia arrived just as Sonya was about to drink her morning cup of coffee. Sonya's head shook a little, she scooped Jasia up and pressed her to her bosom, and they wept in the corridor for a long time.

Then they went to the studio. The body had already been removed to the mortuary. The unnatural, horrible disorder in the studio after the comings and goings first of the medics and then of the mortuary attendants was quickly put to rights.

Sonya stripped the incriminating sheets from the divan and hid them away in her suitcase. Then they went to ring Tanya in Leningrad, but the neighbors said she and Alyosha had gone off somewhere. Jasia was clinging to Sonya's hand the whole time like a little child. She was an orphan and Sonya was her mother.

The concierge had already managed to relate with great pathos to anyone who would listen every detail of old Robert's scandalous death. From midday on, his artist neighbors came to the studio, bringing whatever they thought appropriate in the circumstances: flowers, vodka, money. . . .

In the process, public opinion formed. The public were sorry about Robert, hated and despised Jasia, but found Sonya considerably less straightforward. They waited to see what she would do, watching her with a curiosity that was, however, entirely sympathetic.

Late that evening, when only close friends remained in the studio, Sonya had a quiet tearless weep before suddenly saying firmly, "Get a good-sized hall. I want these pictures hung where the coffin will be standing." She pointed upstairs to the mezzanine, where the canvases were ranged.

The Barbizonian exchanged glances with Gavrilin. They nodded.

And that is what was done.

The Artists' Trust allocated a hall. They hung the pictures the evening before. There were fifty-two of them. Sonya expertly supervised the hanging. The sun suddenly thrust its way in, painfully bright and harsh, hindering and even interfering in Sonya's work. The canvases gleamed in the sunlight and mirrored it, and Sonya asked for the official-looking flounced cream curtains to be lowered. She completed the hanging, the curtains were raised, the sun stopped being awkward, and everything was found to be positioned just right. Robert could not have done the job better himself.

The following day at around noon the flow of people began. No one could have imagined how many people would flock to Robert's funeral. There came the old and venerable who had earned themselves calluses and medals by churning out official portraits of we shan't say whom; the middle-aged and by now only relatively New Wave; and also those whom respectable members of the Artists' Union would never have allowed through the door: the streetwise bohemian riffraff of the avant-garde.

This posthumous exhibition was not the place for critical debate, and indeed Robert had never felt any need to discuss what he was doing.

In the center of the hall stood the coffin. The face of the deceased was dark and looked somehow melted. Only the hands folded on his breast gleamed with an icy hue—what Robert called the whiteness of dead things.

Jasia, wearing a black silk dress, clung to large, shapeless Sonechka, peeping out from under her arm like a fledgling peeping out from under the wing of a penguin. There was no sign of Tanya: it had been impossible to find her on her junketings in Central Asia, whither she and Alyosha had repaired to graze new pastures.

All the whispering and scandalmongering about the death were left behind in the cloakroom. Here in the hall even those most avid to sniff other people's dirty linen kept their counsel. People came up to Sonya to proffer clumsy condolences, and she, pushing Jasia slightly in front of herself, replied mechanically, "Yes, it's a great misfortune . . . a great misfortune for us both. . . ."

Timler, who had come in the company of his young mistress to bid his old friend farewell, said in a thin, quavering voice, "How beautiful! Leah and Rachel. . . . I never realized Leah was so beautiful."

GOD GRANTED Sonechka a long life in her apartment in Likhobory. Long and lonely.

Tanya gradually drifted into matrimony with Alyosha and

received as his wedding gift the sorcerer czar's standoffish city, where only the proud and self-reliant feel at home. She became a native of Petersburg. Her talents blossomed late. She was already past twenty when it became clear that she had an astonishing talent for music, and drawing, and anything else her scatterbrain took a fancy to. She effortlessly learned French, then Italian and German, and only for some reason had a curious aversion to English. She rushed from one enthusiasm to another until in the mid-1970s—by now separated from Alyosha and having seen off a further two short-term husbands—with a six-month-old son in her arms and a bag slung across her shoulder, she emigrated to Israel. Shortly afterward she obtained an excellent job at the United Nations, owed in no small measure to the world renown of her father.

For several years Jasia lived with Sonechka in the apartment in Likhobory. Sonechka looked after her tenderly, feeling a reverent gratitude to providence for sending such an adornment to her dear husband Robert, such a solace in his old age.

Jasia returned to the idea of entering drama school, but somehow not very seriously. She and Sonechka enjoyed taking up various handicrafts, knitting an unusual patterned sweater for Tanya or taking in sewing to order, but for all that they spent most of their time sitting at home, immoderately drinking black coffee and eating Sonechka's honey cakes. When Jasia's health gradually began to fail, Sonechka sought out two of her aunts and a grandmother in Poland by means of an extensive correspondence kept secret from Jasia. They were not in the least aristocratic, of entirely modest social origins. Kitted out by Sonechka, Jasia emigrated to Poland, where a conventional fairy-tale plot soon ran its course. She married a rich young handsome Frenchman and now lives in Paris not far from the Jardin du Luxembourg, a stone's throw from the house where Robert once had his studio, although of course she does not know this.

The house in Petrovsky Park, bereft of its residents, its windows broken, scarred by minor fires caused by youthful arsonists, stood empty and unused for many years more, affording shelter only to stray dogs and stray people. Once someone was found murdered in it. Then the roof fell in. There was no telling why officialdom had been in such a hurry to resettle its former occupants in the soulless suburbs.

Robert's fifty-two white pictures were dispersed all over the world. Each time one turns up at a contemporary art auction, collectors are put at risk of a heart attack. As for his prewar works, when he was living in Paris, these command fabulous prices. Very few of them have survived, however: only eleven.

A fat whiskery old woman, Sophia Yosifovna still lives in Likhobory on the third floor of a five-story building dating from Khrushchev's crash program of apartment-building. She has no wish to move, either to the Jewish homeland, whose citizenship her daughter enjoys, or to Switzerland, where her daughter is currently employed, or even to the Paris that Robert so loved and to which she is constantly being invited by her other daughter, Jasia. Her health is failing with the apparent onset of Parkinson's disease. Her hands shake when she tries to read.

Each spring she goes over to the Vostryakovo Cemetery and plants white flowers on her husband's grave, but they never take root. In the evenings, she perches a pair of lightweight Swiss spectacles on her nose shaped like a pear and plunges into blissful depths, returning to the shady avenues of Bunin or flinging herself headlong once more into the torrents of spring.

# The Queen of Spades

*For Natasha*

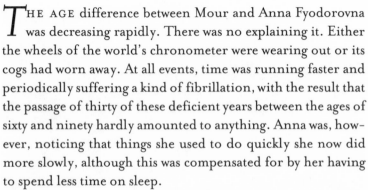

THE AGE difference between Mour and Anna Fyodorovna was decreasing rapidly. There was no explaining it. Either the wheels of the world's chronometer were wearing out or its cogs had worn away. At all events, time was running faster and periodically suffering a kind of fibrillation, with the result that the passage of thirty of these deficient years between the ages of sixty and ninety hardly amounted to anything. Anna was, however, noticing that things she used to do quickly she now did more slowly, although this was compensated for by her having to spend less time on sleep.

Today she had woken early—indeed, in the middle of the night—because of a bad dream. It was not yet four o'clock. A grown man, shrunk to the size of a large doll, was lying in the drawer of her writing desk and complaining, "Mummy, it feels really awful in here." He was her son, and her heart went out to him, but she could do nothing to help.

In reality she didn't have a son, she had a daughter, and she had woken in horror because the dream was more real than reality. For a moment after waking she was convinced she really did have a son she had completely forgotten about. She turned on the light, the delusion was put to flight, and she remembered that the previous evening she had had to search through the drawers of the writing desk for a missing piece of paper. Her ridiculous dream had come about by association with that.

Anna lay in bed a little longer and then decided to get up, the more so since, the day before, she hadn't managed to find the paper she needed.

Now she found it right away. It was the review of a dissertation, written some ten years previously and now suddenly needed again.

The whole house was asleep, and that was a blessing she had been granted—or perhaps stolen. Nobody was making demands of her. Completely out of the blue, two hours entirely her own had materialized, and she wondered what to spend them on: whether to read a book that a patient, a famous philosopher or philologist, had given her long ago or write a letter to her bosom friend in Israel.

She tidied up her sparrow-colored hair and threw an old cardigan over her dressing gown. Casual clothing didn't suit her. In the dressing gown she looked like a dacha landlady from the suburbs. People said she looked best in suits, which she had been wearing since she was a student. Now, in gray or navy blue, she looked every inch the professor that she was.

Anna brewed herself some coffee, opened the book of literary criticism written by her renowned patient, readied a sheet of paper for notes, and put a blue dish of chocolates beside herself, an indulgence not usually allowed. She savored the aroma of the coffee, but Mour appeared in the kitchen before she could take a sip, the wheels of her walker squeaking and her back as straight as a ramrod.

Anna nervously checked the buttons on her cardigan to ensure they were done up correctly, but she never was able to predict exactly what she would be found to have done wrong. If the cardigan was buttoned correctly, you could be sure the stockings she had put on would be deemed hideous, or she would have done her hair all wrong, although it was difficult to see how that was possible when all her life she had worn it in an unvarying braid, coiled like a sausage on her neck. Her morning scolding could, however, relate to anything at all: The curtains might need cleaning, or the variety of coffee might smell revoltingly of boiled cabbage. The only surprising thing was the spontaneity with which Anna always reacted, apologizing, trying to find excuses. Sometimes she even attempted to rebut the complaint, but if so always cursed herself afterward, because it only made things worse. Mour raised even higher the eyebrows that nature had already etched very high, to a point where they disappeared under her pink-blond bangs. She would slowly lower her long eyelids and gaze disapprovingly at Anna with eyes the color of an empty mirror.

On this occasion, Mour wheeled herself to the middle of the kitchen and said nothing. The black kimono hung in empty folds as if there were no body beneath it. Only the bony yellowed hands, with rings that were never removed, and the long neck surmounted by a small head, stuck out puppetlike.

All her life, for as long as she could remember, Anna had rehearsed how she was going to behave with her mother. As a child she used to freeze in front of her door, like a swimmer about to take the plunge. When she reached adulthood she psyched herself up like a boxer before a bout with a stronger opponent, not aiming to win but only to lose with dignity. At this premorning hour her mother had caught her off guard, and, without any time to ready herself, she saw the old lady for the first time as somebody else might see her. An angel stood before her, without sex or age and almost without flesh, a being existing only in the spirit. What kind of spirit that was, Anna knew only too well. Clutching a new book in its hand, the spirit gave utterance.

"What nonsense is scribbled in these memoirs! What imbecile gave me this to read? In 1916 I was still living with my father in Paris. I was a little girl. Caspari gave me the diadem in

1922—I was married to him then—and I lost it at the gaming table in 1924 in Tiflis. There was no more Caspari by that time, I was already with Mikhail. He was a great musician." She gave a sly insinuating giggle and Anna cringed, because there now always followed a stream of utterly vulgar language. Her mother took pleasure in making her cringe. "But he was totally useless when it came to fucking." Mour laughed tenderly. "It really wasn't his day when they were dishing out the dicks. It was there, in Tiflis that I lost the diadem at cards; in the portrait Bakst painted—well, that diadem is completely different, some piece of nonsense, a stage property."

This was the best page of her reminiscences, her famous lovers. Their name was legion. Reams had been written by the best pens in praise of her pale ringlets and the ineffable secrets of her soul, and from the portraits of her that were conserved in museums and private art collections you could have studied the trends of early twentieth-century painting.

She really must have had some mysterious power, because it was not only lovers who would have died for her. Anna was Mour's only daughter, the progeny of a rare virtuous caprice, and she struggled all her life to find an answer to the riddle. What was the source of the power Mour had been given over her father, her younger sisters, men and women, and even those ambivalent creatures who occupied the narrow and tormented margin between the sexes? Apart from ordinary men with completely unsophisticated intentions, she was constantly being fallen in love with by camp homosexuals and by robust lesbians who had struck out from the wearisome path of womanhood. Anna could find no answer to this question but, herself submitting to the unknown force, hastened to humor her mother's latest caprice. And Mour, like a pregnant woman, was constantly wanting something elusive and indefinable. In other words, "Go search to the ends of the earth and bring me back I know not what."

Those who put up any sort of resistance to her superhuman allure simply disappeared from the scene: Anna's husband, long forgotten by all; the husband of her granddaughter, Katya; and the entire family of Mour's last husband. It was as if they had never existed.

"You have coffee." Mour put the mendacious volume down in front of Anna and sniffed the air with her discriminating nose. It smelled good, but she always wanted something different. "I should like a cup of chocolate."

"Cocoa?" Anna readily stood up from the table, without having time even to regret the demise of her little holiday.

"What cocoa? It's muck, that cocoa of yours. Can I really not have even a simple cup of chocolate?"

"I don't think we've got any."

There was no chocolate in the house. Or rather, there was, of course, in the form of masses of chocolates in enormous boxes brought as offerings by patients. There just wasn't any powder or bar chocolate.

"Send Katya or Lenochka. How can we not have any chocolate in the house?" Mour asked incredulously.

"It's four o'clock in the morning," Anna pointed out defensively, but immediately threw up her hands. "We have, for heaven's sake; of course we have."

She pulled an unopened box of chocolates out of the buffet, hastily split open the crackling cellophane, shook out a handful of chocolates, and began to separate the thick soles of the candies from their redundant fillings with a table knife. Mour, who was readying herself for combat, immediately subsided at the sight of such resourcefulness.

"Bring it to my room, will you?"

Carefully protecting her hand with a thick oven glove, Anna warmed the milk in a small dipper. She protected her hands the way a singer protects her throat, and with good reason. Her slender hands had long broad fingers with neatly cut oval nails, their borders stained with iodine. Every day she sank these hands, armed with a manipulator, into the very heart of an eye; carefully made her way around the fibers of tightening muscles, capillaries, Zinn's ligament, the risky Schlemm's canal; and proceeded through many membranes to the ten-layered retina. With those rather coarse fingers she patched and darned and glued together the most delicate of the wonders of the world.

With her mother's little gilded spoon she was skimming the thin milky foam from the thick chocolate when she heard the insistent ringing of Mour's bell, summoning her. Placing the pink cup on a tray, Anna went in to her mother. She was already sitting in front of her card table in the pose of an absinthe drinker. The little bronze bell, its petaled face gazing downward into the faded baize, stood before her.

"Bring me, if you will, just milk, without any of that chocolate of yours."

*One, two, three, four . . . ten.* Anna silently counted out her customary cooling-down period. "You know, Mour, the last of the milk went to make this chocolate."

"Let Katya or Lenochka run out for some."

*One, two, three, four . . . ten. . . .*

"It's half past four in the morning. The shop isn't open yet."

Mour sighed with satisfaction. Her slender brows twitched. Anna got ready to catch the cup. The withered lip with its deep groove, radiating a multiplicity of tiny wrinkles, tightened in a sarcastic smile.

"Well can I get a glass of ordinary tap water in this house?"

"Of course, of course," Anna hastened to assure her. This morning's tantrum seemed not to have happened. Or to have been postponed. *She's getting old, poor dear,* Anna noted to herself.

It was Wednesday. Her surgery at the clinic began at twelve.

She could let Katya lie in today, it was self-service for the grandchildren on Wednesdays. Before she went to the institute, seventeen-year-old Lenochka would take Grisha to the grammar school. Katya would collect him, but Anna needed to be back home no later than half past five. Katya worked from six, teaching English at evening school. She had the food for dinner but needed to buy milk before she left. The bell rang.

*One, two, three, four . . . ten.* "Yes, Mour?"

A thin hand was holding metal-rimmed spectacles elegantly poised, like a lorgnette. "I've remembered. That firm L'Oréal was on the television. A very pretty girl was recommending cream for dry skin. L'Oréal. That is an old firm, I think. Yes, yes. Lilechka ordered their perfume in Paris. She wanted a one-liter bottle, but her poor lover sent a little flacon. He couldn't afford the big one. She made such a scene about it. And Maetsky brought me a liter bottle. Oh, what am I saying? That was L'Origon de Coty, not L'Oréal at all."

This was a new disaster. Mour had proved exceptionally susceptible to advertisements. She wanted to buy everything: a new cream, a new toothpaste, a new super-saucepan.

"Sit down, sit down, do." Mour magnanimously indicated the round piano stool.

Anna sat down. She knew all the circuits, figure-eights, and loops, like those of Grisha's model railway, along which the little engines of the old woman's thoughts would slip and slide, making stops and changing direction at familiar points in her great biography. Now she had started in on perfumes. Next came her friend and rival Lilechka, and then Maetsky—whom she had taken from Lilechka—the famous director. The film career that had made her famous. Her divorce. Parachuting— nobody could believe she was capable of that. Then came the airman, a test pilot, so handsome. Crashed six months later but left wonderful memories. Then there was the architect, terribly famous. They went to Berlin; she created a furor. No, she had never worked for the Cheka or the NKVD; such a silly suggestion. She had slept around, certainly. And how! There were men around in those days, real men. But you and Katya are shaggy-arsed fur stockings.

Forty years ago Anna had wanted to hit her over the head with the furniture. Thirty years ago she would have liked to pull her hair. Now, however, with a feeling of nausea and revulsion in her heart, she let all the boastful soliloquies flow past her, only sad that her morning, which had started so promisingly, had come to nothing.

The telephone rang. It was probably her department. Something must have happened for them to be calling so early. She quickly picked up the receiver.

"Yes, yes, speaking! . . . I don't understand . . . from Johannesburg?"

How had she not recognized that voice immediately, rather high but not at all womanish, the gliding *r*, the pauses as if he had been cured of stammering. Choosing his words. Thirty years . . .

At first everything rushed to her head. She felt flushed, and a moment later broke out in a sweat. She felt ridiculously weak.

"Yes, yes, I recognized your voice. How are you?" What an absurd question, after so many years. "Yes, of course. . . . No, I don't mind at all. Goodbye."

She put down the receiver. The blood had drained from her hand. The pads of her fingertips were weak and sunken as if she had just finished washing a lot of clothes.

"Who was that?"

"Marek." She needed to get up and leave but hadn't the strength.

"Who?"

"My husband."

"Well, what do you know, he's still alive! How old is he?"

"He is five years younger than I," Anna replied curtly.

"Well, what does he want from us?"

"Nothing. He wants to visit me and Katya."

"Nonentity, a complete nonentity. I don't understand how you could—"

"He has a clinic in Johannesburg." Anna tried to deflect the arrow and succeeded.

Mour came to life. "A surgeon? How amusing. Your father was a surgeon. I was involved in a car crash in the Caucasus. If it hadn't been for him I would have lost a leg. He operated brilliantly." Mour sniggered. "I seduced him while I was in plaster."

It was amazing how inexhaustible the details were. Anna had long known that Mour got married for a bet, winning a diamond brooch from a famous friend in the process. This, however, was the first she had heard about the plaster, and she felt a sudden access of dislike for her long-dead father, whom she had fervently loved as a child. He was twenty years older than her mother and the last representative, if you didn't count Anna herself, of a family of German medics. He was devoted to his profession to an extent that was life-threatening, and his survival had been purely fortuitous. In his youth, working as a doctor in a small provincial town, he had performed a trepanation of the skull on a young worker who was dying from a suppurative inflammation of the middle ear. After the Bolshevik Revolution the worker rose to wholly improbable heights, and Dr. Storch, who had forgotten all about him, remained in the grateful patient's memory and was given a kind of safe-conduct pass. At all events, his service as a doctor in the czarist army and subsequently in the anti-Bolshevik Volunteer Army did not prevent him from dying in his own bed, an honest if painful death from cancer.

"Tell me, will you, is this Johannesburg in Germany?"

To some the old woman's thoughts might seem to be jumping about like hungry fleas, but Anna knew her mother had an extraordinary peculiarity of thinking about several things at once, as if she were plaiting a braid of several strands.

"No, it's in Africa, the Republic of South Africa."

"Tell me, will you, the Anglo-Boer War; I remember, I remember. . . . It was so amusing. . . . Well, don't forget to buy me that cream." She ran her frail fingers over her skin, which yielded like an old apricot.

In earlier times Mour had been interested in events and people as the setting for her own life and as extras in her play, but with the years all that was secondary had faded, and now only she and her sundry desires remained in the center of an empty stage.

"What is there for breakfast?" Her left eyebrow arched slightly.

Breakfast, lunch, and dinner were not secondary matters. Her food had to be served strictly on time. She required a full table setting, with a stand for the knife and a napkin in a napkin ring. Increasingly nowadays, however, she would take the fork in her hand only to drop it at the side of her plate.

"I'm not hungry," she would say, sulky and irritated. "I'll have a grated apple, perhaps, or some ice cream."

All her life she had enjoyed wanting and getting what she wanted. Her real misfortune was that she had ceased to want. She was afraid of death only because it meant the end of desires.

THE DAY before Marek was due to arrive, Katya cleaned the apartment till late at night. It was falling to pieces and hadn't been redecorated for such a long time that cleaning it made little difference. The ceilings were yellowed in the corners and their plasterwork was peeling, the antique furniture needed restoring, and the books were dust-laden in their dried-out bookcases. It was the intelligentsia's usual mix of luxury and penury. Late in the evening Katya and Anna, both looking like threadbare plush toys in their cosy old dressing gowns, sat down on the little tapestry sofa. It looked as worn as they did themselves.

Anna slumped against the armrest and Katya tucked her thin legs under herself and squeezed in under her mother's arm like a chick under the wing of a fluffed-up hen. There really was something chicklike about Katya, despite her almost forty years: the round eyes in her pale feathery little head, the thin neck, the long beaky nose. She had a birdlike charm, a birdlike incorporeality. The mother and daugher loved each other infinitely, but that very love got in the way of intimacy, because they were desperately afraid of upsetting each other. Since, however, life consisted chiefly of upsets of one form or another, constantly keeping quiet about things was what they did, instead of quietly complaining to each other, enjoying the pleasures of mutual consolation, or thinking aloud together. Accordingly, more often than not, they would talk about Grisha's cold, Lenochka's exams, or getting more sleeping pills for Mour. When something important did happen in their lives, they just huddled closer together, and for longer than usual, or sat silently in the kitchen over their empty cups.

"Before he emigrated he gave me a microscope, a little brass one. It was just so wonderful." Katya smiled. "I took it and straightaway lent it to Tanya Zavidonova. Do you remember? She was in second grade with me."

"You never told me about the microscope," Anna said and, without raising her eyes, snuggled down more into the dressing gown.

"I thought it would upset you if I brought it back home. Zavidonova never did give it back. Perhaps her father sold it for drink. . . . You know, I loved him terribly. Why did you get divorced anyway?"

It was a hard question, one with too many answers. It was like going down the stairs into a cellar: The deeper you went, the darker it got.

"We got married and rented a room in Ostankino, from a woman who baked communion bread. Her stove was always in use, and there were communion wafers everywhere. That is where you were born. Your first solid food was those wafers. We lived there for four years. Mour was living with her sisters, Eva in town and Beata at the dacha. Aunt Eva served her all her life, starching her blouses. She was an old maid, a secret Catholic. She was exceptionally strict and never forgave anyone anything, but she worshiped Mour. She died suddenly, before she was sixty, and Mother immediately demanded that I come to look after her. She couldn't stand having servants from outside the family."

"Why didn't you simply refuse?" Katya interjected sharply.

"Well, she was nearing seventy, and they had made that diagnosis. I couldn't abandon someone who was dying."

"But she didn't die."

"Marek said at the time that she was as deathless as the theory of Marxism-Leninism."

Katya grunted. "That's good."

"Oh, yes. But as you can see, he was wrong. Mama, thank heaven, has even outlived Marxism. The tumor became encapsulated. It ate part of her lung and then became inactive. I was looking after her, and Aunt Beata was looking after you. She couldn't stand children. You were sent off to Pakhra immediately. You only came back when it was time for you to go to school."

"Why didn't Father move here with you?"

"It was out of the question. She hated him. He kept on living in Ostankino until he left."

"Were they allowing people to emigrate then?"

"He was a special case. It was because of Poland. His mother was a Communist. She fled Poland and brought him and his elder brother to Russia. His father stayed behind and was killed. They were a large family; many of them escaped. Some went to Holland, some to America. I can't remember anymore; Marek did tell me. You have a whole host of relatives all over the world. He himself, as you see, is in South Africa." Anna sighed.

Katya continued her latter-day investigation. "And what about Mour?"

Anna laughed quietly. "She's ordered a manicurist for tomorrow and wants her striped blouse ironed."

"No, I meant then."

"Mour forbade me to write to him. One time an Israeli citizen with Polish antecedents brought me a few hundred dollars and some toys for you, some little clothes. She found out and gave me such a telling off I didn't know what to do. I don't know what I was more afraid of. At that time you were put straight in prison for having dollars. I handed everything back to the Pole and asked him to tell Marek not to put us in danger by sending things."

"How silly all that was," Katya whispered forgivingly, and stroked her mother's face.

"No. It is just life." Anna sighed.

Nevertheless, the conversation left an unpleasant aftertaste: Katya seemed to be hinting that she was living her life all wrong. She didn't recall her holding that view before.


AFTER MANY days of extreme cold, the weather relented and snow began to fall. The Zamoskvorechie region was being blanketed as you watched. From the disproportionately high entrance of a Stalin-era skyscraper perched on a forbidding granite plinth, an elderly gentleman in a thickly padded sheepskin coat emerged. His fur hat had cost not one but two foxes their lives. Some lunatic was coming toward him up the broad steps wearing only a beige jacket and no hat. He had a red scarf tossed over his shoulder and a covering of snow on his curly white hair.

Before the door could slam shut the white-haired man nipped nimbly past the warmly wrapped-up gentleman and into the vestibule.

He rang at the door of the apartment he was seeking and heard footsteps retreating from the door; then a clear woman's voice shouted, "Grisha, give me that plasticine!" After that he heard the tinkle of breaking glass and someone exclaimed irritably, "For heaven's sake, open the door!" The door was opened.

Inside stood a large elderly woman, in the depths of whose ravaged face remembered features could still be discerned. Perhaps the trigger was a sizable mauve bean on her cheek, the fetching little beauty spot of yesteryear. In one hand she was holding the broken neck of a glass jar, and she looked out at him fearfully.

At the end of the corridor, where it turned toward a small room, was a puddle; a girl he didn't know was standing in it with a cloth in her hand. Her age was closer to that of a grand-daughter than of a daughter of the man who had just entered. She was tall and gangly and had narrow shoulders and round eyes. From a far room the shout was again heard: "Grisha, give me that plasticine!"

The visitor trundled his bag in and stopped. Anna, sucking the blood from her cut finger, said "Hello, Marek" to him in a down-to-earth manner.

He took her by the shoulders. "Anelia, I could go mad! The whole world has changed, everything is different, only this house is exactly the same."

From the far room Katya emerged, dragging Grisha behind her.

"Katushka! My bobbin!" the visitor gasped. This was a long-forgotten childhood name, given to Katya back in the days when she was a chubby baby.

Katya looked at his youthful, suntanned face, which was far more handsome than she remembered it. She recalled how ardently she had loved him, how awkward she had felt about it, and how she had hidden it from her mother in order not to cause her pain. Now, suddenly, she found that in the depths of her heart her love was undiminished. She was embarrassed, and blushed.

"These are my children, Grisha and Lenochka."

Katya's little face, he now noticed, was no longer young but wrinkled, and the hands clasped under her chin were not young either. Before he had time to take a close look at his newly acquired grandchildren, a door in the depths of the apartment slowly opened and, in the doorway, the metal rails of her walker clinking delicately, Mour appeared.

"The Queen of Spades," the visitor whispered, in stunned amazement. "It could drive you out of your mind."

For some reason he gave a cheerful laugh and rushed to greet her, and she, grandly proffering her desiccated hand to be kissed, stood before him, frail and magnificent, as if it were she this well-dressed gentleman, this foreign stud, had come to see. With her newly manicured hand the grand old lady swept aside the general awkwardness, and all the members of the family immediately saw clearly how they should behave in this unfamiliar situation.

"You look marvelous, Marek," she commented amicably. "The years have been kind to you."

Marek, without letting go of her redemptive hand, rattled back his response in Polish.

It happened that this was the language of their childhood, the one, born Maria Czarnecka in a narrow semi-Gothic house in Stare Miasto, the other the grandson of a chemist from Krochmalna, a Jewish street in Warsaw known to the whole world for a variety of reasons.

Katya exchanged a glance with her mother. Even here Mour had imposed herself ahead of his daughter, ahead of his grandchildren.

"You may come into my room" was Mour's gracious invitation, as if she had forgotten just how strongly she had disliked Marek thirty years previously. At this point, however, something unexpected happened.

"I thank you, madame. I have only one and a half hours at my disposal today and wish to spend it with the children. I shall come again tomorrow. And now, if you permit, I shall see you to your room."

She had no time to object before he firmly but gaily turned her walker about, together with Mour herself, and ferried her back into the boudoir.

"Everything in your room is just as elegant as ever. Will you permit me to help you to your chair?" he inquired, in a tone that allowed of no alternative.

Anna, Katya, and Lenochka stood at the door like a tableau vivant, waiting for the shrieks, the screams, and broken teacups, but nothing of the sort eventuated. Mour sank meekly into her armchair.

Marek bent down, touched her narrow foot—squeezed into a wizened shoe of old blue leather—and said, rather strictly, "No, really, you must not wear such shoes. I shall send you a pair that will be much more comfortable: a specialist firm. The girls will need to take your measurements." He left her alone and closed the door gently behind him.

"How can you get away with talking to her like that?" Anna asked in total bewilderment.

He gestured casually. "Experience. Eighty percent of the patients in my clinic are over eighty years of age, and all of them are rich and capricious. It took me five years to learn how to deal with them. Your mama, though, is a real Queen of Spades. Pushkin drew his character from her. But enough of that. Let's go, Grisha, and take a look at what we've got in the suitcase."

Grisha promptly forgot all about the plasticine with which he had just so skillfully blocked the drain in the sink, and pulled along the well-made wheeled case that held so much promise.

Anna stood beside the set table. Nothing that was happening seemed to involve her at all. Even loyal Katya could not take her eyes off Marek's tanned face; Anna found her daughter's smile weak and even slightly foolish.

It's just as well, she thought, that I didn't dye my hair from that doubtful bottle I bought the day before yesterday. He might have thought I was trying to look younger for his benefit. All the same, it's a pity to have let myself go so much. When he's gone back to South Africa, I will dye it.

Marek looked over toward her and made a familiar gesture with his hand as if he were playing table tennis, and Anna remembered what a good player he used to be. It had just been catching on during their engagement. He talked easily and freely with the children. He had his arm round Katya's shoulder all the time, and she melted beneath it like a cow.

Yes, like a cow, Anna confirmed to herself.

The presents were splendid: a cordless telephone, a camera, some little pieces of technological wizardry. He produced a small photograph album from the inner pocket of his velvety jacket and showed them his house in Johannesburg, the clinic, and another pleasing two-story house by the sea, which he referred to as his dacha.

Then he looked at his watch, ruffled Grisha's hair, and asked what time he could come tomorrow. He really had only spent an hour and a half in their home.

"I'd like to come fairly early in the day. Is that all right?" He was asking Anna; she had the impression he was a little daunted by her.

"Don't you wear a coat?" Grisha asked admiringly.

"I do have a jacket for outdoors back in the hotel, but what do I need it for? I have a car waiting for me downstairs."

The children gazed at him with such admiration that Anna was quite upset and immediately felt ashamed of herself. It was all entirely understandable. He always had been charming and now, having grown older, he was also handsome. An ache in her heart, however, left her feeling indefinably disgruntled and bewildered.

AS OFTEN happens, a tradition of fatherlessness in their family had grown stronger with each succeeding generation. In effect, the last man in the family, the last father figure, had been old Czarnecki, descendant of a fierce Polish military commander and the doting sire of three beautiful girls: Maria, Evelina, and Beata.

Anna herself was at first left without a mother, when Mour ditched Dr. Storch on the spur of the moment, walking out of the house one day and seemingly forgetting to come back. Several days later she sent for her immediate necessities, but these did not include her eighteen-month-old daughter. Mour's new marriage was not to be her last but represented a step in the right direction, her antennae having sensed that the age of decadent poets and unruly heroes was over.

Mour's first foray into the realm of the new Soviet literature was not one of her more propitious ventures, but her subsequent attempts led ultimately to success. She came up with a truly classical Soviet writer, a genius of duplicity, wearing the mask of an ascetic but with nouveau riche passions raging in his breast. Showing off his porcelain collection, a newly acquired Borisov-Musatov, or a sketch by Vrubel, he would open his arms wide in a most charming gesture and say, "All Mour's whims. I've taken me a lass from the nobility, and now I just have to put up with the consequences."

This last marriage was an excellent match, and little Anna got to stay with her own father until the time came for her to be remembered. Mour was relaunched into the upper reaches of literature, had an affair with the most important playwright of the time, another with a very notable director, and several amusing liaisons in first-class sanatoria in the south of Russia that were well appointed to cater for them. At last a solid residential block was built in Zamoskvorechie where the apartments were allotted not on the basis of a plebeian calculation of so many square feet per head but in accordance with the true dimensions of a writer's soul. Even here, certain bureaucratic requirements needed to be met. Mour had to register both her sisters as living in the apartment, and it was decided to take back the little girl. Mour noticed, moreover, that the great Soviet classical writer who belonged to her was casting a less than platonic eye over plump waitresses and young chambermaids, and she decided the time had come to support the institution of the family and give her classic the opportunity of realizing himself as the parent of a young girl.

Mour took the aged surgeon's seven-year-old daughter away from him. The girl, who adored her father, was removed from the sweet languor of Odessa to the prim newly acquired apartment in Moscow. She was forbidden any further contact with her father and gradually forgot him. At Mour's insistence, Anna had her birdlike German surname changed to a name famous the length and breadth of the Soviet Union. She was instructed to call the fat bald man *Papa* and was entrusted to the care of her second aunt, who lived all year round at the writer's dacha in the countryside.

A few years later came the outbreak of war and evacuation to Kuibyshev, which left Anna with a fear of the cold that remained for the rest of her life. They returned to Moscow in an overheated government railway carriage, and the first months after their happy homecoming to the capital cemented its status as her hometown. She never did see her father again and had only a vague intuition of how deeply similar she was to him.

The memories that Anna's daughter, Katya, retained of her own father were even more tenuous. They were fragmentary images, but taken in close-ups. In one she was ill and had bandages over her ears, and her father was bringing a puppy straight into her bed. In another she was standing on the porch and watching him fish a sunken bucket out of the well, using a long stick with a hook on the end. In yet another they were going out of a little wooden house with an acrid smell of smoke and walking along a snowed-up road to an enormous czarist palace that smelled of forests and summer and had great windows from floor to ceiling, decorative tiled stoves, and oil paintings on the walls.

For some reason, she could hardly remember her father visiting Pakhra, where, like her mother before her, Katya lived until she was ready for school. She retained just one vivid memory: she was walking along a narrow path to the bus stop wearing her spotted cat-fur overcoat and hat, holding Aunt Beata by one hand and her father by the other. The bus was already waiting and she was terribly afraid her father would be too late to get on it. Tearing her hand away, she shouted to him, "Run quickly! Run!"

That very year he acted on Katya's advice.

It was truly amazing how deep down her filial love was buried. For many years she had not thought about her father at all or remembered her honest German instrument for studying the cells of an onion skin or the tiny feet of a flea.

Katya's early daughter Lenochka did not remember her own father at all; Katya had divorced him a year after the baby was born. She never received any alimony from him, and only through mutual acquaintances did she even know he was alive.

Until Grisha was born, the family consisted of four women, but the total absence of men troubled nobody apart from Mour. Mour was used to regarding her daughter, Anna, as a colorless, asexual creature of value only for rushing through the housework, but she was puzzled as to why her granddaughter, Katya, led such a dull life. Mour couldn't imagine how they came to have any children, given such a complete dearth of feminine wiles. These people seemed no better than animals: they fucked purely in order to procreate.

Mour was profoundly unjust in respect to Katya, who was blessed with an unhappy love life of enviable intensity. It had led her to abandon her first dysfunctional husband. She suffered egregious torments with the object of her great love, had Grisha by him, and for thirteen years now had been running to this high-minded lover for stolen rendezvous. She kept putting off from one year to the next the moment when her son and his secret father would become genuinely, rather than one-sidedly, acquainted. The family is sacrosanct, he declared, and Katya could not but agree. Fatherlessness had thus become a deep-rooted inherited condition in their family, firmly established over three generations. It would never have occurred to Anna, Katya, or even Lenochka, who was approaching puberty, to introduce into this house, so completely and utterly the domain of Mour, even the most modest and insignificant male. Mour, filled with a magnificent disdain for her female progeny, had accorded them no such right. Anna and Katya had entirely reconciled themselves both to the ambience of fatherlessness and to their womanly solitude, while Lenochka, who was entirely infantile in precisely the area in which her great-grandmother had most fully displayed her great talents, had never given the matter a thought.

All the more acutely was Anna aware of how the whole house had gone mad after that first visit from Marek. Not only eight-year-old Grisha but even lanky Lenochka, who that winter had reached a height of almost five-foot-eleven, and Katya herself ran out to answer the doorbell. From all the excitement you might have thought it was Father Christmas standing outside. Marek even rather fitted that downmarket red-and-white image. Above his African suntan billowed those dazzling white curls, and in place of the vulgar red tunic with its white cotton-wool collar he had, casually wrapped round his neck, that woolen scarf of a blood-red hue and a quality so superb as almost to turn material values into spiritual ones. As behooved Father Christmas, he was jolly, ruddy, and incredibly generous in dispensing treats and presents and, even more so, promises. Mour herself was displaying an immoderate interest in him.

Anna was suffering from a sense of personal humiliation that she had not experienced for a long time. Three days ago Marek had not even known of the existence of Grisha and Lenochka, yet already he was playing a central role in their lives. Lenochka talked only about where she should go to study abroad, England or America. Grisha was hooked on some Greek island where Marek had a cottage, a two-story villa with its back resting against a pink cliff. It looked out onto a small bay with a white yacht anchored in the midst of it, like an ivory brooch pinned on deep blue silk. Grisha eviscerated Marek's photograph album, and the color prints of someone else's unreal life were spread all over the apartment, even in Mour's room. What was most annoying, however, was that Katya was walking around with a really rather stupid grin on her face and purring slightly, exactly like her grandmother. To add insult to injury, conscientious Anna was tormented by the fact of harboring such mean-spirited feelings and being unable to control them.

Something had upset Anna at work too. One of her most

difficult cases of recent times, a young policeman who had come in as an emergency, had been operated on remarkably successfully. It seemed sure that one eye at least had been saved. A few days ago, however, he had dragged the television set from one corner of the hall to the other, and all the fine craftsmanship she had practiced on his eye had been wrecked. There were new ruptures in the retina, and it now seemed very uncertain whether she would be able to save the oaf's eye a second time.

Marek had come to Moscow on business. This consisted of a single meeting with medical bureaucrats, and the appointment had been on the first evening of his stay. There was a deal concerning special equipment for the postoperative care of patients, and he had some kind of involvement in manufacturing it. He himself later admitted that the negotiations had been a pretext for coming to see his daughter. He had not repeated his first attempt to establish communication with his former family all these years, having had only too much experience of dealing with Soviet power in both its Russian and Polish varieties.

Marek had had no idea what to expect from the trip, but he had certainly not anticipated meeting such direct and lovable children, in effect his own family, who were getting along fine and knew not the first thing about him.

He even felt a hint of interest and liking for old misery guts. He spent several hours with her that day because, as it happened, Grisha had bounced off to yet another New Year's party at a classmate's apartment and Lenochka had gone off to fail yet another exam.

Marek cunningly asked Mour a very well-received question about the Stalin Prize that her husband, the great Soviet writer, had received. This launched her into a spate of agreeable memories. Her husband's final success had coincided with a revival of Mour's fortunes, a string of brilliant successes in her related field. There had been a tempestuous romance with a secret general, who held the entire literary process in his hairy fist; some hanky-panky with her husband's male secretary; an affair with the husband of her dearest friend, an Academician of some description in biology; et cetera, et cetera. All this had been witnessed by her frowning daughter, Anna, who suffered a puritanical sense of outrage and a profound despair at the impossibility of loving and her inability not to love this subtle, improbably beautiful, and always theatrically overdressed woman who happened to be her mother.

Mour told the story disjointedly, selectively, dropping in names and details, but Marek saw the picture she was painting with complete clarity, and in any case he already knew a lot from Anna.

The great Soviet writer died at just the right moment, not surviving his much lauded Leader by very long at all and thereby demonstrating his remarkable perspicacity one last time to his envious colleagues. He was laid beneath a heavy gray stone in Novodevichy Cemetery, and for a time Mour's life became drabber. She did, however, have obscene amounts of money, and it kept flooding in: fees from books, productions, and royalties. A lesser woman might have settled down to living a quiet life, but Mour was restive. Her romances had become wearisome and lost their savor; her desires had lost their old resilience. The years between fifty and sixty she found dreary, later putting this down to the menopause. Her menopause came to a satisfactory conclusion, however, when Mour had two minor but, for the time, unusual operations. Her friend Verochka, a famous film star, gave her the name of her doctor, and Mour was rejuvenated—needless to say, by an affair, dazzling, unprecedented, with a young actor. There was a forty-year difference in their ages. Every record in the crumpling of bedsheets was broken. Her friends were in nursing homes and hospitals, some were living out their last years in exile, but she was alive, with pert breasts, a neat little bum, and an overhauled neck, entertaining her ravishing gypsylike boy while his young wife raged at the front door. Moscow was abuzz; life was back to normal.

Alas, at this point things began to go wrong. The boyish actor descended into alcoholism with incredible rapidity; her old friends were going down like skittles; her daughter Anna left home and married a skinny student, and he was a Jew. Mour had had an aversion to Jews since she was a child. Live and let live, of course. She certainly didn't want them sent to the gas chambers. But really, the thought of marrying one!

Marek was greatly intrigued—who did she think she was talking to?—but asked no questions. He just listened attentively.

Her ex-lovers all died off one after the other, the generals and the civilians. Most annoying of all, her sister Eva died too, loyal devoted Eva, who was ten years younger. She had to bring Anna back to the house, and soon they had Katya living there also. Before you knew it, the place was overrun with children and life was trivial, no fun, nothing of any interest happening.

Coming into her mother's room to take away the teacups, Anna noted to herself that Mour was looking just as happy as the children and was, moreover, ready for action: Her voice was a purr and an octave lower than usual, her eyes were two sizes wider, and her back, if such thing was imaginable, was even straighter. A tigress on the prowl was how Anna characterized her mother at such moments.

Marek was just sitting there, smiling enigmatically.

THE LAST evening of the family's ecstasy was in progress, with Anna trying to take as little part in everything as possible. Grisha was hanging on Marek, unglueing himself from time to time only in order to take a run and jump higher up on him and cling even more tightly. Lenochka was heading full steam ahead to failure in her exams, but in these crucial days she had abandoned her studies and was following her brand-new grandad around like a shadow. Since the allure of England had taken away her appetite for studying in her homeland, she now felt not a twinge of concern at the prospect of tomorrow's exam. As for Katya, Anna did her best not to look her way at all. Her expression was too embarrassing.

It was past eleven when Marek, having said goodbye to all of them, went in to Mour. Her feet clamped on a hot-water bottle, she was watching television and eating chocolate. It was one of her guiding principles that one pleasure should never be allowed to get in the way of another. As regards the hot-water bottle, at which Anna had been protesting for the past thirty years, Mour had been accustomed to go to a warmed bed since she was little, even when a rubber bottle was not her only companion for the night.

As Marek respectfully bowed to her, she graciously held out a slip of paper half covered in spidery letters. "This is for you, my friend. There are one or two things there that I need."

Without glancing at it, Marek put the paper in his pocket. "With the greatest of pleasure."

He knew how to treat old ladies. He went out and Anna lingered, straightening the column of pillows behind Mour's back.

Mour licked a finger smeared with chocolate, smiled mysteriously, and fired a question at her. "Well, now do you see?"

"What?" Anna asked in surprise. "Do I see what?"

"How my lovers treat me." Mour smirked.

First signs of dementia, Anna decided.

The children wanted to see him back to the hotel. He was staying nearby, in what had been the Hotel Balchuga. It had been transformed over the last few years into something quite magnificent, like the crystal bridge in the fairy tale that in a single night spans from shore to shore.

"No, let's decide that we have said goodbye," he announced, with unexpected firmness, and Grisha, who would whine about anything, usually until he got his way, immediately accepted the situation.

Marek wound his unendurably red scarf round his neck and kissed the children for the last time as naturally as if it were not a mere five days before that he had first met them. Then from the hall stand he took Anna's fur coat, which was balding on the breast, and said, in that inexorable voice, "Let's go for one last walk."

For some reason Anna submitted, although a minute before she had had no intention of going down to the street with him. Without a word, she squeezed into the coat and put round her neck a shawl that was a present from Orenburg. She accepted presents if she was offered them: boxes of chocolates, books, envelopes with money. She took them and thanked the givers in a reserved way. She never named the price for her own operations, and in that respect, although she was quite unaware of it, she was following exactly in her late father's footsteps.

In the street he took her arm. From Lavrushinsky Lane they came out onto Ordynka. The street was clean, snowy white and virtually deserted. The few passers-by looked round at the lean foreigner wearing only a light-colored jacket and walking unhurriedly along with an elderly citizen packaged in a thick fur coat. They couldn't relate her to him in any way; she looked too educated to be his cleaner, and she was too old and badly dressed to be his wife.

"What a lovely city. For some reason I was remembering it as gloomy and dirty."

"There are different sides to it," Anna responded politely.

*Why did you come back?* she was wondering. *Turning everything upside down, unsettling everyone.* But she did not say it out loud.

"Let's go and sit down somewhere," he suggested.

"Where? At night?" she asked in surprise.

"There are any number of places open at night. There's a marvelous restaurant quite near here. I had lunch there yesterday with the children."

"You have to be up at the crack of dawn tomorrow," Anna said evasively.

Marek was going back on an early flight, and she herself had to get up at half past six. The reference to tomorrow calmed her. He would leave; everything would get back to normal; all this turmoil in the family would come to an end.

"I would like to invite the children to come to Greece for the summer. Would you mind?"

"Not at all."

"You are an angel, Anelia. And my greatest loss."

Anna said nothing. Why on earth had she come out with him? It could only be because at home she had been used to doing as she was told for so many years. She really should have refused.

He detected her wordless irritation and caught hold of her puffy mittens with his thin glove.

"Anna, do you think I don't see or understand anything? Emigration is a hard school, very hard, and I have experienced it three times. From Polish to Russian, from Russian to Hebrew, and for the last fifteen years I have been speaking English. Each time you have to learn your way into a new life again from scratch. I have been through all sorts of things. I have fought in wars, starved . . . I have even been in prison."

What a sweet boy he used to be, a student in the third year, so different from the hearty males performing the robust ritual of the dog's wedding beside her mother. As part of her duties as a postgraduate she had been conducting an under-graduate seminar at the time, and their romance began among the retorts and the bacilli. For a long time she had meticu-lously concealed their relationship from everyone. It was embarrassing that he was so young, but it was precisely his youthfulness, the absence of aggressive meat, that subcon-sciously attracted her to him. He had a white hairless chest and a constellation of birthmarks, the dipper of Ursa Major to the left, near the nipple. To this day he was the only man there had been in her life, but she never regretted either that or the fact that it had been him. She always knew, though, that marriage was not central to her life. She was around sixteen when she decided never to get married. She knew nothing more repug-nant than the purring voice, the sexually aroused laughter, and the drawn-out moaning proceeding from her mother's bed-room. The eternal sex hunt, animals in heat. For a moment she relapsed into an immensely powerful childish sense of the irredeemable filthiness of sex, when it was an embarrass-ment to look at any married couple because you immediately imagined them, sweating and grunting, getting on with that dirt. How fine to be a nun, dressed all in white, pure, with-out any of this. But what a joy it was, all the same, that Katya existed.

Marek was talking, saying something, but it flew past her like the snow. She was suddenly jolted back to herself by his faltering words.

". . . a real miracle how a curse can turn into a bless-ing. This monster, this demon of egoism, the Queen of Spades, has destroyed everything, has put everyone in their graves. And how do you bear it? You are simply a saint."

"Me? A saint?" Anna stopped in her tracks as if she had walked into a lamppost. "I am afraid of her . . . and there is my duty . . . and I feel sorry for her."

He brought his face close to hers, and she could see that he was not by any means so young. His skin was that of an old man, with little incised wrinkles and senile dark freckles beneath the year-round suntan. "How can I help you? What can I do for you?"

She waved a gray mitten at him. "See me back home."

MAREK CALLED from Johannesburg more frequently than her friends called from Sviblovo. Grisha waited frantically for his calls, pouncing on the telephone and shouting to absolutely anyone who rang, "Marek! Is that you?" Lenochka devoted herself exclusively to the study of English and to readying herself for the journey abroad. She became remarkably businesslike, not an attribute that had been much in evidence up till then. She set about selecting the location for her future studies with intelligence and discernment. Even Katya, always calm and a little indolent, was expecting indefinable changes that would relate in some way to the reappearance of her father. She seemed to have cooled a little toward her secret lover, who for his part began making noncommittal remarks about possibly leaving his family.

Marek enthusiastically set about fulfilling his Christmas promises. The first to materialize was shoes of an uncompromisingly orthopedic appearance for Mour. They were exceptionally ugly and probably no less exceptionally comfortable, and they were brought directly to their home by an old friend of Marek's who was practically a first secretary at the Israeli embassy. Mour did not even try them on, merely muttered something. They had schoolgirl heels and were elasticized, as befitted footwear for the elderly. For the past seventy years, Mour had worn only pumps with heels as elegant as the latest fashion allowed.

The pair of shoes was followed by a pair of small computers, their size in inverse proportion to their cost. He also took time to find computer games for Grisha. Lenochka had yet to get over the amateur ciné camera he had left her before departing. She was still in thrall to that special perspective on the world revealed by a viewfinder when her new present arrived, demanding that she should promptly learn to do all the things that were now possible with its magical assistance.

Finally, six weeks after Marek's departure, there came an invitation from Thessaloniki, signed by a certain Evangelia Daoul who was a close friend of Marek's wife. Of Marek's wife, all that was known was that she had a Greek friend who would send them an invitation.

The wording of the invitation left it open to them to come at any time between June and September.

Grisha, delighted to seventh heaven by the mere sight of the envelope with its rectangular window, rushed around the apartment with it until he collided with Mour, who was steering toward the kitchen in her metal contraption. He waved the envelope in her face.

"Look, Mour, we're going to Greece, to the Island of Séri-phos. Marek has invited us."

"What nonsense!" Mour snorted. She never made concessions of any kind to age. "You're going nowhere."

"We are, we are!" Grisha shouted, jumping up and down in excitement.

Mour wrenched her hand from the rail of her walker and stuck it with great aplomb under the nose of her eight-year-old great-grandson in an obscene gesture, the bright red nail of her thumb jutting out between the fingers of her clenched fist. With her other hand she deftly snatched the invitation from the grasp of the startled boy, who had not been expecting such an audacious attack. Leaning her elbows on the rails, she screwed up the envelope and threw it in a ball as solid as a good snowball straight at the front door.

"You foul old witch!" Grisha howled, and rushed to the door.

Katya jumped out of her room, seized her son, not knowing what had transpired between him and her grandmother. Grisha was straightening out some kind of paper and continuing to shout wholly unexpected words.

"You godforsaken old crow! You fucked-up old bitch!"

Lowering her eyelids, Mour reproached her granddaughter more in sorrow than in anger. "Remove your little bastard, my dear. One really does have to teach children a modicum of good manners." Her wheels squeaking, she proceeded to the kitchen.

Katya, still unaware of what the scrap of paper was that the sobbing Grisha was trying to straighten out, dragged him off to her room, from which his sobs were to be heard for a long time afterward.

That day Anna returned from work more tired than usual. Some things are more draining than work itself. A seriously injured girl had been brought in. They had no suitably qualified doctor in the pediatric department for her. She was about Grisha's age and had a shrapnel wound. The operation had been very distressing.

Putting the blood pressure cuff back in its case, Anna wondered where Mour got her energy from. With those readings she should have been feeling weak and sleepy, but instead she was aggressive and acute in her reactions. Other mechanisms were evidently coming into play. Ah, well, gerontology. . . .

"You're not listening to me! What are you thinking about? I'm against it, do you hear? I was never in Greece. They are going nowhere!" Mour was tugging at Anna's sleeve.

"Yes, yes, of course. Of course, Mama."

"What do you mean, of course? Don't you mama me!" Mour shrieked.

"Everything will be just as you wish," Anna said, in a soothing tone, meanwhile deciding emphatically, for the first time in her life, *No, my dear mother. Not this time!* The word *no* had not yet been uttered but it already existed. It had already broken through like a puny shoot. She decided simply to face her mother with the fact of her family's disobedience without any preliminary discussion. One could only imagine what kind of hullabaloo this bloodless insect would raise when it became apparent that the children had left.


BY EARLY June they had obtained external passports for travel abroad and the necessary visas. Air tickets to Athens had been booked for the twelfth of June. That same day, in accordance with Anna's ingenious plan, had been chosen for the move to the dacha. Everything had been thought through down to the last detail. In the morning Katya and the children would go to Sheremetievo Airport, which should rouse no suspicion because Katya always went on ahead to the dacha in order to prepare it for Mour's arrival. A taxi had been ordered for twelve to take Mour and Anna there. Anna hoped the turmoil of the move would soften the blow, the more so since preparations to go to the dacha would disguise the great escape. Grisha and Lenochka were simply bursting with excitement, especially Grisha. His semi-Greek grandfather had turned up at just the right moment. All Grisha's classmates had been abroad. He was almost the only one who had never been taken farther than Krasnaya Pakhra. A photograph of his grandfather with his curly white hair standing on board a white yacht had been shown to the entire class and successfully made up for the absence of a father of his own.

On the eve of their departure, Anna and Katya hardly slept at all. Marek rang early in the morning to tell them not to bring more luggage than they needed because, as no doubt they knew, they could get everything in Greece, and said he couldn't wait to see them and would meet them at the airport.

At half past seven, Mour demanded her coffee. Her morning coffee she took with milk, while coffee after dinner was required to be black. Anna helped her to dress and made the coffee, at which point she discovered that the milk carton in the refrigerator was empty. This was Lenochka's slovenliness: she was forever putting empty cartons back in the fridge. The time was approaching eight, and the taxi to Sheremetievo was due at half past eight.

Anna popped out of the house wearing an indoor blue dress and bedroom slippers on her bare feet. She ran down to Ordynka to get the milk. It should take no more than ten minutes at the most. She hurried along, almost running at first, but suddenly slowed down. It was an extraordinary morning: the light was bluish and hazy, the sky was shimmering like the iris of an enormous, very deep blue eye, and as she passed the welcoming little rounded Church of All Who Mourn, which she occasionally dropped into, the small well-tended square beside it was of the purest green. She walked slowly and easily, as if in no hurry at all. The shop assistant, Galya, a local Ordynka Tatar who had worked all her life in shops around here, greeted her warmly. Some fifteen years previously Anna had performed an operation on her mother-in-law.

"How is Sophia Ahmetovna?"

It was amazing how, given such a quantity of gold teeth, a smile could be so shy and childlike.

"She's gone completely deaf. Can't hear anything, but her eyes see well!"

Anna took the cool carton of milk. In fifteen minutes' time the children would leave, and in another two hours Mour would learn that they were gone. Most probably by that time Mour would be in Pakhra. She pictured to herself her mother's faded eyes, her quiet croaky voice rising to a shrill glassy shriek, the fragments of broken crockery, and the wholly disgraceful, utterly unbearable swearing to come. Suddenly she saw, as if it had already happened, herself—Anna—taking a long easy swing and giving that old rouged cheek a good hard long-overdue slap. And she didn't care in the slightest what happened after that.

She felt surrounded by a marvelously triumphant sense of freedom and victory, and the light was so intensely bright, so burning bright. But at that very moment it was switched off. Anna had no time even to notice. She fell forward without letting go of the cool carton, and the light slippers came off her strong stoutly Germanic feet.

By this time Mour was already raging. "The house is full of ne'er-do-wells! Is it really too difficult to buy a bottle of milk?" Her voice was transparently shrill with fury.

Katya looked at her watch. The taxi would be here in fifteen minutes' time. Where could her mother be? she wondered in perplexity. There was nothing for it: She ran out to get the milk herself.

Galya, the shop assistant, whom she knew, was running about on the pavement. A small crowd had gathered round the entrance to the shop. There was a woman lying on the pavement in a blue dress with stars on it. The ambulance arrived some twenty minutes later, but by then there was nothing for them to do.

Katya, clutching to her breast the still-cool carton of milk, kept murmuring, "The milk, the milk, the milk," until she was sent to get her mother's passport. As she approached the house, she repeated, "Passport, passport, passport."

Back in the apartment, Katya discovered the place in uproar. The taxi driver, having waited some twenty minutes downstairs for them as arranged, had come up to the apartment to ask why his fares for Sheremetievo had not come down.

Grisha, trembling with impatience like a puppy waiting for its morning walk, yelled joyfully, "Hurray! We're going to Sheremetievo!"

Mour came wobbling out into the hallway in her metal cage

and guessed she was being duped. She forgot all about her coffee and the milk and, in ripe expressions which even the taxi driver did not hear every day, she declared that nobody was going anywhere, and that the driver could take himself off to a most original destination. The driver, a young man who had graduated from a theater institute, was overcome by purely professional admiration and leaned against the wall, reveling in the unexpected theatricality of the situation.

"Where is that cunt-headed turkey? Who is she trying to trick?" Mour raised her bony hand in the air, and the sleeve of her extremely expensive old kimono fell back to reveal the dry bones that, if we are to believe Ezekiel, should at some future time be clothed in new flesh.

Katya went over to Mour, took a long easy swing, and gave her old as yet unpainted cheek a good hard long-overdue slap.

Mour shook in her cage and then was still. She grasped the rail of the captain's bridge from which, for the last ten years, since she broke her hip, she had been steering the course of life in this apartment, and said, quietly and distinctly, "What? What? All the same, everything shall be as I wish."

Katya walked past her to the kitchen, slit open the carton, and slopped the milk into the cold coffee.

# Zurich

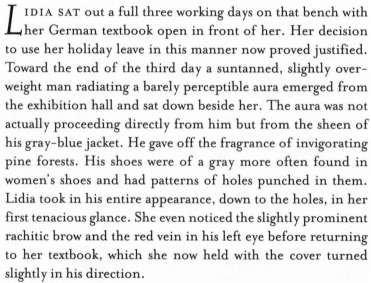

*L*IDIA SAT out a full three working days on that bench with her German textbook open in front of her. Her decision to use her holiday leave in this manner now proved justified. Toward the end of the third day a suntanned, slightly overweight man radiating a barely perceptible aura emerged from the exhibition hall and sat down beside her. The aura was not actually proceeding directly from him but from the sheen of his gray-blue jacket. He gave off the fragrance of invigorating pine forests. His shoes were of a gray more often found in women's shoes and had patterns of holes punched in them. Lidia took in his entire appearance, down to the holes, in her first tenacious glance. She even noticed the slightly prominent rachitic brow and the red vein in his left eye before returning to her textbook, which she now held with the cover turned slightly in his direction.

The man opened his mouth like a fish and promptly swallowed the bait. *"Oh, die deutsche Sprache!"*

After that, he smiled. A thin but confident stream of conversation began to flow. The gentleman informed her that he was a Swiss businessman from Zurich, represented a company manufacturing paint, had a house on the outskirts, and loved animals. Lidia for her part told him about herself. It was a tale she had thought out long ago, learned by heart, and rehearsed. She was a pedagogue. She worked with children. She went to a German class on Mondays, Wednesdays, and Fridays, just out of interest.

"I very much like the orderliness of German. Everything has its right place, especially the verbs."

The Swiss businessman melted. Oh, he also studied foreign languages, and also considered German to be the most logical.

The plainclothes KGB agents were overloaded beyond all reason. This was an international exhibition so the entire Moscow demimonde had converged upon it; those big-bosomed harbingers of spring, the women pioneering international trade, were bringing their fresh goods packaged in pink silk knickers with bad elastic. Lidia had nothing to worry about. It would never have occurred to anyone that she too was here on a manhunt.

She truly had nothing in common with the girls who flocked here, being past thirty and with no pretensions to pulchritude. Quite the reverse, indeed, since her lower lip was pulled forward like a spade and her nose drooped slightly. If she had consorted in the circles of European royalty her lip would have been considered Hapsburgian, but since she was born in the hamlet of Saloslovo her childhood nickname was Liddy-goose. Her two most conspicuous assets, other than the German language, were her luxuriant blond hair, tied up in a layered bun, and her unusually slender waist, constricted by a crude lacquered belt to the point where she appeared to have been half sawed through.

The conversation was proceeding unhurriedly and all in the right direction, but a time came when the Swiss businessman glanced at his Swiss watch and Lidia was afraid he was just going to stand up and leave, bidding her *Auf Wiedersehen.* He didn't. On the contrary, he invited her to come and see his stand and have a cup of coffee.

Lidia smiled demurely, flashing the two gold teeth in the depths of her thin-lipped mouth, put the textbook away, and for a moment was in a quandary. She had a pair of white nylon gloves in her handbag, and the edging on them exactly matched that on her blouse. Should she put them on? Gloves were smart, but might she be overdoing it? Unable to make her mind up, in the end she just pulled them out and clutched them in her hand.

"My guest." The Swiss nodded to the security guard, and Lidia, toying with her gloves, followed him in.

He took her to the little room at the back of his stand. Lidia was ecstatic. She found it such tremendous fun to look at samples of the house paint in which the overweight Swiss businessman traded.

"How lovely!" she exclaimed, and no one could have doubted her sincerity. Although she had many merits, including a certain forthrightness, sincerity was not one of them. More than that, she was really rather devious. That summed her up: forthright, but just a bit devious. As far as implementing her life strategy was concerned, on this occasion she had had every intention of being devious, of deceiving, even of duping. None of this was proving necessary, however. She really very much fancied the gentleman.

*Just don't lower your guard, don't lower your guard,* Lidia instructed herself.

He invited her to sit down, sat down himself, slightly hunched, in a splendid red plastic armchair, and smiled vaguely. Why could he have invited this unknown woman into the hall, who hardly seemed a prospective customer and was not pretty?

"You need a massage. You have osteochondrosis!" Lidia

announced decisively and, without giving him time to gather his wits, sank her fingers into his neck and began working her small powerful hands over his fat withers. He froze in horror. His eyes bulged and he gasped for air.

Lidia was catastrophically short of German vocabulary. She did not know the word for *relax*, but she recognized that in no way could she allow herself to lose the initiative or remain silent. She must say something, so talk she did. First she repeated what her textbook had to say about the history of Moscow, then the biography of Pushkin. In passing, she removed his shimmering jacket, praising the material. He tried to protest but soon succumbed to her onslaught and, did in the end, relax.

"I have a diploma in massage: sports massage, therapeutic massage; I have even studied Chinese massage," she declared, and she was evidently not lying; her movements were assured and vigorous.

In Switzerland he had had occasion to be massaged, and it did not come cheap. As regards her diagnosis, she was perfectly right: He did have osteochondrosis.

She plied him with her small fingers for fifteen minutes or so and very pleasant it was too, only the door was ajar and he was a little anxious that other people might see them. Nobody intruded, however, and when she had finished, giving him an agreeable pounding through his shirt, there was nothing for it but to thank her. She was an extremely strange lady but very nice, he decided.

It was time for the coffee. He rotated his warm neck and decided that besides coffee he should offer her some chocolate. He had a supply both of bars of chocolate and of chocolates in boxes for regaling good customers.

*The main thing is not to lose the initiative,* Lidia thought, focusing, and while he was making the coffee she was wording an invitation in her head.

"I will be glad to invite you to my home for dinner. I have a diploma in cooking," Lidia announced. "European cuisine, cuisine of the peoples of the USSR, dietary cooking. I have a permit to work as a chef in a restaurant."

This hit the bull's-eye. The Swiss businessman had long been thinking about starting his own restaurant but had been prevented by his circumstances.

"Are you then a masseuse or a cook?" he asked, entirely genuinely.

"Both. Although at the present time I am teaching the history of our city," she said, with modest pride. "I am a pedagogue."

This was all perfectly true. Lidia was in her second year of conducting a local history class at her neighborhood Pioneers' Club. The pay was wretched, but the job left plenty of time for her many other interests, and she earned money by sewing and knitting and simply by selling odds and ends. What did money matter anyway? It was the root of all evil. Lidia had lived to do whatever she found interesting since she was a child, and her main interest in life was studying.

"Oh, I shall be very happy to come to have dinner with you!" The Swiss beamed and brought out a larger box of chocolates than the one he had been going to produce. He found Lidia very interesting.

LIDIA MADE a start with the curtains. As soon as she got home she took them all down and put them in the washbasin. She enjoyed doing laundry more than any other housework. She found it a calming occupation, and if something unpleasant happened, or if she was just in a bad mood, she would go and do some washing. Right now, however, she was in a very positive, competitive mood, as if she were about to take an important exam. Something told her that, like all her other exams—and she had taken hundreds of them—she would pass

this very important one too. Just as long as her Swiss businessman turned up.

Even before she got back home, Lidia recognized that she
had made a mistake with the arrangements. She should have
promised to collect him; otherwise all sorts of things could go
wrong. He might forget, or he might have business to attend
to, a visit to the Bolshoy or the restaurant at the Hotel
Nationale. What else did foreigners do in Moscow? Oh, well,
yes, the Tretyakov Art Gallery.

In the time it took to wash the curtains, Lidia thought out
the entire program. She could not possibly get by without help
from Emilia Karlovna. There were a number of things she
needed to borrow from her for the meal. No need to go over-
board on the *zakuski* to start with. She should buy caviar, of
course, and perhaps half a pound of smoked sturgeon, but
basically what this called for was a real Russian meal: fish soup,
piroshkis, perhaps *kurnik* chicken pie. Beef Stroganoff might
be good, but you didn't want to make things too complicated;
just get the right balance. And what should she wear? That
really was a primary consideration. She mustn't overlook the
main point of the exercise.

Lidia toiled unstintingly for two days. She found time to fit
in everything. She went to the Prague Hotel's food hall and the
Central Market and to Emilia for the silverware. Emilia raised
an eyebrow as if to say, I'm sure I don't know what this can be
for, but she did not turn Lidia down. She took two silver table
settings from the dresser, two pie servers, two dessert forks, and
a two-tier fruit stand with a pike on top. Lidia knew how to
present it properly: You arranged the grapes on top, one
bunch, and draped them down like a little curtain. On the
lower tier, of course, you put two peaches, a pear, and five
or six plums. And no apples. In winter of course you would
have Antonov apples, but then not in a stand. You would have
them steeped with pickled cabbage and cranberries. She also

asked to borrow the enameled caviar dish—that should really impress him.

How did Lidia know all this, all these subtleties about how to set a table, how to launder, to blue and starch, and how to fold a man's shirt, how to safeguard linen from moths over the winter, how to crush a pill for a child and put it in cranberry mousse, and all the rest? Partly it came from Emilia, who had taught her all sorts of things, partly from courses she had taken, and the rest she had conjured out of thin air using her imagination. Lidia might not be pretty, but she was formidably intelligent, something she had known for a long time. Of all the people of her acquaintance, only Emilia was cleverer. As for the others, she had sometimes thought she had met a really clever woman, but she subsequently turned out to be no cleverer than Lidia. Lidia recognized she had made a few blunders in her dealings with the male sex, both with Kolya and with Gennady, but that was a long time ago. Now she had seen the light and realized that all her life she had been looking in the wrong direction. As they say, better late than never.

Martin was half an hour late already, and Lidia, in her immaculate apartment, wearing a dazzlingly white blouse, standing beside the laid table, kept rushing from the door to the window and cursing herself for a fool. What a stupid thing to do! She should have known this would happen. The smart thing would have been to go to Sokolniki, find him at the exhibition, and drag him here.

Hover as Lidia might by the window, she failed to spot her visitor coming because he didn't approach the apartment from the lane. The twit had walked off in the wrong direction from the Bauman metro station and tramped this way and that for forty minutes in the heat, until two schoolgirls brought him to his destination.

He rang the doorbell and came bearing flowers. Roses, and not just three, five, or seven as a Russian might have, but twelve. He stood in the doorway all wet, the sweat dripping from his forehead, his mouth open, out of breath. *His heart's not up to much,* Lidia immediately thought with alarm. Hers was a practiced eye, and she had also taken courses in medicine. At that time you couldn't go on to massage courses unless you'd been through medical college, and she was desperate to learn massage.

*"Ich warte Ihnen so lang,"* Lidia said.

He started apologizing, but his eyes were all over the place. A good start.

"Do you allow me," he said, "to remove my jacket?"

The jacket was still gray, but a different one, without the sheen. He removed it. Lidia took it for him, and it was as smooth as silk. Perhaps it *was* silk. Switzerland is an extremely rich country. Emilia had told her long ago, "They have more banks than we have bars." Martin's light-blue shirt was dark blue under the arms and on the back. He really had been sweating, poor lamb, and she didn't even have a bathroom of her own. This was a decidedly proletarian apartment building. She could think herself lucky she had at least her own separate toilet.

Then Lidia had a moment of inspiration. "Sit down here a moment." He sat in the armchair she indicated and looked at her table as if it were a museum exhibit. His mouth gaped slightly, evidently a habit of his.

Lidia meanwhile darted to the kitchen and half filled a bowl with water. She brought it through, holding it out, and set it on the floor directly in front of him. Then she sat nimbly down. "Allow me . . . excuse me. . . ." She took off his gray shoes and his socks, which were also gray.

The Swiss businessman's eyes were out on stalks and he flapped his lips. *"Was? Was?"*

"It's what we do in Russia," Lidia said. "If you're too hot, a cold footbath is extremely good for you. And a cold compress on the forehead. With my medical training I know all about these things."

Her German might not have been too elegant, but he understood and nodded his bald head. *"Ja, ja."*

What feet he had, what dainty little feet, what little toes. Did he have them pedicured? When she thought back to Kolya's hooves, the fermenting muck in his toenails, which it was impossible to get out. . . . "It's the boots," he would say. That smell came from the boots, and washing or not washing his feet wouldn't make the slightest difference. Whether he wore tarpaulin boots or chrome leather, any guy in boots, you could bet, would have smelly feet, said Kolya.

The moment Lidia saw his little toes she saw her future. This was her moment of destiny.

Lidia had a subtle smile. Smiling made her drooping nose touch her lip. This did not improve her looks, but she was clever enough to know that, and when she smiled she would lower her head and turn a little to one side. "We live in the East," she said, "and this is what we do in Russia."

He said something in reply which seemed to register approval, but the language was too complicated and she couldn't understand the words. Never mind, she would learn all those words, no problem. There was the dictionary lying on the shelf. It was no big deal.

She placed one foot on a towel, dried it, tugged the toes to straighten them, then the second foot. His shoes were soft and smooth. What did they make them from? You could wear leather like that anywhere on your body. His face expressed surprise and bewilderment. She had shocked him. Good!

The napkin was encircled in a silver napkin ring, the fork had a German monogram. "Oh! Gothic script: *CR.*"

"Yes. Christine Runge, my grandmother from Riga." (Christine Runge was actually Emilia Karlovna's grandmother. What difference did it make?) The Swiss raised his eyebrow. She really was a most interesting woman.

"Bon appetit! Do have some hors d'oeuvres" (in faultless German). Lidia had learned all these little mealtime expressions by heart the first year she went to work as Emilia's maid. Emilia was looking after five children at that time, in a kind of private nursery. She remembered them perfectly. Little Jewish children, all of them, as sweet as could be: two sisters, Masha and Anya, and Shurik, Grisha, and Milochka. They were brought in the morning with their little covered dishes, all of them for nine o'clock, but Milochka was brought at half-past nine by her great-grandfather, who was as old as the moss on a tree stump. Emilia took them out to the square for a walk and back for half past eleven. Lidia removed their coats, washed their hands, and took them into the room. There was half an hour until lunch. While Lidia warmed up the food they had brought, they played German bingo and spoke only German. *"Ich habe Nummer einundzwanzig."* They spoke German at lunch too: *"Geben Sie mir, bitte"; "Danke . . . Entschuldigung. . . . Das hat mir geschmeckt."*

After that Lidia washed the dishes while the children had a rest hour: the three girls were put in the big bed together; Shurik on the couch; Grisha on the two-seater settee. Whether they actually slept was neither here nor there, but they mustn't say a word. It was the rest hour. That was the rule. Then they all got up, washed, and had tea. There was cake at teatime, which Emilia provided. Lidia could make that cake with her eyes shut: two egg yolks mixed with half a cup of sugar, add four ounces of chocolate-flavored butter. . . .

"Oh, caviar!"

"Yes, please take some. We have Astrakhan and Caspian caviar. This is Astrakhan. I prefer it. It is not black but gray, and the grains are smaller. It's very creamy. Please, please. Take some butter. It's Vologda butter. Try it. Can you taste the nutty flavor? It's the best butter in Russia. I know Swiss dairy products are very good, but this Russian butter is also excellent. *Perfekt. Sehr perfekt. Kalach* is a special kind of Russian bread roll. *Ein russische Brötchen.* A little glass of vodka? Just a little one. Good health! *Prosit!*"

He took just a little of everything, tested it on his tongue, pressed it against his gums, his expression tentative, exactly like Emilia. Perhaps he was a Lett as well? He nodded his head, moving his arm to one side.

"Eels." The first word in any German dictionary: *Aal.* "They live in the Baltic Sea. You don't have eels in Switzerland, do you?

"Tomato stuffed with sheep's cheese. It's a Bulgarian recipe. I learned it from a course about cuisine of the peoples of the world. What is a popular Swiss dish? Fondue? Lasagne?"

"No, that is in French Switzerland. We live in the German part. In my region people like potato pudding. I'll have to look that up in the dictionary." An exceptional woman. Such beautiful hair. If you let it down it would be truly magnificent. It would probably come below her waist.

And the way he ate his food! Slowly, precisely, the napkin on his knees, no clattering about with his knife and fork, as if he had been taught by Emilia herself. Eating not in order to satisfy hunger but purely in the service of beauty, the way people play the piano or dance. Russians can't eat like that to save their lives. Actually, Lidia can because she has been taught by Emilia.

She took the dishes with the hors d'oeuvres out to the kitchen. On the way she turned toward the hall stand and sniffed his jacket. She breathed in, and her loins caught fire.

While she was out in the kitchen, ladling fish soup out of the pan and into the soup tureen, Martin was trying to find the answer to a riddle. It didn't add up for him, this unheard-of hospitality. He had never tried caviar in his life; he had never dreamed he would. The table settings were fit for a czar. They wouldn't be out of place in a museum. In spite of all that, the apartment was beggarly, a slum. What a mysterious woman! And his feet? How she had washed his feet for him! One could expect a lot from her. He had been going to see a certain Polish woman for eight years before he got married to Elise. He paid her two hundred francs, and she had never given him so much as a bottle of mineral water. He had to take everything there himself: water, coffee, cake. Not for nothing do they talk about the mystery of the Russian soul.

He subsequently turned out not to be all that young. Despite being fresh-looking and plump, he was already about forty-eight. His face, though, was very smooth, quite without wrinkles, his suntan was even, and it was only the top of his head that was bald. For the rest, he was a very, very nice man. Over there in Switzerland everyone was like that—clean, respectable, nice—but Lidia only discovered this later.

At the moment she knew just one thing: You didn't meet people like Martin in Moscow; if she searched for a hundred years she would not get anyone like him here. Perhaps actresses or singers had such husbands, but she personally had never seen any, either in Emilia's house or at the clinic, in the teacher training institute or at the University of Marxism-Leninism. Nowhere.

The fish course. You weren't going to impress someone from Switzerland with meat. Sterlet soup with fish tartlets, but not too much. *Kabachok,* a light vegetable marrow dish. Béchamel sauce.

With a partner like this Lidia, a man could open a restaurant tomorrow. Not in the center of Zurich, of course, but in some agreeable location like Zollikon or Kilchberg. Lidia, a pleasant name, an elegant name. And an elegant figure. Her waist . . . Undoubtedly there is a charm in smaller women.

Elise with her size, her girth, could never look elegant. He frowned.

Lidia was alert: "Don't you like vegetables?"

"Very much. Especially potatoes. Do you know, I grew up in the countryside, and it was during the war. Don't imagine that because Switzerland didn't take part in the war we lived very well. We had a hard life during the war. We ate potatoes and milk. It is a healthy diet, but for peasants. Simple, and there wasn't much of it. Your cooking is fantastic. Have you never worked in a restaurant? You could be a chef."

"No, I cook only for friends. I very much enjoy having friends round for a meal. . . . Here, have some of this, it's called *nemchura*. In Russia people visit each other very often, cook for each other, bake *pirog*, it's a bit like sponge cake, but it doesn't have to be sweet."

"Do you have many friends?"

"Not very many. I like only the very best quality, so I don't have very many friends."

"Oh, yes. Quality is very important. That is the basis of everything, quality. The firm I represent has been in existence for sixty years because it manufactures paint of very high quality."

The firm belonged to Elise, and that was the cause of all his troubles. If only the firm had belonged to someone else, or to no one, or was just private. Indeed, if it had belonged to him. . . . But he was so firmly in the embrace of his paint-and-varnish wife that he sometimes woke up from a terrifying dream in which he was stuck in paint and couldn't get his feet out of it. He would try, he would tug desperately, only to see that his feet were those of a fly.

"May I?" Her cool arm touched his forearm as she collected his plate. "Coffee? Tea?"

He had intended even before leaving to find himself a Russian prostitute in Moscow. Alas, such institutions as he had

found, for example, in Amsterdam, where he had once enjoyed the services of a very interesting Chinese girl, simply
did not exist here, and he hadn't the courage to pick up a
woman in the street, although there were plenty of them wandering around the exhibition, and not a few around the Hotel
Moskva, where he was staying. All of them somehow seemed
too young and raised the suspicion that if you went with them
you might land yourself in a scandal. He had been briefed
about that before he left Zurich. Lidia, however, was plainly a
respectable woman, with caviar and table silver. When, nevertheless, her bare arm touched his bare forearm, he guessed that
just maybe. . . . The thought was enough to arouse him. He
asked where the toilet was, and Lidia showed him through.
Everything was spotless but desperately poor. But then, what
about the caviar? He had to wait some time before he was able
to urinate. He fancied this woman. That much stuck out a
mile.

The washbasin was the sink in the kitchen. He went there.
Lidia was standing with her back to him, and her long neck,
bending over the cooktop making the coffee. Two little
ringlets of hair twisted on her neck. Her legs were a delight,
with slender ankles and calves firm as a ballerina's. On high
heels. He waited while she turned off the gas and took off the
coffee, then put his left hand on her waist and with the right
drew her to him. She lowered her face onto his shoulder, and
he realized he was going to get lucky and even more, because he
had his way with Elise but just any old how, while here there was
such inspiration.

He labored over Lidia until late in the evening. He achieved
his output target for a month ahead. He had never felt himself
to be a giant in sex, but that night he discovered something of
the giant in himself because of this woman with the slender
waist, this extraordinary woman of mystery, with gray caviar
but no bathroom or even a shower, with silver place settings

and unshaven armpits. And so educated, too. On all the walls there were framed diplomas, at the very least eight of them, and she had a grandmother whose initials were *CR* in Gothic script, yet she did not even have a telephone.

Yes, yes, of course, Swiss women were just cows, Poles were greedy, Chinese were venal; but this Russian Lidia was a miracle. She really was a mysterious Russian soul. Where had he got that from? Who had said that? It might have been their great writer Leo Tolstoy, or perhaps it was his schoolmaster in Niederdorf.

Then, late in the night, they fed once more on caviar with butter and *kalach,* and drank champagne, entirely respectable champagne. If she was a schoolteacher, how could she afford champagne? And tomorrow—today, already—he had to leave and he could not even give her a decent present. Everything suggested she was from a very good family, perhaps even from the aristocracy. Such an interesting appearance in every particular, you could tell she was a person with good taste. And she could cook, as well! This was not Switzerland. In Russia there had been a lot of aristocrats; they had counts and princes and barons. But then again, perhaps she was a KGB secret agent under instructions to investigate him. His testicles contracted at the thought. No, that was impossible.

Lidia fearlessly went to see him off at Sheremetievo. Everything there was very impressive and had a strong odor of foreignness. They exchanged addresses, of course, but that was vapor, the stuff of dreams, without substance. The only substantial thing was that Lidia had been happy as never before in her life. She was already aware that the last seconds of her happiness were ticking away, and she would never again in her life see this Martin, who was so unusual. Such men simply did not exist. Even his sweat did not smell. It was as if he were an angel.

In the plane, Martin immediately fell asleep and slept all the way to Zurich. Lidia, however, from the moment she got onto the bus taking her back to the airport reception center in Moscow, cried all the way home, even in the metro and as she was walking through the side streets to her apartment.

Back home, Lidia got washed. She really was not one for weeping. She finished what little remained of the caviar. She washed and cleaned; she took Emilia's china and silver, wrapped each piece separately, and placed screws of newspaper between the items to make sure they wouldn't get chipped or damaged. She put everything in a bag so that tomorrow it would be ready for her to take to Emilia before going on to school.

AS SOON as Martin left, she was inundated with work. She got two new customers for massage; the director of the Pioneers' Club wanted her to knit a dress in mohair. All summer she had sat yawning in the after-school tuition office, but now that the holidays were ending the children started preparing themselves and came in every day. Her main preoccupations, however, were the German language and postcards. Lidia had decided first to enroll in a new course and second to start collecting postcards with reproductions of Russian paintings or views of the Russian countryside.

She mailed them every day. She would write a few sentences on the postcard along the lines of

This depicts one of the most beautiful views of our North Russian countryside. I wish you happiness, good health, and success in your work.

*Lidia*

Or,

A painting by the famous Russian artist Vasily Surikov, *The Morning of the Execution of the Streltsy*. It depicts a historical event when the young Czar Peter the First foiled a plot by his sister Sophia. I wish you happiness, health, and success in your work.

*Lidia*

She would put the postcard in an envelope and affix a pretty commemorative stamp. It was both civilized and not importunate, just a reminder that she existed.

The postcards were being sent not to his home address but to a post office box number. By some caprice of the postal service, Lidia's postcards took just two weeks to reach their addressee, while she received the first letter from him almost two months after it was sent. Although she was sure she would get it, she felt it was a miracle when it arrived. More exactly, she was sure a miracle would happen and that she would get a letter from Martik. Martik was what she had called him to herself from the first day she met him.

Lidia remembered, as if she had seen it in a film, every detail of the day—the morning—when she removed from her letterbox an envelope as white as a fainting fit, with a stamp depicting somewhere in the mountains and the address finely written in black ink. She pulled off her leather glove and, with her bare hand, extracted the envelope. Even though she had allowed just enough time to get to work, she went back up to her apartment, took off her coat and overshoes, and sat down at the table to read the letter. The first thing to come out of the envelope, however, was a photograph of Martik wearing white shorts, which came down to his knees, and a white vest, standing beside a fence with a tennis racquet in his hands. Her heart fairly stopped beating.

And what a letter there was inside! What a letter: the greeting precisely in the middle—*Meine liebe Lidia!*—the margins as if invisibly delimited, every sentence beginning on a new line. Oddly, however, although everything was written very clearly she couldn't make out a single word. None of the letters seemed to have been formed normally. In the end she wrapped it in paper, slipped it into a paper bag, and rushed off to work, because that morning they had a local history excursion for sixth-graders to the Red October candy factory.

In the evening, Emilia Karlovna first spent a while turning the letter over in her hands, studying it from every angle, and viewing Lidia with a new interest. It would not be too much to say that she had brought this girl up with her own hands. She had rented a dacha in the Moscow Region around 1958. Her husband, Ivan, was still alive, so yes, it was 1958. The landlady's niece, an orphan called Liddy from somewhere in Belorussia, was serving in the guesthouse. She was a quiet girl, cowed and with no abilities whatsoever, or so it had seemed to Emilia Karlovna at first. On the last day, just before leaving, she nevertheless decided to take her with her. She suggested it to the landlady. What was she called? She couldn't remember. . . . No, she was called Nastya, and she was perfectly happy to let the girl go. Liddy wasn't yet sixteen and was already in Moscow by the time she received her internal passport; Ivan Savelievich was a retired colonel and able to arrange it through his personnel department. He registered her address as a factory hostel, but in fact she lived with them, next to the kitchen.

Now, as Emilia held the letter, she looked at Lidia with new respect. Well done! Well done, girl! From completely dire circumstances, out of nothing at all, she had really done very well. She had got herself an education and an apartment of her own. She had even managed to make something rather aristocratic out of her unprepossessing appearance. She had style, there was no denying it. The fact of the matter was that, in relative terms, her own daughter, Laura, had not done half as well.

Emilia Karlovna wanted to tell Lidia that she used to go to Zurich before the war with her grandmother and had been

taken to Geneva and Paris, but the habit of never telling anyone anything about herself proved too strong. Since 1945,
when she had met Ivan Savelievich, she had understood that
the main thing in modern life was to keep quiet. Ivan really
had completely fallen for her but even to him, a captain in the
NKVD, Emilia said nothing whatever about herself. She was
merely a girl from a poor Latvian family, her father a skilled
worker. Oh, in Latvia we always had great respect for profes-
sionals; he was an instrument maker and first class at his job.
Ivan, himself from the working class, was impressed by that.
That her father had been assassinated by partisans while serving the Germans as commander of a Latvian *Sonderkommando,*
energetically implementing the Judenfrei program, was something she omitted to mention.

Liddy was also good at keeping her mouth shut. She knew
things she didn't talk about. She too had skeletons in her cupboard. Her father had been arrested after Belorussia was liber-
ated by the Red Army and shot in 1944 for sins of some
description that he had committed against Soviet power. It
wasn't entirely clear whether Lidia had forgotten or had never
known anything about it. He left eleven children and a
burned-out hut. Of the eleven, only three survived, and they
did not want to keep in contact. They dispersed and disappeared. She had heard that her elder brother was in the army
and that her sister lived somewhere like Nalchik or Pyatigorsk.
Everything in the past had been forgotten for all time, both for
Emilia and for Lidia.

Emilia, however, had been almost beautiful, tall, with bub-
ble breasts, a fringe of dyed hair over her forehead, and a
backside like a pear. Like two pears, in fact. Ivan Savelievich was
billeted in her apartment until he was allotted his own place by
the state. When he did get it, he moved in together with
Emilia. He took in Emilia's daughter, Laura, too, and later
gave her his surname.

Every paper that documented the past—photographs, cer-
tificates of any description, diplomas, letters—burned to ashes
in conflagrations large and small, accidental or deliberate.
Only the silver and the good china survived from the old
times; Ivan Savelievich had no objection to them. He adapted
rapidly. It is not so difficult to make the transition from using
an aluminum bowl to using a silver one. The reverse transition
would have been considerably more problematical, but he
didn't have to endure that. Emilia humored him to the day he
died, not because of any great love for him but because she was
a respectable woman. She taught Lidia to do the same. Things
didn't work out quite so well with Laura.

The letter was clearly from a respectable man, there was no
doubt about that. He thanked Lidia for her exceptionally generous hospitality, confessed that he had never before had the
pleasure of meeting such a cultured woman, hinted also at her
incomparable feminine charms, and went on to inform her
that he had not immediately opened her eyes to his married
status because at first it had seemed entirely irrelevant and
afterward he had been afraid of upsetting her. He had never
imagined that after returning to Switzerland he would think
about her all the time. She was so much in his thoughts that his
relationship with his wife had completely fallen apart, and now
he was thinking about his future. There were some important
decisions he needed to make, but this was very difficult. His
head was going round in circles.

After Emilia had read the letter out, Lidia was also able to
decipher his writing. He had an odd way of writing *r, n,* and *k.*
*l* looked like *t.* Once you got used to that, however, it was perfectly readable. In conclusion, Lidia played her trump: the
photograph. Emilia examined it closely before reaching her
verdict. "Lidia, you must take this very seriously. You will have
to work hard without any great hope of success. These matters
are far from straightforward."

*What a fool my Laura is,* Emilia Karlovna thought tetchily. *In spite of all her advantages, the best she can manage is that wretched Jew, Yevgeny.* She told Lidia to write the reply in Russian, and she would translate it in order to make the best impression.

Lidia spent three days writing it, and the letter that resulted took Emilia aback; it was more than passable, it was positively elegant.

Even more did it take Martin's wife aback. She was looking in a drawer in her husband's desk for a copy of a missing receipt when she found a stack of twelve picture postcards and the very same elegant letter, from which it appeared that Martin had got himself a woman in Russia. This was something Elise had already begun to suspect for a number of reasons. An enormous domestic row erupted over what had taken place. Martin might perhaps have got over his amorous adventure. It might of its own accord have taken its place as one of the episodes of his (on the whole, rather modest) sexual biography, with Lidia being relegated to a place in a series that began with the Pole, continued with his one-night stand with the Chinese girl, and concluded with his one-night stand with a Russian—her. Elise, however, escalated the row by unworthily accusing Martin of being useless in every respect and impugning his masculine prowess when, as he now knew for a fact, all he needed to be capable of great things was for a lady to be bowled over by him and to plunge his overworked feet into a bowl of cooling water. Succumbing to an unfamiliar masculine assertiveness, which felt as if he had it on hire, he told Elise with quiet dignity that, yes, he had fallen in love with a Russian woman. He had been prepared to suppress his feelings but if she, Elise, now wished for a divorce, he, Martin, had no objection.

Pulling out from her revolting crocodile-skin handbag the edge of a stack of postcards with their incriminating Russian views and the envelope with Lidia's elegant letter, Elise raised a meaningful eyebrow and made vague mention of a lawyer. Even without a lawyer, Martin had little doubt that the twelve years he had been toiling in paints and varnishes would simply be stolen from him. The fact that he had built up the business and paid off the debts that hung over the company after Elise bought out her brother would count not a franc to his credit. All his labors would have been in vain. Perhaps he would get only a part of the money for the house, and even then it was unclear what use Elise might make of the letter. That same evening Martin wrote Lidia an unplanned letter, informing her that he would come to Russia for Christmas, and a second letter to a lawyer requesting an appointment.

The divorce proceedings and the division of their property took more than a year, but the outcome was more advantageous for Martin than could have been foreseen. He was not the joint owner of the company, but neither had Elise paid him a salary. She was now obliged to pay compensation, and very substantial compensation at that, for his labors over the past twelve years.

In the two and a half years that preceded the solemnization of his new marriage, Martin saw Lidia for a total of six days, divided between two trips. He confirmed his belief that she was indeed a living treasure, providing top quality massage, care, food, and sex.

He and Lidia agreed to restrict their meetings for the greater good of their future together. Martin saved money furiously. After the divorce, Elise unexpectedly invited him to continue working for her as an employee. Martin thought it over carefully and agreed. He was now earning a very fair salary. If you took the compensation and added to it as much again, after his new marriage it would be possible to open a small restaurant.

Lidia for her part also prepared purposefully for her new life. With a mysterious smile, she handed in her notice and abruptly switched her allegiance from the cultural sphere to public catering. She got herself taken on in the restaurant of the Central Hotel as an assistant chef. The hotel served Russian food but, as Lidia soon found out, on a very primitive level. What was it, after all, that foreigners ordered? Pancakes and caviar, borscht, vodka. Nothing too ambitious. Perhaps such primitiveness was all that was needed? At the same time, Lidia was able to check out the finer points of the production process. After three months there was no point in staying on at the Central; everything there was to know she had already learned. A new goal suggested itself: to earn as much money as she could for her dowry, so that she could arrive in Zurich in style, not as a downtrodden waif but as a grand Russian lady.

She needed to buy an Astrakhan fur coat like Emilia's, gray, and a diamond ring, and a pair of earrings. She also wanted to buy gold and red Khokhloma tableware for her future restaurant. She liked the idea. The only problem was how to get it out of the country. She stopped sending Martik views of the north of Russia and instead sent him a collection of postcards depicting Khokhloma ducks and spoons. He approved.

A fairy tale is soon told, however, and the day came for Lidia to pack into two suitcases all her best clothes, which she wouldn't be ashamed to wear in Switzerland. (In fact, she was wrong. The only clothes she would wear afterward were what Martik bought her. All her own clothes ended up being used for rags.) She bought a train ticket to save money. Lidia departed from the Belorussky Station, on her way to the legendary city of Zurich, where the cellars are full of gold and where Lenin once lived, sitting in the Odeon Café on the bank of the River Limmat, eating *Apfelstrudel* and dropping sweet crumbs onto his volume of Marx. Zurich. The very name made you want to salivate.

In the compartment Lidia sat very straight, mechanically rubbing the end of her nose with her finger, with her head, weighed down by its heavy bun, thrown backward. When she opened her mouth wide to take a bite of something, her lipstick would leave a mark on the tip of her nose and she periodically took measures to put things right. Through the window the scenery of her Russian homeland flashed by, and Lidia, who for the last two and a half years had dreamed only of the moment when this train would move out, was suddenly overwhelmed and started thinking nostalgic thoughts about Russian birch trees, although for the moment all that stretched beyond the window was scrub and suburban garbage dumps. She thought she might be feeling homesick, although why should she feel homesick when this was all there was to Russia, a million Kolyas in tarpaulin boots, a million old women like Aunt Nastya, who had never once inquired how her niece was getting on in the city, or even whether she was alive or dead. The one person she felt close to was Emilia Karlovna. Only she understood Lidia. Of course she did. *Selbstverständig.*

Two elderly commercially active Polish women with whom she was sharing the compartment asked her a question in mid-Slavonic, but Lidia was in such a turmoil that, to her own surprise, she answered them, very confidently, *"Entschuldigen bitte. Ich verstehe nicht."* The Poles immediately recognized their mistake in taking her for a Russian, when it was obvious she was a German. Her suit of jersey material was of bourgeois quality, and she had rings on her fingers.

Oh, Martik, Martik! He was the reward for all she had gone through, especially after two changes of train. He met her at the station in Zurich in a hirsute dark-green overcoat and an equally hairy hat with a narrow brim, cocked up at the back and with a brightly colored little feather to the side. He looked so sweet and even smelled of eau de cologne. He didn't grab her suitcases as a Russian man would have, but signaled for a porter, kissed Lidia, and walked off arm in arm with her. All around was a foreign world the like of which had never been shown in Soviet films. There had been a film about Rome, for example, which Lidia well remembered. It was very dirty there, with rubbish dumps and ruins. They weren't that far ahead of us, and they ate cheap food, just like in Russia—the same macaroni—and even thought it was worth filming. She could see now why the Soviet authorities didn't show the real world abroad. There had been good reason for Lidia's two-year stint at the University of Marxism-Leninism, where they filled everyone's heads with nonsense.

Her first year in Zurich was the happiest. They were still just a bit too short of capital to rent suitable premises for their restaurant, so they lived on a shoestring, renting the tiniest studio rather than an apartment. But how high the rent was! Lidia had not been expecting everything to be so expensive in wealthy Switzerland. She was very capable and well able to adapt, but they were hard pressed to get by. Martin checked all the outgoing money himself. He was a trained accountant. Lidia wanted to get a job straight away. He wouldn't let her at first, but later he did. She translated all her diplomas into German and was taken on as a manicurist. Martin was amazed at how quickly she got established. By the end of the year they had signed a contract to rent a marvelous building for a restaurant. There had been some kind of canteen there before, which was good, because when people are used to getting fed in a particular place, they keep coming back from force of habit.

Martin invited his country cousin to come and work for them. She was a very simple woman, almost rustic, but she dressed like a town dweller. Although only just. Lidia was beginning to understand a few things, perhaps even more than Emilia Karlovna: which shops were for the less well-off, which were for those who are a bit more prosperous. Martin was already very knowledgeable about this because his rich ex-wife, Elise, had taught him. By now Lidia knew that not all foreign goods were equal, but there were, of course, still some things she didn't understand in detail. Why, for example, the English Shop was even more expensive than Swiss shops, even though there was not the slightest discernible difference in quality. She was aware that French items were very pretty but risky; the quality was not up to much. That was even more true of Italian goods.

Before the restaurant's opening, Martin advertised it, sent invitations to his acquaintances, and hung up posters all over the district announcing, *The Russian House Restaurant invites you to a Russian meal.* They hired one Russian waiter, a slightly odd man, displaced and not entirely Russian. Nevertheless, he pronounced the word *borscht* very satisfactorily. A second, a local lad, they hired for one night only.

The restaurant's first evening was a great success. It was the last happy day of Lidia's life. The next morning it was all over. Martin did not wake at six, which was when they usually got up; he just slept on and on. At first Lidia did not want to wake him. He must be tired, let him rest. At ten she did try to wake him but was unable to. He lay on his side, and one arm was twisted awkwardly. Lidia touched it. It was cold. He was breathing, at least, but he did not wake up and he was very heavy. The doctor was called and Martin was immediately taken to the hospital. He'd had a stroke. It was the end. She immediately calculated that her happy life had lasted one year and twenty-one days, from her arrival until his stroke. Now she faced a nightmare.

One thing at least was good. All the hospitals in Switzerland were on the level of the Kremlin Clinic in Moscow. The nurses did everything themselves: changed diapers and fed their patients. You didn't even have to pay to have someone on duty during the night. When Ivan Savelievich was in hospital with cancer, the three of them, she, Emilia, and Laura, had been run off their feet. Lidia recognized how lucky she had been in coming to Switzerland. At first they fed him intravenously; then the nurses began feeding him normally.

For three months there was little change. You couldn't even really tell whether or not he recognized Lidia. One time it seemed as if he did, the next it seemed that he didn't. He couldn't walk, but they moved him to a chair. Lidia would visit him in the mornings. She had to change buses, and it took three and a half hours. Meanwhile, she had a restaurant to run; she had food to buy and cook. When was it to be done? She enrolled at a driving school. They had a car but Lidia didn't have a driving license. What a fool! She cursed herself. How much unnecessary knowledge had she accumulated over the years, while she hadn't even got round to learning to drive. The lessons extended over three months and lasted for four hours, three times a week. It was a sentence of hard labor, not a life. She managed five hours' sleep if she was lucky, but when she was out of luck she didn't even manage three. She was sorry for Martik, but she didn't even really have time for that. He was like a little baby. The down on the back of his head was pressed flat, and as soon as Lidia got him home she slicked it back into place and started giving him an hour's massage every day. The doctors said he would never recover, but the left leg, which had been affected, began gradually to grow stronger. After three months he could stand. He held on to the back of a chair and stood by himself.

Business in the restaurant, meanwhile, was going well. Lidia did not give up on it. She had to simplify things, of course, introducing something akin to set menus. But life in Switzerland proved, oh, so hard. You had to pay for everything—electricity, water, gasoline, garbage removal—and the taxes were something else. She had to start taking courses again. Nobody would tell you anything unless you paid them. At first Lidia had greatly liked the Swiss for their good manners and cleanliness, but they were very canny. Back in Russia she had always thought of herself as clever, but here everyone turned out to be just as clever, working everything out in advance.

The Swiss took to her Russian restaurant precisely because they soon calculated that for the money they paid they were being very well fed. If Lidia had not been on her own she would have enlarged the premises after a year. There was a summer terrace she could have adapted. Indeed, she would not have been afraid to rent a larger building, if only Martik had been a human being rather than a chronic invalid.

She had no time to grieve or think about anything, however, because there was just so much to get through. In the morning she had to wash Martik, give him his massage, put him on the bedpan, and then feed him. Every two days she went to Frau Temke's farm for vegetables, and every two days to the butcher's. Fish was delivered to her door, but for groceries she went to the wholesalers. That was only once in two weeks. All the cooking she did herself. Of course, everything was carefully planned. She had to buy an industrial refrigerator. She froze a lot, although she would never have admitted it to anyone; the Swiss looked down on frozen food. She prepared the pancake filling for the blini once a week and froze that; not the fish, of course, because it would have spoiled the flavor. To be perfectly honest, the Swiss didn't really know all that much about cooking. They appreciated the fact that she gave them large helpings.

Lidia was terrified the whole year that she would not make ends meet, but at year's end it turned out that she had made them meet very nicely and even had a bit to spare. She banked the profit under her own name. At that moment she understood the meaning of life for the Swiss. If Martik had been well, she might not have come to the realization through the haze of marital bliss, but since that was now at an end, Lidia came to the realization that in Switzerland happiness was expressed in numbers. The greater the number, the greater the happiness. It was not nakedly a matter of money. There were subtleties. You needed people to appreciate your success, to be made aware that you were smart and had talent by barely perceptible pointers. She painted the fence twice a year. She planted new flowers on the terrace. She hung English curtains. For those with eyes to see, she wore Bally shoes and a Loden coat. There was no Emilia Karlovna here, but she would have noticed.

Lidia sacked Martik's rustic cousin. She just got under her feet and, although she was a true-born Swiss, knew nothing. In her place she hired other assistants: a Yugoslav girl who had a good head on her shoulders and was also married to a Swiss, and another helper, a crippled, very ugly woman who was, however, brisk and businesslike. Lidia even entrusted her with some of the more straightforward jobs at the stove. She too later turned out to be not a real Swiss but of Jewish origin. One more waiter was Italian. Everybody knows that Italians are born waiters, courteous, smiling, and full of jokes, but inclined to pilfer. Nobody pilfered from Lidia. She ran a tight ship. A business reputation is no small matter; you can't buy it for money. It is like a seed of grain. You sow it in a pot, water and fertilize it, and it grows. One year, a second, a third. And then the same all over again.

Martik grew thinner and more debilitated and turned into an old man. Lidia, on the other hand, who in Russia had been close to being regarded as ugly, was here considered an interesting lady. Sometimes she was even taken for a Frenchwoman. She taught her husband to walk again. Now he could hobble around the house with a stick and walk in their garden. Lidia bought him a pedigreed dog, a gray toy poodle, and called it Milok. Milok cost next to nothing for vaccinations and vet's fees, but here too Lidia had picked a winner. The Swiss loved animals. Families would come to the restaurant to dine; the children would play with Milok and later ask their parents to take them to play with the Russian dog again. These were good customers. The children called Martik "the doggy's grandad."

When Lidia had got the management of the Russian restaurant and looking after her invalid husband completely sorted out and running smoothly, for old times' sake she again enrolled in a course. For two years she studied French and, of course, succeeded in mastering it. She thought about English. She would have liked to learn to ski, but it was out of the question to leave the restaurant, Martik, and Milok for several days, even though now she was no longer standing at the stove. She had two chefs whom she herself had trained to do everything. Twice a week she went to a swimming pool, and occasionally to a women's club where she met other businesswomen. She met them once, she met them twice, and decided that what was lacking in her personal life was recognition. These women too wore Bally shoes, mink coats, and Orient watches. Lidia was irritated that for them it was only what they expected. She wanted to tell them they were all foolish domesticated hens while she, Lidia, was a soaring eagle. They had been born in Switzerland on a lump of butter, while she was born in a peasant hut with an earthen floor and a thatched roof. Until she was fifteen she had worn felt boots in winter and gone barefoot in summer and had acquired her first underclothes in Moscow when, by a stroke of luck, she was taken to work as a maid for a good mistress. Before that, like any other Belorussian peasant girl, she had not even worn a pair of drawers. A feeling of dissatisfaction developed, and an old, suppressed, and unformed dream, like the beginnings of an illness, began to grow and take form and acquire definite contours. Lidia started keeping a list in her business diary, in the last section reserved for personal matters in which the businesswomen entered the details of their meetings with lovers, gynecologists, or plastic surgeons. What she listed, however, was how much she needed to buy for a trip back to Moscow. In Moscow there lived the only person in the world who could properly recognize the magnitude of her achievement.

As with all her other enterprises, Lidia first thought everything through thoroughly. She had kept up no links with Moscow at all. When Emilia Karlovna was bidding her farewell, she had wished her every success but asked her not to write letters or to telephone. At that time the first unpleasantnesses had begun for Laura because her husband, Yevgeny, had signed some protest, was shooting his mouth off left and right, and had brought the predictable disagreeable consequences down on the whole family. Laura listened to his every word spellbound. She seemed not to have a brain of her own and ignored her mother's advice. Emilia Karlovna hated Soviet power but hid her feelings in the depths of her soul, which the state had long since abolished by decree. At the same time, she vehemently despised that idiot Yevgeny who was squawking like an imprudent parrot. Lidia's friends from the Pioneers' Club and the other places where she had studied or worked were not even worth the cost of a postage stamp. The only friend she trusted was her old neighbor, Varya, and at first Lidia maintained a tenuous link, but after Martik's misfortune she stopped writing to her. What was the point?

Now Lidia wrote to Varya and asked her to call Emilia and find out how she was doing. Varya did so, and informed her that they were living as they always had, still in the same place.

Lidia bought herself a good travel bag. Until then she had been on no travels and had no luggage. She began buying the presents for Emilia that she had listed. She decided to dress her anew from head to toe in clothes of the highest quality. She should be completely outfitted, like a new baby. Lidia now spent her spare time shopping. After Christmas, when the

January sales began, she completed her campaign of purchases on which she had spent more than six months. The bag received into its checked interior top-quality items worth a total of all but three thousand Swiss francs: lingerie, panty hose, sandals, shoes, boots, a jersey suit and a silk suit, a jacket, a hat and scarf, a handbag, and a pair of gloves. And all of it matched, because Lidia had taste. She had learned it from Emilia.

Inside the handbag nestled an Orient gold watch, in a case that was a work of Swiss art in its own right.

Lidia then bought herself a three-day individual tour to Moscow, capital of the Soviet Motherland, with accommodation in the Hotel Moskva.

More than ten years had passed since she had first seen Martik off to Zurich, after the memorable and life-changing dinner when his feet were washed and he was fed gray caviar. Sheremetievo had not changed. Liddy-goose had not turned into a beautiful swan, but of her former self nothing remained. She was Frau Gropius, a citizen of Switzerland, wearing an apparently modest raincoat with a soft lining of kangaroo fur. A porter walked behind, carrying her small suitcase and travel bag, and she was met by an Intourist translator, a minor KGB lieutenant with a standard-issue smile bearing a sheet of paper with Lidia's surname on it. A taxi took them to Manège Square. Lidia felt sick with excitement on the way. The interpreter spoke to her in bad German, and Lidia did not reveal her knowledge of Russian. Why should she? In the second-floor restaurant she ordered Stolichnyi salad and galantine but, after trying it, put the fork down. She felt sick.

The next day she was taken on a tour of the city, shown the Borodino Panorama and Moscow State University on the Lenin Hills. She lunched in the restaurant of the Central Hotel with its Russian cuisine. The maître d'hotel was the same person but, of course, didn't recognize her. In the evening she was taken to *Swan Lake* at the Bolshoy Ballet. She sat in the third row of the orchestra wearing a purple silk suit and a diamond brooch shaped like an arrow. She had Americans sitting next to her. One of the women was wearing curlers under a nylon cap. They were going on to a restaurant after the theater, and evidently she needed to have her curls in order for the meal. The ballet was admirable. She and Martik had not gone to the theater in Zurich very often. In Moscow she used to manage to get tickets quite regularly, even for the Taganka and Malaya Bronnaya theaters.

The next day, a Sunday, she told the interpreter she had a headache and didn't want to go on the excursions. The girl offered to send a doctor but Lidia declined, although she really did have a headache and was feeling sick again. At two in the afternoon she took her travel bag and left the hotel. It was a five-minute taxi ride. Emilia lived nearby on Mayakovsky Square. She got out at a gray brick building on Second Tver-skaya Yamskaya Street. The oddly positioned cornerwise building had been constructed for the country's most important ministry after the war. Shortly before his retirement Ivan Savelievich had been allocated a two-room apartment here. She went up to the fourth floor, remembering how—it must have been thirty years ago—she had entered this palatial mansion for the first time. It was connected to the gas mains; it had electricity, a hot-water heater, a bathroom, and a toilet. It was the first time she had seen these things.

The bell hadn't changed, a white button on a black wooden circle. She pressed it, and its ring hadn't changed either. The door was opened, without anyone asking who it was, by Laura.

"Who are you looking for?"

"You. Emilia Karlovna. It's me, Lidia. Laura, do you not recognize me?"

"Lidia! Lidochka! You've been sent by heaven!" Laura exclaimed in delight.

In those years foreigners were immensely useful. You sent out letters and documents with them, since anything sent by post was read by the KGB. Lidia, however, didn't take kindly to her reception. *Here I've arrived from Zurich carrying a bag, so now I'm dear sweet Lidochka. She never had any time for me before.* There was nothing in the bag for Laura.

Then Lidia breathed in the familiar air of the old apartment. She took off her shoes and couldn't believe she still recognized all the footwear in the shoe stand, the brown indoors slippers for visitors, two pairs for children, bygones of the professional past.

"Do you still have children coming here?" Lidia asked, with a smile.

Laura shrugged. "How could we now?"

Lidia went through to the main room where the private nursery school used to assemble. There was the long table with its six chairs, and the piano on which Emilia Karlovna would play a polka or a waltz, not too exuberantly, while the children danced, and the side table by the big sofa covered with a hand-woven rug. In the bay window, with its back to the door, stood a wheelchair, not collapsible, institutional, its iron framework painted white, and above the back of it rose a head of luxuriant piebald hair à la Pompadour. Laura walked to the window, turned the wheelchair round, and wheeled Emilia Karlovna out for public inspection.

She looked just like Martik, as if she were his sister or his mother or grandmother: the magnificently snow-white puffy skin, the little chin from behind which a second chin, flowing and almost transparent, emerged like a ruff, the pale blue eyes in round folds of soft skin, and the apologetic smile sliding down to one side. The only difference was that Martik's nose was short with pronounced nostrils, while Emilia's was long and hooked and pointed at the end.

"Mama, look who has come! Lidia has come! Do you remember Lidia?"

Emilia Karlovna was clutching a deck of cards in her right hand, and it wasn't clear whether she was running through them or simply feeling them. Lidia had completely forgotten that more than anything else in the world her old mistress loved playing solitaire. For heaven's sake, I should have bought some cards. How could I not have thought of that? was her first thought.

"Emilia Karlovna, it's me, Lidia. Do you recognize me?"

Emilia Karlovna smiled Martik's tactful smile, and a round bead of saliva gathered in the corner of her mouth.

"How long ago?" Lidia asked.

"Almost a year," Laura replied quietly. "It's a nightmare. We submitted applications for all of us to emigrate, but we can't think how she's going to travel. When I saw you I immediately thought, There's someone who can help us. We are flying via Vienna. That's not far from you. Who knows how long we shall have to wait there. If you could meet us, or even take out a letter with you for the Jewish Agency to meet us there with a wheelchair. I am sure permission to emigrate is coming any day. There are signs. My husband is completely against going to America. Only Israel is acceptable. I would have preferred America myself. . . ."

Lidia said nothing, taking in the situation. Laura chattered on without a break, twisting and cracking her fingers.

"Mama, Mama." Laura recollected the purpose of Lidia's visit periodically and shook Emilia Karlovna's shoulder. "Look who's come, Mama. Lidia. Do you recognize Lidia? You see, Lidochka, we would have applied long ago, but Mama refused to go to Israel. She wouldn't hear of it, but it was only Israel that Yevgeny wanted. Many of our friends actually prefer America. Perhaps you don't know it, but for all her good points Mama is a bit of an anti-Semite. She absolutely dug her heels in over Israel: no way. After she was ill, though, we applied anyway. It's all the same to her now, isn't it? But when are you going back, Lidochka?"

Laura went out to put on the kettle and Lidia sat down beside Emilia and took her hand.

"Emilia Karlovna, I'm so glad to see you. You are still very beautiful. Are you feeling all right? My Martik, you know, had a stroke too. Seven years ago, but now he is a lot better. He is walking. He used to be sitting in a wheelchair all the time too, but now he can walk and I have bought him a little dog."

Emilia Karlovna seemed to be listening and to understand. Laura came back with the tea tray. The sugar bowl, the milk jug, the pink teacups; everything was just the same. Even the cakes were the same: two egg yolks mixed with half a cup of sugar, four ounces of chocolate-flavored butter. . . . Laura had learned how to make them. She hadn't been able to do that before. Emilia moved her fingers and opened her mouth. She said something that sounded like "U-at."

"Right away, Mama." Laura pressed a piece of cake into the agitated right hand.

Emilia shoved it in her mouth and chewed it contentedly.

"There, you see how it is. All she wants to do all day is eat and eat. She gets cross if I don't let her, but then she has stomach problems. For the past year she hasn't gone once without an enema."

Lidia opened her handbag and took out a bar of chocolate she had been keeping for the maid in the hotel. After a moment's further reflection she took out a small vial of Chanel No. 5. It was her own perfume but she had only just started it.

"Here is a little present for you, Laura."

Emilia Karlovna ate the cakes one after another, completely heedless of the proprieties of swallowing food that for years she had sought to inculcate in her charges. She rammed the cake far into her mouth, pushing it with her broken nails. Crumbs fell on her dirty collar and the worn front of her old blouse. Lidia's head was splitting and she felt really sick. She had yet to learn that this was a first sign of high blood pressure.

"I must go, Laura. I'll call you tomorrow morning. See you again before I fly out."

"Do stay a bit longer. Yevgeny will be back soon," Laura urged her, but Lidia was desperate to get out, spend her last night at the hotel, and leave once and for all just as soon as she could.

She pulled on her shoes, put on her mantlelike coat with its Australian animal lining discreetly concealed from public view, and with an effort lifted the checked bag.

"I have somewhere else I have to go. Some friends have asked me to take this for them."

As a good businesswoman she had all the receipts, just in case, in a separate envelope in the top drawer of the writing desk at home. She could take it all back. It's a good policy to buy items in expensive shops where you can take them back or exchange them if need be, especially if they already know you quite well.

She asked the interpreter to order the taxi a bit earlier than was really necessary. The poor woman was struck dumb when Lidia instructed the driver in perfect Russian, "On the way to Sheremetievo I need to stop off at Spartak Street. I'll show you the turning."

They drove there. The house stood where it always had, a regal four-story ship among the single-story timber huts, but for all that unambiguously a slum. She smiled, imagining to herself Martik's reaction when he had first entered her sad squalid little apartment. She thought for a moment of going up to the third floor, ringing the doorbell, and asking to see what her old residence looked like now. Then she thought better of it.

She told the driver to take her on to Sheremetievo. She checked in her suitcase and the bag, having forgotten her promise to call Laura.

All the way back in the plane, Lidia was dying of impatience. She couldn't wait to get back home and kiss Martik on the sagging corner of his mouth. He was a lot better, a lot better than Emilia. He could at least walk. He was better at smiling. He smiled more convincingly and had a certain number of words he could say entirely meaningfully. In any case, how had her business been getting on without her for the past three days?

She still had the headache and couldn't shake off the nausea. Lidia whispered, almost to herself, but nevertheless just audibly, "Zurich . . . Zurich . . ." and dozed off with the thought that she really had done better than any of them.

*The Beast*

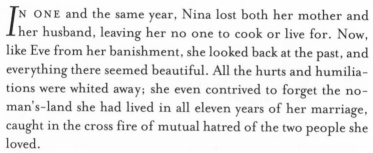

*I*N ONE and the same year, Nina lost both her mother and her husband, leaving her no one to cook or live for. Now, like Eve from her banishment, she looked back at the past, and everything there seemed beautiful. All the hurts and humiliations were whited away; she even contrived to forget the no-man's-land she had lived in all eleven years of her marriage, caught in the cross fire of mutual hatred of the two people she loved.

Now, with the passing of time, she was inclined to remember it all as a drama between complex characters rather than pathetic routine squabbling, day in, day out, inexcusable mutual goading, irritation that sometimes boiled over, and outbursts of rage that recurred every time Nina succeeded in getting them to sit down at the same white tablecloth in the insane hope of reconciling the irreconcilable.

Never had Nina lived in Paradise, however, unless perhaps when she was young and still a student at the Conservatory, before she met Seryozha and suffered her first misfortune. Now they were all dead. It seemed as if life was being rerun and the past, stagily lit with a cinematic aura of happiness, was greedily swallowing up both the desolate present and a future that had lost all meaning.

Her thoughts and feelings now revolved solely around the dead, who looked down at her from every wall. Mama with her harp, Mama wearing a hat, Mama holding a monkey. Seryozha as a boy on a wooden horse, Seryozha as a schoolboy with a translucent shock of hair, Seryozha as a yachtsman with rock-like shoulders. Then the penultimate Seryozha, with jowly cheeks, sly and dangerous, and the ultimate Seryozha, with the thin face, sunken temples, and look of doubt, or perhaps of insight, in his eyes—or perhaps a thought he had finally been able to formulate but that now would never be expressed. And there was Grandma Mzia, who had died before Nina was born, her face stern and belonging to a bygone age, wearing a round bonnet under a dark shawl, a renowned performer of songs that nobody now remembered.

Almost two years had passed since her mother died and eleven months since the death of Seryozha, and things hadn't got any easier, only worse. She was tormented by dreams. Not nightmares, but gray scenes set against a sepia background, lifeless and faded and moldering, so that you couldn't really call them dreams. In these enfeebled scenes, Nina told herself to wake up, but the drab cobweb of shadows would not release her. When at last she did come out of it, she brought to the daylight a mood of indescribable wretchedness as unrelenting as a toothache.

Like a pressure cooker, Nina kept all these unpleasant nocturnal experiences boiling away inside herself and, when she could stand it no longer, complained to her friends. She had two. The elder, Susanna Borisovna, was a highly educated lady with mystical gifts who even belonged to the Anthroposophical Society. The younger was Tomochka, who was very timid, not very bright, and so God-fearing that in the years of their friendship Nina had taken a considerable dislike to this God who demanded so much from her and gave her nothing at all in return. And even that which by birth Tomochka did have, rather pallid good looks, had been taken away from her: her mother had scalded her when she was a child, and her right cheek was disfigured as a result.

Both Nina's friends helped a great deal in her times of trial, but they did not get on well with each other. They were jealous. When meek Tomochka spoke about Susanna she flushed with anemic petulance, not having enough spirit to manage anything more dramatic. She would go pink in the face and hiss, "She will give herself away yet, mark my words. I can feel her devilish wiles in my water. . . ."

Susanna appeared to regard Tomochka with tolerant condescension. Only occasionally would she pass some incidental comment on Tomochka's ignorance, bizarre pagan misconceptions, and overall primitiveness. Nina's late husband could stand neither of them. He considered Tomochka a sad little thing and, recalling Ilf and Petrov's tale of the twelve chairs, referred to Susanna behind her back as "the widow Gritsatsueva."

When primitive Tomochka heard from Nina about her torments in the night, she announced that she would pray for her even more fervently and urged Nina to go and take communion, because these trials were being sent to her solely in order to guide her back to God.

Susanna was a physician of sorts in that she possessed a cosmetological cabinet. She prescribed for Nina a tranquilizer and a sedative and explained her trying dreams as being caused by the incomplete destruction of the astral bodies of her dear departed and by unpropitious circumstances attending their path in the afterlife. She recommended that Nina embark on the path of self-improvement without delay and, to this end, left her a quite exceptionally tedious book about spiritual hierarchies and their reflection in the physical world.

Whether it was the medicine working or Tomochka's prayers, she did for a time begin to sleep better. The shadows of gray and brown ceased to flit before her. Weirdly, however, she now began to dream about a really vile stench. She would be wakened by an intolerable smell so supernaturally powerful it filled her with horror and would then fall asleep again. She began to have the feeling that there was something in her home—a shade, a specter, an unclean spirit—and this stench. It was unlike anything she had ever known, probably related to those chemicals which drive people out of their minds.

After a few days, the stench in her dreams seemed to materialize. One day when she came home from work, Nina found the place filled with a pungent smell of cats. It was revolting, but nothing that went beyond the bounds of respectable realism. With her long sensitive nose Nina soon homed in on the epicenter of the smell: Seryozha's house slippers, which all this time had been lying on the shoe shelf by the front door. Nina meticulously washed them with detergent, but a number of recalcitrant molecules evidently remained, since she also had to spray the apartment with air freshener. The smell of cats still managed to force its way through the fragrances of lavender and jasmine. She rang Susanna to tell her about the problem.

There was a long silence before Susanna unexpectedly said, "You know, Ninochka, you just must give up smoking."

"What on earth for?" Nina asked in amazement.

"You are under attack from occult forces, and smoking blunts mystical awareness," Susanna explained. "There are inauspicious forces at work in your apartment."

*Inauspicious* was putting it mildly. Her apartment was cursed. It was thrice cursed. She had never liked the place. Immediately after her mother died, Seryozha had taken it into his head to exchange their cosy little apartment on Begovaya Street and her mother's one-room studio for this mansion, and nothing Nina could say would stop him. He brushed aside her protests that it was on the top floor and that there were leak

marks on the ceiling. That year things were going so well for
him that a leaky roof was no deterrent. He would replace it if
need be. That was the kind of man he was.

In the course of six months he did all he had planned:
knocked down walls, raised the floor in half the apartment by
almost a foot, and transformed a moderately sized kitchen and
one of the rooms into a refectory. Their entire living space
became a hall with two chambers, cold and drafty. An interior
door led to a large en-suite bathroom, the only place Nina
liked in the whole apartment. Now she had installed a small
table in there and in the mornings drank coffee while sitting
on a stool between the bath and the toilet pedestal.

It was this accursed apartment that had sapped Seryozha's
strength and put him in his grave. Nina particularly hated the
fireplace. From a technical viewpoint it was a failure, the flue
having been designed by a Candidate of Physics and Mathe-
matical Sciences rather than a competent stove setter. Smoke
immediately filled the apartment and billowed in acrid clouds
for ages afterward. Sergey had been unable to put it right
because, by the time his makeover was nearing completion,
he was in thrall to analyses, diagnoses, consultations, and
clinics.

He suffered from a malignant cancer for only six months
or so before dying and leaving the doctors baffled. He had
been eaten away by metastases, but they never did find the primary site. For Nina this no longer mattered. She was left completely alone, and by her very nature loneliness was something
she could not endure. She felt like a fly with its wings torn off,
driven out of its mind. She circled round and round the same
spot while the world collapsed beneath her or fell away to one
side. And now there was this devilry.

The mystical attack predicted by Susanna manifested itself
in the most disgusting manner shortly afterward. Returning
from work, Nina discovered in the middle of her ottoman, on

her knitted beige divan cover, a revolting pile of something
of a completely and unambiguously material nature. The
stench filling the flat was so foul that the very air in her home
seemed to have taken on that gray-brown tinge of unendurable wretchedness with which she was so familiar from her
dreams. She put her head on her arms, let her sad Caucasian
hair fall down, and cried. Not for long, however, because
Tomochka arrived. She gasped, busied herself with removing
the pile, and explained its provenance.

"Don't leave the quarter-light in the window open. Some
stray tomcat from the roof has got into the habit of visiting
you."

"What do you mean, tomcat?" Nina protested.

"What do you mean, what do I mean? A big tomcat—a very
big tomcat, indeed—made that mess," Tomochka elaborated
confidently. She knew what she was talking about. She had
been a cat-lover for the whole of her life.

Nina laundered the cover and swabbed the floors, and
they were able to breathe more easily. They didn't manage to
dispel the smell completely, however, and went to sleep at
Tomochka's. Before leaving, they closed the quarter-lights
firmly.

When Nina came home from work the next day, a pile
was lying in just the previous location, directly on the blanket.
The quarter-lights were shut. It really was something occult.
Susanna was right. No tomcat could climb in through a closed
window.

She set about washing and scrubbing again, used up a bottle
of air freshener, and, trembling from an attack of nerves, went
to bed on the desecrated ottoman. She had learned to put up
with the smell, but now she couldn't sleep because of vague
noises coming from a source she couldn't identify.

"This is what going mad must feel like," Nina surmised.

When she went to work in the morning, she again took care

to lock the windows and the door to the balcony. Despite this, she didn't feel brave enough to return home alone and went round to collect Tomochka. It was after eight in the evening when the two of them arrived. Nina opened the complicated lock on the double doors and went in. Tomochka followed. He was waiting for them, as if he had decided that the time had come to introduce himself. He was sitting in the armchair, huge, self-assured, with his pouchy cheeks and muzzle turned toward the door. Nina was taken aback. Tomochka seemed positively delighted.

"Wow, what an enormous cat!"

"What are we going to do?" Nina asked in a whisper.

"Do? Feed him, of course."

"Are you out of your mind? We'll never get rid of him! Look, he's fouled again, over there." A new pile of muck was lying in the middle of the hallway.

He certainly was a character, and with a practiced eye too. He unerringly selected the exact midpoint of his target.

"First, we need to give him something to eat, and then we'll see," Tomochka decided.

He was not fluffy. On the contrary, his fur was as smooth as asphalt. He sat there without stirring, his head slightly lowered. He fixed them with a feral stare and, as far as one could judge, totally without remorse.

"How can he be so brazen!" Nina exclaimed indignantly, but took out of the fridge a saucepan of old soup which, obedient to habits of many years' standing, she still boiled up. She dropped in two rissoles and banged it down on the cooktop.

Tomochka put a bowl of the warmed-up soup down by the door, right on the doormat, and called, "Pussy, pussy!" He was versed in the language of humans, jumped heavily down from the armchair, and strolled over to the saucer. He was an imposing creature. If he had been human you might have said he walked like a retired weight lifter or wrestler, stooped by the combined weight of his muscles, physical attrition, and reputation. He stopped in front of the bowl, sniffed it, crouched down, and, pressing one ear to his head while the other, a torn lop-ear, drooped, began lapping it up rapidly, as Tomochka exhorted him in tones of supplication.

"Eat up, kitty, kitty! Eat up and then off you go. Off you go, there's nothing to keep you here. Eat up and off you go home, please."

He glanced around, turning his broad chest, and gave her a knowing look, then stuck his head into the bowl of soup again. When he had finished, he licked the bowl clean.

Tomochka opened the front door for him and said firmly, "And now, off you go!"

He understood the situation precisely, walked craftily in the direction of the door, did a volte-face at the shoe tray, and, executing a lightning-fast semicircular detour around the flat, squeezed in under the bookcase.

"He doesn't want to leave," Nina said despairingly. "I knew we shouldn't have fed him."

"Pussy, pussy," Toma hissed heatedly, but the cat did not respond.

Nina brought the mop from the bathroom and rammed it viciously under the bookcase. The cat hurtled out, rushed around the apartment a couple of times, and disappeared under the little sofa, which had its back pressed up against the raised kitchen area. Nina prodded under the sofa, then moved it away. The tomcat was not there. He had vanished. The friends looked at each other.

They stood in silence for a moment, taking in what had happened. Then Tomochka leaned down and began not very happily to feel along the baseboard. She pressed slightly and it shifted. It was the entrance to a flat little basement underneath the kitchen floor.

"So that's where you've got him living," Tomochka said, with artless satisfaction. "And you thought it was something mystical!"

"How dreadful. We'll never be able to get him out of there."

"That baseboard has got to be hammered back in place right away," Tomochka said with idiotic certainty, as she jumped to her feet.

"What do you mean?" Nina said, imagining the consequences. "Supposing he dies in there? Can you imagine what it would be like having a dead cat in the house?" Oh, if only Seryozha were alive, none of this nonsense would be happening.

"We need to buy some valerian drops. That's it! We'll lure him out with valerian and then board it up," Tomochka exclaimed. "Only it'll take quite a lot of valerian."

They bought a lot of valerian, filled a saucer with it, and hid. Tomochka clearly had a deep understanding of feline psychology, because within five minutes the tomcat crept out through the loose board, padded friskily over to the saucer, and lapped it all up in a single session. He moved away from the saucer to return to his hole, swaying like a sailor on board ship. He staggered, having plainly lost his sense of direction, turned round awkwardly, and headed toward the ottoman on which the two friends were hiding. The first glimmerings of a sense of humor appeared in Nina.

"In a minute he's going to ask us for a cigarette."

When she had finished giggling, Tomochka instructed, "That's it. Now we catch him and put him outside. And board that hole up pronto."

She again hissed "Pussy, pussy" and held out her arms to the cat, but he darted to one side. Nina grabbed him, but he wriggled free and fell heavily to the floor. He might be drunk but he wasn't giving in. The cat was evidently trying to struggle back to his hole, but Nina, like the Second World War hero Alexander Matrosov, covered the enemy gun embrasure with her own body, holding the loose board in place with her bluish fingers.

"Tomochka, get the cardboard box in the bathroom," she shrieked, but the cat seemed to have guessed what they were planning and decided on a retreat to the balcony. With every minute that passed he was getting more inebriated. "The door! Shut the balcony door! He'll fall off!"

Tomochka beat the cat to it and slammed the door in front of his nose. With considerable difficulty they crammed him into the cardboard box the juicer had come in. He snarled something in a deep voice that sounded like swearing, possibly even impugning their mothers' virtue. They lugged the box down to the courtyard, set it next to the garbage container, and opened the lid. He continued yowling but did not come out. The women hurried home to nail up the gap. They had a little celebration to mark their deliverance from the enemy, toasting it in good Georgian wine, but their rejoicing was to prove premature.

A particular strength of this itinerant cat was the ease with which he transformed himself from a shameless animal, which behaved in ways not even the most backward female cat would countenance in her own home, into an ethereal specter. He could slip in and out of Nina's dreams and her everyday life, leaving in both of them an appalling stink, fear, and a special cat quality that seemed to become detached from him and to disperse, to settle on everything and penetrate Nina through the air, through the pores of her skin, so deeply that she used up bottles of shampoo and soap trying to wash away its pervasive loathsomeness. The cat himself did not physically reappear, but she now dreamed of him almost every night. He could change his appearance deftly, but Nina learned to recognize him in a dark cloud creeping up from a corner, in a landscape that unquestionably related to him, and even in a gentleman she identified in the crowd, as in former times one might have identified a secret agent.

Susanna, informed of all these peripeteias as she was leaving for some colloquium or symposium in Germany, promised Nina to discuss the situation with the most authoritative specialist in the whole of Europe.

One night the tomcat again appeared in the flesh. How he had got into the apartment remained a mystery. The loose baseboard was nailed down, and the balcony door and windows were tight shut. The fireplace was above suspicion, since its straight flue went directly up to the roof and no cat, unless possessed of the physiology of a flea, could have leaped the more than ten feet of absolutely vertical chimney stack. In any case, the fireplace had a fire screen pressed against it. Probably the only way to discover the cat's secret passage would have been to demolish the old house in its entirety. He jumped up onto a high shelf, capsized it, and brought down all the delicate black pottery, a marvel of Georgian applied art, that Nina had collected in her student years.

Having just survived the horrors of the end of the world, which in her dream had been accompanied by an avalanche with a matte black tinkling sound, Nina turned on the lamp to find the floor covered in pottery fragments. The tomcat, not having had time to dissolve as only he knew how, had retreated to a corner and was baring his teeth like a dog on a chain. This was such a natural continuation of her dream that she wasn't immediately sure whether she was now in a new dream or in her own home.

Nina picked up the shards of pottery and, without turning around, complained disconsolately, "What sort of bastard are you? Where do the likes of you come from? Why do you keep coming here? What is it you want from me? Just tell me, will you?" She took half a chicken from the fridge and carried it out to the landing. "Here, go and eat that, and I never want to set eyes on you again!"

He hadn't actually been demanding food, but neither was he going to turn up his nose at it. He strolled indolently out after the chicken. Nina closed the door behind him, well aware that she couldn't get rid of him that easily.

Four days later he was back. He was sitting in the armchair entirely at his ease, as if it were his place. In the center of the beige cover, which had been laundered and aired on the balcony, lay proof positive of his dominance over both this apartment and Nina herself.

Susanna, meanwhile, returned from Germany and invited Nina for dinner. Susanna was now serene and calm. Her home was redolent of wealth, ecclesiastical odors, and burning candles. For dinner she served something completely insubstantial that Nina would have been ashamed to offer to a guest. In contrast, Susanna herself was like a widowed queen. She was cloaked in a lilac vestment, her head bound round with a turbanlike violet scarf, and her makeup was so dark and monstrous that no one could have accused her of coquettishness.

They ate a dark blue salad of red cabbage before drinking claret-colored rose-hip tea, all color-coordinated. Susanna then explained to Nina something that could have occurred only to her. She stressed that this was not only her personal opinion but a particular insight of her teacher. It seemed that a human being is set certain specific tasks that he or she must complete, and that higher powers, angels and the like, and also our teachers in this world, help us to do so. If, however, a person rebels, these tasks become transformed into something nightmarish: an illness, for example. A tomcat, even. Nina's cat was nothing less than a manifestation on the physical plane of some spiritual disharmony. It was even possible that this was not something caused by Nina herself but to be found in the relationships of relatives who had already passed on.

"This is very serious, Nina. Much work will be required. I am prepared to help you myself, to the extent of my abilities, and to introduce you to advanced people," Susanna concluded.

This conversation and all the lilac coloration left Nina feeling even worse, and she began to wonder whether after all she shouldn't go to church with Tomochka, since she was after all an Orthodox Christian, baptized as an infant in the old Church of Saint Nina in Tbilisi. She even had godparents.

Nina could not sleep again that night, and pills did not help.

The following day Mirkas, her boss and a friend of the late Seryozha, called her into his office after lunch. He had taken her on in his office after Seryozha died and offered her a good salary, even though at that time he had no idea how exact and meticulous she always was. In practice, her record keeping couldn't be bettered.

Now Nina was worried that she might have made a mistake. Last week they had put through a very complicated contract, and she might well have muddled something up.

When she entered his office, however, he took her aback by saying, "Look, Nina, you're not ill, are you? You don't look at all well."

There was an awkwardness in their relationship. When Seryozha was alive they had been on straightforward friendly terms, but now this was in conflict with their new business relationship.

Nina went to some lengths to keep the mood neutral. "It's nothing serious. I'm having trouble sleeping."

He looked her over as if appraising a new consignment of goods. Not his type, but undeniably stylish. She was thin with an early, frank graying of her hair, and always wore black. Her chin was too long, of course, and her cheeks hollow; she had rings under her eyes; but there was certainly something about her. . . .

"Get yourself a lover," he advised her bluntly.

"Is that an instruction from the boss or a piece of friendly advice?" She looked down, but her chin wanted to rise. Silly girl. So proud of herself.

"Insomnia is an illness too. Perhaps you need a holiday. Tunisia, the Canaries, or wherever it is that girls go on holiday nowadays. The firm will pay for it. Take a week, ten days. You look dreadful."

He sounded irritated, perhaps even disdainful. Nina raised her chin higher and higher.

Then he pulled a wry face and said, in a kindly, direct voice, "Come on, what's happened? What's troubling you?"

At that, proud Nina's eyes filled with tears. "Oh, Mirkas, you won't believe it. There's this tomcat that's driving me crazy."

Haltingly and not entirely coherently, Nina told him the whole story. The more he heard the more his sympathy seemed to evaporate, until at the end he cut her short with his routine senior-management voice. "Okay, fine. Next time it shows up, call my pager straight away. I'll sort it out."

There were rumors circulating to the effect that Mirkas was well able to sort out troublemakers.

Those rumors may possibly also have reached the cat, because there was neither sight nor sound of him for several days, although he did not leave Nina's apartment without his attentions. One time she went off to work without closing the wardrobe door, and the unconscionable creature naturally took advantage of her oversight to foul in there. Poor Nina had to take all her considerable collection of clothes to the cleaners, and even then she still seemed to detect that catty smell. It was too awful.

The day did come, however, when she discovered the cat sitting, as if it were the most natural thing in the world, in her armchair. She immediately called Mirkas. He arrived precisely twenty minutes later, all of which time Nina spent sitting dejectedly on a stool in the bathroom.

Without a word, Mirkas made straight for the armchair, but the two sides proved evenly matched. He grabbed the cat by the scruff of its neck and it sank its claws into his arm. A visceral roar was heard, and there was no way of telling who it had come from.

"Goodness me!" Nina gasped, when she saw the bloody stripes on Mirkas's arm.

"The balcony!" Mirkas barked.

Nina ran ahead of him and opened the balcony door. Well, that's not going to do any good, she reflected, not yet having read Mirkas's mind. He'll just come back again.

The bloodied Mirkas held the tomcat by the scruff of its neck while it scratched at him with all its claws. Nina pressed herself against the door in horror. She couldn't stand the sight of blood. Growling a low ominous curse, Mirkas took a swing and hurled the cat over the balustrade of the balcony. Nina distinctly registered a moment when the cat's trajectory took it upward for an instant. As it flew, it straightened its forepaws and lowered its head. It seemed then to freeze like a weightless cosmonaut in the emptiness of space, before disappearing from view. A sound was immediately heard from below as if somebody had emptied out a bowl of water. In the darkness of the courtyard nothing could be seen. Nina, still traumatized, rinsed Mirkas's scratch wounds as he shook his head.

"That was some beast. . . . Animals like that should be shot." He looked as if he had just killed an old woman with an ax.

For the whole of that night, Nina slept like a log. It was a long time since she had felt so completely rested. As she was about to leave the house in the morning, however, she was suddenly horrified at the thought that the dead cat might be lying beneath her balcony. How could she possibly walk past it? Of course, everyone knows a cat can keep its balance while flying through the air, rotate its tail like a propeller, and land on all four paws.

There was no dead cat by the house; in fact, there was nobody around at all. Nina left Chisty Lane and walked toward Zubovskaya Square.

The cat had disappeared, either for the present or forever. Nina's mood went from bad to worse. Mirkas probably had killed it, and although it was undeniably a terrible rogue, Nina had only wanted it removed, not dispatched. Now, however, after all the upset, there did seem to be some relief, although each day when Nina came back from work she was half expecting to find the wretched brute sitting in her chair.

Meanwhile, the anniversary of Seryozha's death was approaching. She needed to hold a reception for thirty people or so, and to do it not just anyhow but in a fit and proper manner. Mirkas was remembering the anniversary too. The whole week he had been walking around looking grumpy as hell. His arm had gone septic and he was having antibiotic injections. As he walked past Nina's desk, however, he put down an envelope.

"Are you inviting people to a restaurant or having it at home?"

Nina's pride was wounded. Nobody would have humiliated her like that when Seryozha was alive, but she snapped out of her absurd fit of pride, tossed her incomparable hair back from her face, and said, "Thank you, Mirkas." She bought another suckling pig, some eels, and half a kilogram of caviar.

Early in the morning, Tomochka went off to church and commissioned a requiem for the dead. Nina didn't go with her; Seryozha could never stand that kind of thing when he was alive. Instead, she took some flowers to the cemetery. The headstone had already been erected. Nina had made all the arrangements early in the spring. It was a large black-and-gray stone, rough and simple.

In the evening, everything went off perfectly. The tables were generously laden and beautifully set, just the way Seryozha liked. Everybody came whom Nina wanted to see: his friends, his cousin and his cousin's family, Seryozha's single sister who didn't much like Nina. Mirkas came with his old wife, Vika, whom he didn't usually treat very well, rather than with any of his more recent acquisitions, of whom there had been a good few lately. Nina was pleased about that. Even Mikhail Abramovich came, a lawyer who had defended Seryozha long ago when he got into serious trouble. The lawyer had since become famous and was forever appearing on television, but even he hadn't forgotten the first anniversary of the death.

Everybody had good things to say about Seryozha, some of which were even true: about his strength of character, his courage, his fortitude, and his talent. Valentina, the sister, did manage to slip in a reference to the fact that Nina had never borne him any children, but Nina didn't bat an eyelid. This aspect of their life was something she had mourned long ago. She had forgiven him for forcing her, fool that she was, so passionately in love with him. . . . It was her mother who could never forgive him. What was the point of remembering it now, when she was thirty-nine?

The guests were late in leaving. They carried away Nina's exceptional fare in their stomachs and left behind them a table that still retained something of its festive splendor and the aroma of expensive cigarettes. Nina packed Tomochka off home; Toma had got herself as tipsy as a schoolgirl and kept wanting to say something special and deeply felt about God, which just embarrassed everybody else. Left alone, Nina took her time clearing everything up, talking under her breath to Seryozha, as she often did. Entirely predictably, she got no more response back from him now than she had when he was alive.

At about four in the morning, she climbed into her clean cold bed, with the blue-and-green checked bed linen she had bought three years ago in Berlin, when she and Seryozha had been there on their last trip together. Even though this time she had taken no pills, she fell asleep just as soon as she was warm and slept deeply, her eyeballs moving to and fro beneath her dark eyelids. Toward morning, when the branches of the great lime tree began coming to life and quietly rustling in the first breeze of the day as they touched the railing of the balcony, she had the most amazing dream of her entire life.

She was standing on the top floor of a large dachalike building that was not yet complete, because looking down you could see the accommodations on the lower stories, rafters and staircases, and all this on several levels that weren't clearly separated. She suddenly heard singing. A woman's voice was singing an old Georgian song. Her grandmother, Nina guessed, and immediately saw her. She was sitting on a little stool, on a cushion with a brown tassel. Her black hat was pulled over her hair, and dark cloth cascaded down the sides of her glowing face. She was singing but her mouth was firmly shut, the lips unmoving, and Nina again very easily guessed that this was a different singing, which proceeded not from the vocal cords but from a different organ, one unrelated to the throat but without which no singing is possible. As soon as she guessed which point in the solar plexus the singing was coming from, she heard the song divide into two voices: her grandmother's low alto and a second soprano voice, her own lost soprano, her irretrievable joy but even more wonderful, purer, more silken than it had been when she was studying at the Conservatory. The sound of her voice, restored to her and rejuvenated, had an otherworldly quality that drew others to it as a magnet draws iron, and the light unfinished house began suddenly to fill up with people. There were no strangers among them, even though Nina did not know all of their names. These were her gray-brown shades, but the sound of this mysterious singing made them become lighter, and they developed like images on photographic paper. Among them she first made out her mother and then also Seryozha.

Nina was descending a staircase toward them just as they recognized each other in the crowd and embraced, as if one had been waiting for the other on a station platform and the train had finally arrrived. Her mother, slim and very young, still half hidden behind Seryozha's wide embrace, suddenly caught sight of her, laughed, and cried out, "Niniko!"

The sound of her mother's voice was not as it usually was. It too was part of the Georgian song, although the song had ceased to be in Georgian and its words, although wholly understandable, were in a different language.

Seryozha put his arm around Nina's shoulder, and the smell of his skin and his hair burned her, and she saw that his nostrils were flared, and he lowered his head to her hair.

Something gently butted her below the knee, and turning she saw an enormous cat rubbing against her legs and demanding to be stroked. It was him, the accursed tomcat that had given her so much grief. Seryozha bent down and stroked its asphalt back. Her mother, with a gesture of friendly familiarity, straightened the side of Seryozha's jacket. But that was not all. From somewhere to one side, arm in arm, her two friends, Tomochka and Susanna, were coming toward her. Their faces too were so lovely that Nina laughed as she realized that, although the two of them had been the most terrible idiots, that had only been for a while.

*Angel*

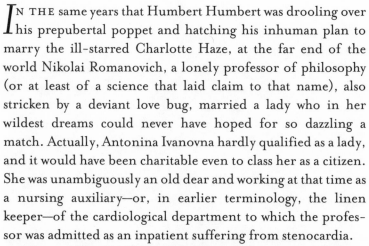

*I*N THE same years that Humbert Humbert was drooling over his prepubertal poppet and hatching his inhuman plan to marry the ill-starred Charlotte Haze, at the far end of the world Nikolai Romanovich, a lonely professor of philosophy (or at least of a science that laid claim to that name), also stricken by a deviant love bug, married a lady who in her wildest dreams could never have hoped for so dazzling a match. Actually, Antonina Ivanovna hardly qualified as a lady, and it would have been charitable even to class her as a citizen. She was unambiguously an old dear and working at that time as a nursing auxiliary—or, in earlier terminology, the linen keeper—of the cardiological department to which the professor was admitted as an inpatient suffering from stenocardia.

The amiable Antonina, who resembled less a hen than a rather gray turkey, expanded downward from her small head to her obese legs. She was divorced, a secret drinker, and she lived in a room one hundred feet square with her young son.

Her salary was derisory and she readily pilfered what she could, although she was ashamed of doing so. In short, she was a perfectly respectable woman. Early in January, as it was the school holidays, she began bringing the boy with her to work. The fair-haired lad, sitting in the linen room peeping out from behind his mother's back, his brow white as milk and with blond brushes beneath his eyebrows, struck the professor right in his sick and disordered heart.

We shall leave a potential digression here on the connection between sickness and sin—their subtle points of contact and overlap—to the psychoanalysts and reverend fathers, both of whom have grazed to their hearts' content on these treacherous terrains.

Nikolai Romanovich would wander down the hospital corridor for hours and peep in the half-open door of the linen room, catching with a targeted gaze a glimpse of a gawky elbow in a mended blue sweater moving lightly over the table (if drawing something) or just a cursory view of items of institutional laundry, yellowed from sterilization in the hospital's autoclaves. Then again, he might suddenly behold, full height in the doorway, a radiant elegant being, a boy from the harem, perhaps not quite fully grown, just needing another two or three years. Twelve is the sweetest age.

Sometimes the boy was fed in the canteen for patients who could walk, and he would sit at the corner table where the doctors ate their rushed meals. His back was straight; he was grave and frightened. Nikolai Romanovich saw clearly his pale blue eyes, which squinted a little when he looked to the right, and his blond eyelashes, as downy as a ripe dandelion head.

"Tonya! Tonya!" the ward sister would call the linen keeper, looking into the canteen; and Antonina would respond in her kind flabby voice, "Over hee-er!"

It was upon hearing that voice one time that Nikolai Romanovich was riven by an insight: Should he not try to arrange a different life for himself? She was, of course, a domestic sort of person, just a linen keeper, a nanny, so why not draw up an honest matrimonial contract? You scratch my back, I scratch yours.

Nikolai Romanovich was approaching fifty-five, a fair age.

The provisions would accordingly include no expectation or assurance of matrimonial delights but would include a room of her own, full board and lodging, and, needless to say, all proper respect. Your own contribution, dear Xantippe Ivanovna, will be to run the household, to maintain hearth and home: that is, to do the laundry, cooking, and cleaning. For my part, I shall adopt your young son and rear him in the best possible way. I shall give him an education, oh, yes, including music and gymnastics. A lightly running Ganymede, redolent of olive oil and young sweat. Calm down, calm down. Don't frighten away a lovely melody. Gradually, miraculously, a tender child will grow up in his house, turn into a boy, a young friend, a pupil, his beloved. In these halcyon days he will weave the nest of his future happiness with his diligent beak.

Linen-keeping Antonina was at first thrown into confusion. How could this be? But happiness, like the wind, comes and goes unaccountably. Here she had landed a two-hundred-square-foot room with a balcony, on the fifth floor, with windows looking into the courtyard, in a smart building on Gorky Street, where your neighbors were actresses and generals and heaven knows who. Everything was good quality and solid. Her new husband was not greedy; he gave her a generous housekeeping allowance for food. And what food it was, from the Kremlin distribution center, no less, though he had said not to tell anyone that. And he never asked for the change. He was clean, changed his underwear every three days, and his socks nearly every day. He doused himself in the bathroom like a duck, and even so went to the bathhouse on Saturdays and spent half the day there. He was smartly dressed, brushed his own shoes, and ironed his own trousers. You wouldn't do it right, said he.

To friends who really very much wanted to know, she would reply in all simplicity: As far as that goes, no, I can't say there is. But how many years is it since I last saw a live . . . ? And

anyway, who cares about that? I'm used to it by now. I really
don't know why I have been so lucky. He looks after little
Slava as if he were the boy's father. To tell the truth, he doesn't
have much to say to me at all. But what would we have to talk
about anyway, when you think about it? He's very educated,
obviously, a professor. . . .

On this point, it has to be said, she was not deluding herself. He was both a professor and educated. Classical philoso-
phers, like pedigreed dogs, did not thrive on the meager fruits
of socialism, but Nikolai Romanovich himself had happened
upon just the right border to cultivate in that garden, and
dug it and watered and manured in it the scrawny tree of
Marxist-Leninist aesthetics. On the very eve of the Revolution
he managed to complete his university education and almost
to defend his dissertation on the topic, "The essence of Plato's
dialectic as interpreted by Albinus and Anonym. Vales."
It was the magic word *dialectic* that opened before Nikolai
Romanovich the royal doors to the new life: namely, the posi-
tion of Lecturer in Classical Philosophy in the Socialist
Academy. There he was the only member who actually knew
Ancient Greek and Latin, so he was constantly in demand as a
supplier of quotations to highly placed leaders, including
Lunacharsky himself.

For decades thereafter he sifted through Plato and Aristo-
tle, Kant and Hegel, looking for the correct scientific resolu-
tion of aesthetic questions before which all these pre-Marxian
philosophers had been as helpless as blind kittens. He also
became so adept in the theory of art and the criteria of artistic
quality that not a single decree of the Central Committee of
the All-Union Communist Party (Bolsheviks) was compiled
without his complicity, whether the matter at issue was Vano
Muradeli's opera *The Great Friendship* or Shostakovich's *Katerina
Izmailova*. He was not schizophrenic in the least. The flexible

dialectic, like a knowledgeable guide in the mountains, led him by tortuous paths through the most insalubrious places.

Alas, however, Nikolai Romanovich was indeed the servant of two masters. His second master, imperious and secretive, was his unhappy predilection for the male sex. From his earliest years it bore down on his head like a migraine, raising his blood pressure and causing tachycardia. The dread Article 120 of the Soviet Constitution hung over him. No enemy of the people, real or set up, no opportunist or oppositionist, experienced the same abyss of fear as those who lived under the threat of this seemingly unremarkable article. Theirs was a real, not fictive, secret society of men who, like freemasons with their secret signs and special handshakes, recognized each other in a crowd by the anguish in their eyes and the anxiety etched on their brows. The Leaden Age that replaced the Silver Age sent on their way the sophisticated youths, smutty schoolboys, and good-looking novices, leaving for Nikolai Romanovich and his ilk dangerous liaisons with heartless, greedy young men with whom you had constantly to be on your guard. They could betray, expose, or slander you. They could have you thrown into prison. Only once in Nikolai Romanovich's adult life did he experience a deep and lasting relationship, with a young historian, a boy from a good family who died at the front in the Second World War and who, before doing so, brutally humiliated Nikolai Romanovich with the derisive letters, full of offensive allusions, of a complete psychopath.

The arrival of Slava opened a new era in the life of Nikolai Romanovich. The professor's cherished dream looked as though it was about to come true. He would rear himself a beloved, and the boy would benefit from the love of a wise educator. Oh, yes, he would benefit rationally. Nikolai Romanovich would mold him in his own image, bringing him up

lovingly and chastely. Nikolai Romanovich would be a true
pedagogue, a slave not sparing even his own life to protect and
educate his beloved.

"I swear by the dog!" Nikolai Romanovich vowed to himself. He leaned over the sleeping boy who now lived in his
apartment, if admittedly in his mother's room, on a couch
upholstered in pale orange plush. "These things shall be!" he
declared, by the flickering light of a bulbous standard lamp.
"My little angel," he murmured, as he tucked in the blanket at
the sides.

In these evening hours, Antonina was allowed to take a glass
or two of something strong to help her sleep, in moderation
and under his supervision. He was truly a pedagogue who
overlooked nothing.

In that first year of their family life, Nikolai Romanovich
sent the boy to music school, to the wind department. Slava
didn't become a flute player, but he came to feel at home in
music as if that was where he had always belonged. His great
gift proved to be an ability to listen to music with godlike
discrimination, so that even in this rarefied area Nikolai Romanovich received a partner. Stepfather and stepson now went
to the Conservatory together to enjoy that art which least lent
itself to analysis from a class standpoint.

The Conservatory's habitués of those years grew accustomed to the sight of this couple, the slender elderly man with
large spectacles on his small-boned face and the lissom youth
with the neatly cut blond hair, in a black sweater with the collar of his white Pioneer's shirt turned over the round neckline. The Moscow melohomophiles, a correlation as yet
unexplained, writhed with envy when Nikolai Romanovich
bought two lemonades and two cakes in the buffet. Nobody
wrote any denunciations of him, however. They were all too
scared for themselves.

In those years a circle of cognoscenti formed at the Conservatory. There was no formal membership, but their faces were recognizable and stood out. Apart from secret coreligionists of Nikolai Romanovich and ordinary music lovers, the circle naturally also included professional musicians and also some of Slava's fellow pupils from the music school, like Zhenya, a young cellist, who usually came with her mother and father. Zhenya was forever whispering in Slava's ear and pulling him by the sleeve over to one side with her.

"A sweet girl," Nikolai Romanovich said to his protégé, "but not at all prepossessing in appearance."

This was not true. She was entirely prepossessing, with dark little eyes and curls restrained by a checkered hairband. It was just that Nikolai Romanovich's heart suffered a pang of dark jealousy for a moment. We can quite do without these girls.

He was granted all that Humbert Humbert ever dreamed of: a golden childhood that developed before his eyes into youth; the respectful friendship of a pupil; and a complete and trusting intimacy, carefully nurtured by one who proved to be a master of affectionate touching, breathing, and mellifluous movement.

In the sixty-third year of his life, Nikolai Romanovich died in his own bed from an aortic embolism. He died suffused with the youthful love of his angel and in perfect harmony with his daemon, never having read the novel charged with Nabokov's high-voltage electricity and recognized his profound relatedness to its unhappy hero.

The orphaned Slava, by now a first-year student in the philosophical faculty of Moscow State University, was left in a state of complete bewilderment after the death of his mentor. While the course continued, analyzing the logic and propaedeutic of dialectical materialism in the old building of the philosophical faculty, whose windows looked out onto the anatomical theater of the First Medical Institute, he did not have too much of a problem. But then the summer vacation arrived. Slava was used to spending this with his stepfather in Estonia, at a guesthouse in Pjarnu, and at this point he became deeply depressed. He took to his bed in his stepfather's study, listening to his favorite records, and had difficulty getting up to turn them over or to put on a new one.

Slava had been done no favors by the old aesthete, whose angel now had no idea how to go on living. Without his mentor, Slava was lost. He had no friends. The scrupulously kept secret of his relations with his stepfather had erected an impenetrable barrier between him and other people. He was remote from his mother and had long been treating her exactly as Nikolai Romanovich did: courteously and manipulatively. For the past four years he and his orange couch had migrated to Nikolai Romanovich's study to escape from his mother's snoring.

His stepfather left what by the standards of those times was a staggeringly large amount of money. There was a whole stack of savings books, some of which provided cash to the bearer on demand, while others were in Nikolai Romanovich's name and had been bequeathed to Slava. One humble little gray booklet with three thousand rubles in it was left to Antonina. Slava passed it to his mother, who threw up her hands in delight. She had never expected to be so rich and went completely off the rails. Instead of the double vodka Nikolai Romanovich had permitted her, she now downed a third of a bottle, and not only in the evening either. By nine o'clock or so Antonina would, as always, be sleeping the sleep of the just, and Slava would go out for a walk, to fill his lungs with the heavy petrol-laden air and to sit on a dusty bench on Tverskoy Boulevard not far from the amateur chess club. As evening approached, it drew those addicted to the checkered board, old-age pensioners and failed chess prodigies. One muggy evening Zhenya from the music school also found her way there.

Zhenya came from a good, thoroughly musical family, whose talents passed from generation to generation in the same way that some families pass on a congenital disorder like hypertonia or diabetes. Among their forebears they numbered an Italian prima donna, a Czech organist, and a German conductor. The main Bach of the family was, however, Zhenya's grandfather. To this day his name can be found in the company of Skryabin, inscribed in the roll of honor of gold medalists of the Moscow Conservatory.

Grandfather's composing was no more than mediocre, in line with the spirit and culture of the times. He was captivated by modernism but had been granted neither the audacity of Debussy nor the originality of Mussorgsky. His fame was as a performer, a cellist, a teacher and public figure in the world of music. He chaired a variety of musical societies and committees and distributed stipends to poor but talented children and allowances to elderly orchestra musicians. He was, in short, a true Russian intellectual of mixed blood—none of it, as it happened, Russian. The family was large, and everything revolved around music. His elder brother was a concert violinist, while his younger brother, less successful, transcribed music.

Zhenya never knew her grandfather. They were separated by three decades, which had included two world wars. Her grandfather died at forty-two years of age on the same day as Archduke Franz Ferdinand, at the beginning of the First World War, while she was born on the last day of the Second.

As an act of rebellion or a sport, the family would suddenly throw up an apostate, like Uncle Lyova, who decamped to the accountants, and Aunt Vera, who was unfaithful to music in favor of agriculture. Zhenya's father, Rudolf Petrovich, was another apostate, seduced by a career in the army. Under the tall Astrakhan *papakha* of a colonel, he pined for music all his life. He was infatuated with it but never touched a musical instrument. He decided, however, to be sure that his daughter returned to the family tradition and chose the cello for her. Their home, already full of signed photographs of all sorts of great people, with dusty sheet music, and with the scores of unburied operas, was filled with the living sound of scales and exercises. The little Zhenya showed promise of developing into a real performer. Daniil Shafran himself took an interest in her and supported her. Her grandfather's renown in the music world put the wind in her sails, but her diligence and assiduousness were entirely her own, and as a girl she spent many hours with her legs spread and a diminutive cello, a learner's toy, clenched between her knees. As she grew older something miraculous grew with her. Her cello proved highly responsive. She had barely to put the bow to it for it to respond with sounds more rich and velvety than anything she knew. And what comparison could there be between the broad sinuous voice of the cello and the scratchy unevenness of a violin, the simplemindedness of a viola, or the glum monotony of a double bass?

That summer she was alone in the city for the first time. Her parents were living out at the dacha, and she was preparing for her first concert program. In the evenings she would go out for a stroll.

They were both delighted by their chance meeting at the bench on Tverskoy Boulevard. Each was feeling lonely. For Zhenya it was an acute but temporary state, since she was alone at home for the first time in her life. It seemed to Slava that for him the condition was absolute and would be lifelong. They talked, however, only about music. They had in addition a shared source of memories in the music school on Pushkin Square, which both of them had attended for so long and of which no trace now remained. On its site there rose the hideous *Izvestiya* building. They recalled the lessons of solfeggio, the choirs, the student concerts, and talked till late in the evening.

He saw her home to Spiridonovka Street and told her on the way, to his own surprise, "My stepfather has died."

It was the first time he had said this aloud, and he was struck by how the words sounded. Something in the air seemed to change. Because these words had been uttered, Nikolai Romanovich's death became irrevocable.

Zhenya, detecting something, felt her heart beat faster.

"Did you love him very much?"

"He was more than a father to me."

This sounded so elegiac it would surely have gladdened Nikolai Romanovich's heart.

"Poor Slava. I would go crazy if my father—if something like that happened to him." At the age of eighteen, she was so far removed from death she couldn't even bring herself to say the word *died*. She shook her head to drive away the shadow of death and her lips pursed in sympathy, but she said something silly and childish. "Let's go and eat some ice cream! A whole great lot of it."

Slava smiled, touched by such total fellow feeling. "But where can we get it at this time of night?"

"I've got some in the fridge. My parents are at the dacha, and it's the only thing I buy."

The ice cream was excellent, with pieces of frozen strawberry or icy blackberries. The downstairs neighbor brought it in a saucepan with dry ice. She was a waitress at Café North. Everybody was stealing, provided only that there was something for them to get their hands on. After the ice cream, Zhenya produced from her father's room an imposing record in a black-and-white sleeve.

"Karajan. They brought it back from Germany. You have never heard Wagner like this."

She reverently lowered the gleaming record onto the turntable of the record player. It was the orchestral version of *Tristan and Isolde*. You would have thought the musicians in the orchestra were not human beings but demons. The two of them listened to it twice from beginning to end, and to the accompaniment of the towering music, Zhenya fell in love with Slava just at the point where Isolde dies. She had never, even with her father, listened so discriminatingly, so much in harmony with the perceptions of another person. And he was drawn to her with all his soul, such a sweet girl, so loving, with her dark clever eyes, her lively curls trembling above her forehead.

"What powerful, masculine music!" Zhenya commented, when Karajan had thundered his last.

"Wow, yes," Slava agreed, wondering how she could know that. The tang of the wild strawberry ice cream lingered in his mouth, the blackberry seeds lodged in his gums, and a flavor of something remained in his heart from their shared experiencing of the dark colors of the tumultuous music.

He visited her throughout August. Late in the evening, when the heat had died down and the nocturnal chess players had gathered on Tverskoy Boulevard, he would go back home feeling cheered. His depression had lifted. The combined sensations of the boulevard at night, Wagner, and melting ice cream were firmly associated with Zhenya.

When autumn came and Zhenya's parents returned to the city, it was time to study again and they began to meet less often, although every day they would talk at length on the telephone about a Richter concert or a marvelous album by Somov that Slava had bought at the secondhand shop on the Arbat, following his late stepfather's habit of browsing in antique and secondhand shops with money in his pocket. Nikolai Romanovich had never been a genuine collector but had gradually learned a thing or two about objets d'art from

the material world, the payoff, no doubt, for being such a convinced materialist.

By the end of the summer it had seemed to Zhenya that she
finally had the beginnings of a real romance, but for some
reason everything got stuck at the stage of a delightful friendship and just would not develop further. She very much
wanted something more than little bits of frozen strawberry or
icy blackberries.

Slava could feel the constant expectation emanating from
her, and it made him nervous. He very much appreciated
being with her, the admirable home he found himself in, and
indeed Zhenya herself, who was so receptive toward literature
and music and even toward him. He felt as much desire for her
as he might have for a lamppost, and there seemed to be nothing he could do about that.

At the age of nineteen, he was well aware that he belonged to
a rare and special breed of men condemned to furtiveness and
secrecy because those soft protuberances enveloped in fabric
disgusted him. He associated them with a large white sow, its
nether side besieged by sucking piglets. The actual structure of
women, the hairy nest with the unfortunately placed vertical
slit, seemed dreadfully unattractive. Whether he had reached
that conclusion himself or whether the professor of aesthetics,
Nikolai Romanovich, had subtly suggested the idea, was imma-
terial. He liked Zhenya very much and she kept him from feeling lonely, but his physical longings had not only not gone
away, they were growing stronger.

After bidding Zhenya good night, he would usually go to sit
on the same bench on Tverskoy Boulevard not far from the
chess players. He would look at the few passers-by, timidly
wondering, *Him? Not him?* One time a well-built handsome
blond man locked eyes with him and he became tense, because
the gaze seemed very pointed, but the man walked on, leaving
Slava in a delicious sweat with his heart pounding and seeming

strangely to be echoing that other heart, which had suffered from angina. *We share that too,* Slava noted. *Music lovers, dicky hearts, aesthetes.*

He was wrong. The true picture was a good deal more complicated, but the error was perfectly understandable. The age of supermen clad in leather and wearing metal chains, homosexuals with bulging pumped-up muscles, contemptuously looking down on "straights," had not yet arrived. Cowboys were sex symbols to excite the female half of the world, bullet-riddled, lustful creatures, not cow boys, cowherds with rear ends battered by coarse saddles, engaging in same-sex love because of a total dearth of women in their environment.

Slava belonged wholly to the Classical World, as romantically imagined by the superficial scholars of the nineteenth century. Even Marx jotted some nonsense about the "golden childhood of mankind."

No doubt, from the immense distance of several thousand years, the picture had become distorted, and the reality was totally bloody and unbridled paganism. In its lurid polytheism, all that existed was deified, inspired, and set to guiltless lechery not only as nymphs, naiads, satyrs, and petty gods of puddles and roadside ditches but also as swans, cows, eagles, shepherds, and shepherdesses. All these engaged in an unending orgy of copulation that knew no bounds, and for some reason this heaving paganism came to be called Classical Materialism. This fallacy was what the beliefs of Nikolai Romanovich consisted of. He passed them on in full measure to his alumnus even as he inserted more personal predilections, cautiously and patiently, with the assistance of his experienced fingers, his sensitive tongue with its discerning tastebuds, and his old withered lance.

He was a brilliant teacher and he had found a brilliant pupil, whose hypersensitive body could no longer bear this indissoluble loneliness. His fair youthful hair, his mouth, his chest and belly, his loins and buttocks were begging for love. The Garden of Eden and the Rose of Sodom, Nikolai Romanovich had called them. The trout was truly breaking through the ice.

In early October, on one of the dark but still warm evenings of a long Indian summer, Slava's nights of sitting on Tverskoy Boulevard were rewarded with a new teacher. From a group of dark figures clustered beneath a lamppost that illuminated the chessboards, a man of around forty in a canvas cap came over to him. He had a handsome, possibly Jewish, face and was wearing an old-fashioned checked shirt. He took the cap off his bulbous skull and sat down carefully on the rickety bench. All of him seemed to be pressurized: his eyes were slightly protruding, and his beard was bursting forth with such force that only his nose provided a clearing free from undergrowth. (Nikolai Romanovich, in contrast, had always seemed a bit depressurized, like a slightly deflated balloon.)

The new arrival grasped the edge of the bench with his hairy fists and addressed himself very familiarly to Slava. "I know your face. You don't by any chance play chess, do you?"

Slava's heart pounded unevenly, dancing to sleazy music. Was this him? "I do a bit."

The man laughed. "Even my grandmother did a bit. At least, she thought she did. We'll soon find out."

The man pulled a small leather case out of his pocket and opened it. The chessboard was already set up. Sharp little pins were inserted in holes punched in leather. "Your move."

Slava's hands were trembling so much he could barely take hold of the chesspiece. He made the first move, E2 to E4, and felt a sense of relief. There was no longer any doubt: this was him. The chess player lightly pulled out a black pawn with its sharp prong, held it between thumb and middle finger, and murmured, "It's getting dark so early now," before ramming it into a white square.

That evening the chess player supposed that Slava's eyes were mirror-black, like the sunglasses that had just become fashionable, but it was a false impression. It was just that his pupils were so dilated that the blue iris was pressed out to the edge of his eyes.

"Let's finish our game at my place. It really is far too dark." The chess player folded up the chessboard and pulled his cap over his forehead, and they headed toward the trolley bus.

Slava did not ask how far they were going. His heart was thumping with anticipation, and the chess player periodically put a hand on his shoulder or on his knee. They reached Tsvetnoy Boulevard, alighted, and turned up a dark alley. They entered the neglected entrance of a three-story building, and as they were going up the stairs the chess player explained that he lived with his mother. She had been a great beauty in her youth, an actress, but was now almost blind and completely out of her mind.

The apartment was small and very dirty. From time to time the mother's querulous voice was heard on the other side of the wall, and then she started singing a ballad. They did not finish their game of chess. They made love, strong masculine love, of which Slava had had only an inkling before. The place smelled of vaseline and blood. It was what Slava had been wanting and what Nikolai Romanovich had been unable to give him. It was a night of nuptials, of initiation, and of ecstasy beyond the reach of music. A new life began for Slava.

VALITA WAS buried at state expense, if indeed he was buried at all. It is possible that he was dissected for his organs, that they were doused with formaldehyde and given, to be torn apart, to the students whose windows looked out toward the philoso-phers, or perhaps to some other students, but it's not very likely. The postmortem established that the body had been lying for fifteen to seventeen days before it was discovered in a secluded corner of Izmailovo Park by a citizen of sporting appearance who was taking his fox terrier for a walk.

It is difficult to explain what made Yevgenia Rudolfovna start a missing persons inquiry. In the forty years and more that she had known him, he had disappeared often and for different stretches of time. The first stretch was particularly long. He got five years, and then in the camps it was extended. That time he disappeared for almost ten years, but not from choice. Then he turned up again, but no longer as Slava. Now he was Valita. Such was the nickname he had acquired. He did tell Yevgenia a few things, but nothing to frighten or embarrass her. He did his best to spare her

It was not exactly that she loved Slava, of course not, but she loved the memories of her youth and recalled how much she had loved an inspired fair-haired boy, how wonderfully they had listened to music together, and how he had suffered from the imperfections of the recording technology of the time. Karajan had six bars piano and eight forte, but everything was evened out. She had felt sorry for this poor man, a pariah who had lost every last thing it is possible to lose: his property, his teeth, his fair hair, even his right to live in Moscow. He wrested that back from the clenched teeth of the world by marrying some irredeemable alcoholic and getting registered as living with her in a street poetically named Deerbank. Of his former riches, all that remained was his rare talent for listening to music and his aristocratic hands with their oval nails.

For many years he came to see Yevgenia at the theater, in her vast office with its MUSICAL DIRECTOR brass plate on the solid door. The other employees who worked there knew him, and the people in the cloakroom let him in. She would usually give him a little money, make coffee, and get some chocolates from a remote corner of the cupboard. He had a sweet tooth. Sometimes when there was time she would put on some music for him, although he admitted that he had long ago ceased to love it. Now he loved only sounds. She was not entirely sure what he meant by that, but in these matters he was better qualified than she was herself, the director of the musical department of a very famous Moscow theater. Unquestionably. She was fully aware of that.

He didn't stay in her office for long. He embarrassed himself, as once his late mother, Antonina, had been embarrassed by herself.

For a couple of months he did not come to visit her, and Yevgenia thought nothing of it. Then one Saturday evening she went to the Conservatory. They were playing Brahms's opus 115, the clarinet quintet, a piece unbelievably difficult to perform. In the last movement, when the soul has almost expired and you fly away into the empyrean, she suddenly remembered Slava. She remembered him sitting with his recorder in a little corner class being taught by Xenia Feofanovna, a fat, florid, coarse lady in a silk shift, and she, Zhenya, came barging into the classroom for some reason and stopped, shocked at her own impertinence. Forty years ago, in the music school, of which not a brick remained standing. The Brahms ended, and with the last sounds she sensed that Slava was no longer in this world.

She made an inquiry through the information bureau. Slava was neither to be found living at Deerbank nor in any other street, and she rang the police. She got a boorish reply, but a day later they called her in themselves, to identify his body. There was virtually nothing left to identify, just a heap of black rags, almost clay, a particularly dreadful kind of clay. Only the hand was human, with its aristocratic oval nails.

She spoke to the investigating officer. He was past his prime, rather flabby, and so knowing he might have been better off knowing less. Yevgenia told him nothing that interested him. The crime would have been fairly straightforward to clear up but the police did not take much interest in homosexual killings. They would snoop around for a while and then pin it on some maniac they already had under arrest. Anyway, who other than a maniac could have wanted to kill Valita, a man who had nothing other than a desperate longing to be loved by a man?

Back home, Yevgenia searched for a long time through the photographs of her childhood until she found the one she was looking for. All the others depicted a little girl called Zhenya with her cello, but this was a picture of the audience during a school concert. Her father had taken it. In the second row you could see both of them quite clearly: Nikolai Romanovich in his gray suit and striped tie with the twelve-year-old Slava in his white Pioneer's shirt with the top button undone. Such a sweet face, as radiant as an angel. And how Nikolai Romanovich had loved him. How he had loved him.

# The Orlov-Sokolovs

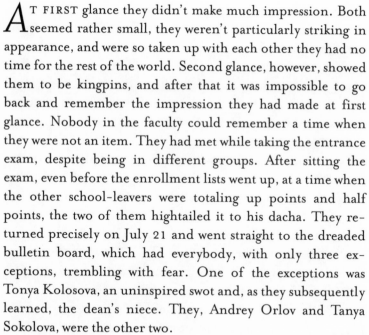

$A$<small>T FIRST</small> glance they didn't make much impression. Both seemed rather small, they weren't particularly striking in appearance, and were so taken up with each other they had no time for the rest of the world. Second glance, however, showed them to be kingpins, and after that it was impossible to go back and remember the impression they had made at first glance. Nobody in the faculty could remember a time when they were not an item. They had met while taking the entrance exam, despite being in different groups. After sitting the exam, even before the enrollment lists went up, at a time when the other school-leavers were totaling up points and half points, the two of them hightailed it to his dacha. They returned precisely on July 21 and went straight to the dreaded bulletin board, which had everybody, with only three exceptions, trembling with fear. One of the exceptions was Tonya Kolosova, an uninspired swot and, as they subsequently learned, the dean's niece. They, Andrey Orlov and Tanya Sokolova, were the other two.

Their surnames derived from the Russian words for eagle and falcon and suited them marvelously. They were soon so inseparably associated that before long people were calling them the Orlov-Sokolovs.

During those five days at the dacha, where they crawled out of bed only long enough to slip down to the village store for wine and suchlike basics, they ascertained that their differences could be counted on the fingers of two hands. Tanya liked classical music; Andrey liked jazz. He liked Mayakovsky's poetry, which she couldn't stand. They laughed over their final difference: he had a sweet tooth, while her favorite treat was a pickled gherkin.

On all other counts they discovered total coincidence. Both were mixed-race, Jewish on the mother's side. Both mothers were doctors, which they also found a laugh. Admittedly, Tanya's mother was a single parent and had brought her up in fairly straitened circumstances, while Andrey's family had had no worries along those lines. Even this was compensated for by the fact that, in place of Tanya's absent father, Andrey had a present stepfather he didn't get on with. The family's prosperity and the good things that his mother showered down upon Andrey in what, for those times, was great abundance, were accordingly an affront to his precocious masculine pride. From the age of fifteen the professor's son was out earning illegal pocket money on Gorky Street, trading in ladies' metal bracelet wristwatches and American jeans, which at that time were just beginning their triumphal progress from Brest-Litovsk to Vladivostok.

At this point in Andrey's confession, Tanya chortled. "The conflict between Labor and Capital!" Her own business had been in an adjacent market segment. While Andrey was hawking jeans, she had been running up button-down shirts, complete with the all-important brand labels, calculating that young people who aspired to wear jeans would sooner or later face the dilemma of where to buy the requisite shirt, which had to have not two but four buttonholes on the collar and a loop at the back.

Tanya made her shirts in three standard sizes. If she worked from morning till evening without a break, which usually meant on a Sunday, she could finish four shirts. Four times five rubles makes twenty, so by the time she was fifteen she did not need to ask her mother for money. The concept of self-service had just arrived, and she followed the trend.

How about sports? Oh, yes, they were both into sport. Andrey had been a boxer and Tanya a gymnast, and they both gave up when the decision had to be made on whether to become a professional. Andrey achieved first category, became a candidate master of sport, and joined the Moscow junior team as a flyweight. Tanya dropped out slightly earlier, on the verge of first category. She was satisfied with that.

At the start of the fourth day, or night, of their life together, they confessed to each other that they had always preferred well-built partners, both of them being fairly diminutive, especially when compared with their fellow sportsmen and sportswomen.

"Are you saying you don't fancy me?" Tanya snorted.

"Absolutely. I've always liked terrible Amazons."

"Well, you aren't my type either. Too skinny." Tanya laughed. They were showing off their sometimes rather alarming directness.

To listen to them, you might have imagined they had both been through fire and water. In fact, although they did have some experience, it was very circumscribed: indeed, barely sketched. They had, however, had enough to recognize the rarity of their sense of identity, which was more what might have been expected between twins: all the sighs and gasps, the soaring and tumbling down, their movements while half asleep or just as they were waking. They would wake in the night and head for the fridge, even assailed by the pangs of hunger at precisely the same moment. And they clung to each other and fused with each other like two drops of mercury, or even better than that, because complete union would have killed the wonderful difference of the potentials that produced those crackling discharges, the blinding flashes of lightning, the moment of death when the world stands still in a void of bliss.

They didn't know how lucky they were. They had everything they could wish for: two small athletic bodies charged with power and lightning-fast reactions, quick rigorous brains, and the self-confidence of the winner who has never suffered so much as a scratch. How deeply all this was ingrained in them! They had retired from their sports just as they were approaching the limit of their capabilities, just a step ahead of the inevitable defeat. They were readying themselves to joust on the new field of their scientific careers, in the country's best educational institution and in one of its most demanding faculties. The world, it seemed, was their oyster and had agreed in advance to spill its pearls at their feet.

The first-year course was heavy going and overloaded with general subjects, an enormous number of lectures, and sessions in the laboratory. They passed all the exams in their first semester with top marks, confirmed their elite status, and had their grants increased.

By now, nobody in their year was indifferent to them. Some they irritated, some they attracted, but everybody they intrigued. They even had their own uniquely individual style of dressing.

During the winter vacation, Tanya had her first abortion, carried out professionally, expertly, and with much more effective anesthesia than was usual at the time. It was the first negative experience they had shared, but they emerged from it without evident damage and became if anything even closer to each other. No thoughts about the baby entered their highly organized minds. It had been an absurdity—indeed, a sickness—of which one needed to be cured as promptly as possible. Andrey's mother, Alla Semyonovna, a good and unpretentious woman who had played an active part in the medical undertaking, had greater qualms about it than the young people. She and her second husband had no children, and Alla was more aware than most of the amazing powers and capricious fragility of this feminine equipment, with its microscopic gaps in the tiniest of tubes. Their pink-napped epithelium would at one moment avidly accept and at another implacably reject the one and only cell from which both her Andrey had been formed, and she herself, and from which some day the baby would be formed who was to be her grandson.

Alla Semyonovna liked Tanya, although she was alarmed by her strength of mind, by her independent manner, and also by the benign indifference she showed toward Alla herself and toward her famous husband. Boris Ivanovich was almost an academician, yet it seemed to be a matter of complete indifference to Tanya what he and Alla thought about her.

"They really do have such a lot in common, the two of them," Alla confided to her husband. "They are a perfect couple, Boris, a perfect couple."

Boris, raising his sexless white face from the newspaper, agreed, slightly deforming his wife's thought in the process. "Well, yes, two boots make a pair."

He had never brought himself to love Alla's son and in truth had not tried all that hard. Himself the son of a poor peasant, the eighth child in the family, he found all this Jewish doting over children fairly wearying.

As for Tanya's mother, Galina Yefimovna, she too knew all about the abortion, but in her eyes her daughter could do no wrong. She never attempted to instruct Tanya and couldn't imagine where her strong character and remarkable giftedness could have come from. Only from Sokolov, she supposed, although she had never noticed any such virtues in him before he abandoned her, long ago.

Galina was privately upset for a couple of months. Stealing occasional hangdog glances at her daughter, she could not understand how Tanya, not yet nineteen, could be so bold, so unabashed. When Galina hinted to her that it might perhaps be a good idea to formalize her relations with Andrey, she gave a curt shrug and said, "Why should we want to do that?"

Their vacation was spoiled, of course. Instead of the planned ski trip they spent a week at the dacha, opening their embraces to each other very carefully indeed. Their negative experience had no moral stigma attached to it for them, but it did entail a number of inconveniences that they would prefer to avoid in future.

The course recommenced, and it was far from easy. They had studied together during the first semester, either in the library or at Andrey's home, and although both of them scored straight top grades, Andrey did nevertheless prove to have the better mind. He solved problems more elegantly, more interestingly, with greater mental agility. His superiority rankled with Tanya more than once, particularly when he expressed surprise at her slowness and sluggishness. Tanya would be a bit offended, and then there would be a reconciliation, but she took to studying without him, in her communal flat with her mother by her side and to the quiet murmur of a music program on the radio.

They both achieved a grade of excellent in the spring exams also, and by now their fame had spread beyond the other first-year students. The professors too were seeing them as rising stars. The only thing that could blight the prospect of a brilliant future was that both neglected the obligatory "social activism." What was worse, they were not discreetly neglectful, in what could have been seen as a passive manner, but overtly and indiscreetly. Here too they were in complete agreement; the Soviet state was beyond redemption and Soviet society was degenerate.

It was, however, the society in which they were going to have to live, and they wanted to live their lives at full throttle, doing justice to their egregious abilities. The question was how far they would have to accommodate themselves to the system, and at which point they would draw the line and refuse any further retreat. Both had joined the Young Communist League and supposed, for no very good reason, that this was where the line could be drawn. Theirs were the problems of the 1960s generation, problems that had not appeared from nowhere but seeped down to them from people like Andrey's stepfather. Boris was a former front-line soldier, an honest but prudent man enthused by atomic energy, which in those years seemed to hold out the prospect of power and prosperity, rather than catastrophe and disgrace. To such people a career in science seemed to promise the least amount of ideological interference in their lives, a hope that had yet to be disappointed. Solzhenitsyn was already being read over hostile radio stations, Samizdat was being passed from hand to hand, and Tanya and Andrey slipped boldly into living the double life typical of the masters and doctors of miscellaneous sciences.

Having done their stint of factory work experience, the two stars rollicked off to vacation in the Baltic states and for a month and a half swam in the cold sea, fell asleep on the distilled white sands beneath stately pines, drank the revolting Riga Balsam, and danced in the dangerous dance palaces of Jurmala. Then it was the turn of Vilnius to receive them and they found Lithuania more agreeable than Latvia, perhaps because they met up there with a lively group from Moscow who were five years or so older than they. Out of sociable cardplaying on the beach, friendly relationships developed that were to prove long-lasting. From then until they graduated, every New Year and every birthday was celebrated with this new circle of acquaintances: a young doctor, a beginning writer, a scientist from the faculty of physics and technology who already was what Andrey hoped someday to become, a young actress who was rapidly becoming (but never did quite become) famous, a very bright philosopher who later turned out to be a KGB informer, and a married couple who lodged in their memory as the ideal family.

In the autumn Tanya had another abortion, all very quickly and smoothly done. This time Alla made her disapproval clear but arranged everything for them. Tanya was regarded as part of the family by now, and even Boris Ivanovich, who paid attention to nothing other than his beloved Alla and his meals, took a liking to her; she had a good brain. He went to America for a conference and brought back presents for everyone, including white jeans for Tanya. Amazingly enough, they fitted perfectly. Tanya was very pleased and twirled in front of the mirror, prompting Andrey to grunt and concede jokingly, "That's the last straw. Now I'm going to have to marry you!"

Tanya stopped wiggling her backside, turned her little head on its long slender neck, and said, perhaps even a little tartly, "No, you aren't."

They were into the third year of sharing life together, and there had been no talk of marriage because there was no need for it. They were enjoying all the advantages of matrimony in full measure and had no interest in the drawbacks associated with responsibilities and obligations toward each other.

By now, Andrey was drawing confidently ahead of Tanya. She followed a short distance behind in his wake and had almost reconciled herself to the fact. Grades no longer mattered as much as they had in the earlier years of their course. Everybody had been allocated to different departments and laboratories, and the first publications had begun to appear from the most active students. Those who had committed themselves to a more direct career ladder were already sitting on Communist Party committees, local committees, and trade union committees, taking minutes and voting and allotting tickets to the New Year Party in the Kremlin, or sturgeon, or places on group tours.

The goodies being handed out for free held no allure for Tanya Sokolova and Andrey Orlov. Everything they needed they already had. Indeed, each of them had a scholarly article to their credit—coauthored, of course, in an entirely fair manner by the director of their laboratory. Their closeness, despite the independently written articles, grew even closer because both of them, against all expectation, chose to work in a slightly backwater discipline, crystallography, rather than anything trendy like theoretical or nuclear physics.

Crystallography reposed at the interstices of physics, chemistry, and even mathematics. Tanya busied herself with spectrophotometers, while Andrey worked at night in the Computing Center at an enormous computer, which at that time filled one entire story of the building.

At the end of their fourth year, tickets were bought for a holiday at Golden Sands in Bulgaria, and the two couples, one young and the other old, went off for a holiday together.

They occupied a hotel room next to that of Andrey's parents without needing to produce any documents other than their passports for travel abroad, which contained no confirmation that they were legally married. When they had holidayed and sunbathed to their hearts' content in Bulgaria, they returned to Moscow. Tanya underwent what had become her annual autumn abortion and they returned to their studies. Tanya's mother on this occasion ventured to express her view that Andrey was a complete bastard. Tanya did not take up the subject, only grunting, "I'll work it out by myself, okay?"

With the coming of their final year, and with postgraduate studies looming, they needed to accumulate a sufficient number of credits to obtain a recommendation from those very representatives of Soviet public opinion whom the Orlov-Sokolovs had so studiously disregarded. Tanya's synthetic leather skirts, knee boots, and other fashion accessories were also going to have a bearing, and not to her advantage. Tolya Poroshko, the Young Communist League organizer for their course and the third signature required, along with those of representatives of their trade union and the university administration, on their references, announced for all to hear that he was prepared to sign anything just as long as the text included in black and white: "Takes no part whatsoever in the social and political life of the faculty."

Tolya was a rustic lad from Western Ukraine. He had completed his army service and was a good-looking, ill-natured idiot. What was more, he could scent blood in a way that any personnel section could only dream of. He got the measure of the Orlov-Sokolovs at first sight; by insisting on his formulation, he could have them automatically debarred from postgraduate study of any description.

True to their origins, however, the Orlov-Sokolovs now revealed their diabolical cunning. Andrey, a qualified boxing referee, had been providing his services to the physical education department, and Tanya, even more cunningly, had been running a gymnastics club for the past two years at a school affiliated to the university. All this had been for a purpose, of course, but the sports department wrote them effusive references on headed notepaper testifying to their valued contribution to social activities. Poroshko got egg on his face and a simultaneous lesson in the omnipotence of the Jewish-Masonic conspiracy.

As far as the crystals were concerned, things could not have been better. Andrey and Tanya were researching symmetry, which was just then coming into fashion, and crystals displayed all manner of symmetrical delights. Andrey duly constructed models, mirrored them, superimposed them, and where the right should have coincided with the left there was always a slight defect, the subtlest discrepancy. This phenomenon had been picked up in times past by the head of their department, and it now greatly exercised the Orlov-Sokolovs, who sat working on the problem till late at night, motivated not by personal considerations but by their passion and enthusiasm for the subject.

Both the postgraduate places allotted to the department were plainly theirs by right, as everybody agreed. In late May, however, when they had already defended their degrees, one of the places was taken away. The head of department, a decent and intelligent man, called in the Orlov-Sokolovs. He had a high regard for them and knew how difficult this was going to be. He had already arranged a good temporary placement in one of the institutes of the Academy of Sciences. The probationer would be working on the same topic and, in effect, also under his wing. He had decided to let them choose for themselves who went where, although his personal preference was for Andrey to get the postgraduate place.

They heard him out, exchanged glances, thanked him, and asked for a day to think about it. They walked to the metro in silence. Both knew that the postgraduate place had to go to Andrey, but each left the other to make the first move. When they reached the metro station Andrey gave in.

"It's for you to choose." This appeared to be very noble.

"I already have." Tanya smiled.

"Well, fine. I'll take what's left."

Each was as good as the other, neither giving an inch.

At Park of Culture station she butted him in the ear with her crew cut, their secret gesture, and stood up. "I'm going home."

"I thought we were going to—" They had been planning to visit friends that evening.

"I'll see you there a bit later," she said, and walked off the train on her improbably high heels.

The pointed toes of her shoes were, Andrey knew, stuffed with triangular wads of cotton wool because her shoes were always too big for her. Her unusually small size was difficult to come by.

Her feet were small, she had a deep scar beneath her knee, a narrow trail of hair down her flat stomach, large nipples that took up half her small breasts, and arms and legs that were a bit too short. So were her fingers and toes. Her neck was exquisite. She had a wonderful oval face.

She went off taking all that with her, and he went home in a bad mood, annoyed and hurt. It really was about time she understood that he . . . it was the one thing they never talked about.

They met up that evening at their friends' apartment. It wasn't a great evening. Andrey suffered an attack of malicious wit and several times floored the mistress of the house, which didn't improve matters. They left late, feeling grumpy. Andrey got a taxi, and they rode to his place. The Orlovs' apartment was large but inconvenient. His parents occupied two large adjacent rooms, while Andrey had a hundred square feet to himself. Boris Ivanovich suffered from insomnia, and the water pipes were subject to the Pompidou Center effect, which meant they began squealing piteously if you turned on a tap. Accordingly, it would be very inconsiderate to try to wash after his parents had gone to bed.

As they lay together in the darkness on a narrow little divan bed that left no room for sulking, he began talking as soon as he sensed that he was being refused nothing.

"You are silly, Tanya. I am the man, for heaven's sake. Rely

on me. Don't feel bad about it. I love you. We share everything. We have everything in common."

She said nothing, and they shared everything fully. When
they had finished, Tanya said in a sad, desolate voice, "I think
I'm up the creek again."

He put on the light and lit a cigarette. She hid her face from
the light in her pillow.

"Well, it's time to go for it, I reckon. Have the baby this
time. A girl, okay?"

"Oh, I get it. You go for the postgraduate place and I go for
a baby and changing diapers."

She never cried, but if she had been going to it would have
been then. As he realized.

Tanya filled in the forms for the job at the Academy's institute, had an abortion, and took off for the south. Andrey
stayed behind to sit the qualifying exams for the postgraduate
studentship. Before she left, they filled in an application to
have their relationship officially recognized at the registry
office, which Andrey considered to be essential. They still felt
dreadful. Neither had done quite what they meant to, and
both still harbored a certain amount of resentment toward the
other.

Andrey saw her off at the station. She would not be traveling alone. Part of their group was already in Koktebel, and
now the remainder were going to join them. They were having themselves a good time and traveling in style, paying an
unbelievably high supplement to have two compartments to
themselves.

Andrey and Tanya kissed on the platform, and she climbed
onto the steps of the train car. Stooping down, she waved to
him. That was the way he was to remember her in this last
moment of their life together: wearing a man's red shirt with
the cuffs unbuttoned and a ridiculously long scarf draped

round her slender neck. It was her personal chic. She would start wearing something unusual, specifically her own, and then others would follow her lead.

The train moved off and he shouted to her, "Don't go falling in love there with Vitya!"

It was a standing joke in their group. Vitya, the beginning writer, was starting to be fashionable and had girls buzzing around him like bees round a honeypot.

"If I do I'll tell you straight away! By telegram!" Tanya shouted, already moving away toward the south.

SOKOLOVA, Tanya, never did come back to Orlov, Andrey. She rang him some ten days later in the early hours of the morning, waking up Boris Ivanovich, who in the morning told Andrey exactly what he thought of him. By then it was too late.

Tanya told Andrey she would not be coming back to him, and indeed might not even be coming back to Moscow. She was moving to a completely different city now and, all in all, see you around!

Understanding very well what had happened and why, Andrey said in a sleepy voice, "Thank you for phoning, Tanya."

She was silent at the end of the telephone for a time before giving in. "How did the exams go?"

"Fine."

She was silent again, because she really had not been expecting him to take it so coolly. "Well, so long."

"So long."

He hung up first.

Andrey's mother ran round to see Tanya's mother. They already knew each other slightly but had not hit it off all that well. Galina did not much care for Andrey, and Alla, who had been anticipating a close friendship between their families, seeing so little enthusiasm on the part of his future mother-in-law, took umbrage. Boris Ivanovich had just managed to clarify the situation regarding the housing cooperative in the Academy of Sciences and things really looked quite promising. Tanya could be allocated an apartment since now she too was an employee of the Academy. Then, just when everything had been arranged and they had even put in the application, there suddenly came this telephone call. Now Andrey just spent days at a time lying on the divan, smoking and reflecting that it was hardly his fault there had only been one postgraduate place available.

"Well, Tanya with her abilities will defend her dissertation even before Andryushka does" Alla was blathering on.

Galina just raised her eyes to heaven. She had known nothing either about the telephone call or about Tanya's change of plans. She was so genuinely and deeply upset that kindly Alla Semyonovna instantly made it up with her. What was there, in any case, to keep them apart? They had bringing up their grandchildren to look forward to, it was all practically. . . . They agreed Galina would let Alla know just as soon as Tanya resurfaced.

She resurfaced some days later, on the phone. Tanya informed her mother that everything was splendid, and that she was calling not from the Crimea but from Astrakhan. The line was poor. She promised to write a long and utterly amazing letter. Galina tried to shout something to her about Andrey, but the line went dead.

We lost the connection, that's all, Galina thought, but she feared for Tanya. How quickly she changed direction. How recklessly she was living. What was she doing in Astrakhan anyway? What was there for her?

NOT FAR from Astrakhan, in a fishing village hidden away among the marshes, lived the relatives of Vitya the writer. His father had been deputy director of the marvelous Askaniya-

Nova nature reserve. A local workingman who had enjoyed accelerated promotion to the top, he had died a few years previously, but any number of his rustic relatives remained. Vitya had fished out his first stories and a novella in these parts, from the waters of the River Akhtuba.

Their village was a poacher's dream, a realm of fish and caviar, shallow waters, and dense reed beds. All the local lads got around on motorboats instead of bicycles, and Tanya and her writer, with a sharp tug on the outboard motor, would take off in early morning and head for a remote sandbank upstream. She could only wonder at how he managed to find the way between the dense reeds and up the ill-defined and seemingly indistinguishable armlets of the river, to bring her unerringly to the rounded sandy beach of an islet shaped like a narrow-handled spoon dipped in the waters of the Volga.

She gloried in the hot golden sand, the myriad fry on the sandbars, and in her new love with this huge man, who was not far off six foot three. His entire physique was different, which was fine, which was excellent, if a bit awkward. They could seem a little out of sync, but that detail would come right with time. He was constantly amazed at how small she was. He would cup her short little foot in the palm of his hand, and it seemed quite lost. He was only thirty but already fairly jaded, having got through a whole succession of women because of a not wholly unjustified lack of trust. With this small person, however, he was a giant, and their fling was the more piquant for her having dumped her fiancé in favor of him. The fact that Vitya knew Andrey well, felt protective toward him as a younger colleague, always lost to him at cards, and had got drunk more than once in his house only added to the spice.

Even before the hair had grown back on Tanya's shaved pubis, she could tell that she was pregnant again. "And this time I am going to have the baby," she exulted, with a sense of triumphant vengeance.

She lolled on the sand with her writer for the best part of a month but then began to find the smell of fish intolerable, and in these parts potatoes cost far more than sturgeon.

He put his hand on her taut athletic belly and anxiously wondered aloud, "How will everything fit in? This is going to be a big baby!"

He was incredibly curious about the goings-on in her belly, already loved what was living there, and felt concern for it. He would fall asleep, fitting all of Tanya onto his shoulder and with his hand sealing her prickly-ticklish muscular entrance and exit.

They registered their union at the village registry office in five minutes flat. The director of this modest institution was the friend of a cousin. No advance application was needed. They just took in their passports, paid one ruble twenty, and in return received a marriage certificate with a violet rubber stamp on it.

It was the day she was supposed to have been marrying Andrey.

Tanya chased the thought of Andrey away but did keep thinking that she must remember to tell him.

Having sunbathed, got sunburned, shed her sunburned skin, and gained a suntan, Tanya returned to Moscow only in mid-August. Without warning, straight from the station, she took Victor home and announced to Galina, "Mum, this is my husband, Victor."

Galina was dumbfounded. Heavens above! The girl really just did whatever came into her head.

He was not particularly good-looking, this husband of hers. He had a plebeian face, thin hair parted down the center that flopped over his forehead, and a coarse prominent brow. He was a large man, which makes a big impression on small women, but was also unexpectedly well-spoken and had good manners.

Galina went out to the kitchen with the kettle and did not return for a long time. When Tanya went to see what had happened to her and the kettle, she found her mother weeping bitterly on a stool beside the bathroom, she was so sorry to have lost Andrey.

She had forgotten to light the gas under the kettle.

Real life began in earnest. Tanya started her first job. That day Andrey came to the institute to see her, not yet knowing she was married. Tanya and Victor had said nothing to their mutual friends, and so far the marriage was a secret.

"Let's go and sit somewhere," Andrey suggested.

"Here's a bench." Tanya sat down on the nearest one.

He told her to stop playing the fool. She told him she was married.

"To Vitya?" he guessed astutely. They were both well versed in the laws of symmetry.

"Yes."

"Well, fine. Let's go round to his house right now and collect your things so there are no grounds for misunderstanding." He made the suggestion so confidently that for a moment Tanya thought that was just what she was going to do.

"I'm pregnant, Andrey."

"That doesn't matter. You'll have to have another abortion. One last time." Andrey shrugged.

That was the breaking point. "No," Tanya said gently. "I can't do that anymore."

He took out a cigarette and lit up. "And all because of that shitty studentship?" he asked viciously.

Tanya had already thought this over only too many times. She already knew she would soon be leaving this institute; her interest in crystals was dependent on having Andrey by her side. Now everything was shattered and she had no interest at all in finding out why the crystals in the druse of one rock were dextrogyre while those in another were levogyre. What she did not yet know was that one of the twin boys she would give birth to would be left-handed. It was to be a strange and delightful surprise.

Something had, quite unpredictably, gone wrong. If Andrey were now to say to her, "You can have the studentship, I'll take the temporary post," would her interest in crystals revive? There had been a glitch, a malfunction of some kind in their destiny but . . . by now it had happened. There was no more to be said.

She stood up, placed her finger on the top of his head, and ran it down across his forehead to his chin, where she put a full stop. "No, Andrey, no. *Amour perdu.*"

THEY WERE next to meet eleven years later, at the seaside in the Crimea, in the place they used to go to when they were young. They were there with what was left of the old crowd, although the physicist had emigrated to America, the ideal married couple was no more since he had died in a car crash and she now had another, even more ideal family. In their place, though, were other perfectly agreeable people. Through mutual friends they had advance warning that they would meet up again on this holiday.

Andrey came with his wife and five-year-old daughter. Tanya was with her ten-year-old twins, scrawny bespectacled boys who were already taller than she was. Her husband was staying in Moscow to write a novel about being a fish, having already written about being all the other animals. It was his way of fighting against the Soviet system but fell considerably short of *Animal Farm*.

Tanya had changed less than Andrey, who had put on a lot of weight. This was not something a person of his height could afford to do. He was now a doctor of science. Tanya had exchanged bikinis for one-piece swimsuits, because her once bewitching belly was crisscrossed with coarse Soviet stitching left behind by her cesarean section. Otherwise she was just the same: she walked on her hands on the beach, wore extravagant outfits, and, as before, stuffed wedges of cotton wool in the toes of her shoes.

Everyone had brought their kids. They walked to coves near and far and taught the children to swim and play card games. Andrey and Tanya met only when other people were present, at large gatherings, and said nothing the least bit meaningful to each other. From time to time Tanya caught the anxious gaze of Andrey's wife, Olga, resting on her, but found that merely amusing. Olga was tall. She had a good figure, was almost pretty, and belonged firmly in the bimbo category. Andrey would occasionally shut her up, and she would flap eyelashes heavy with mascara and pout. Their daughter was a sweet little thing.

A few days before it was time to return home, everybody decided to camp out at Seagull Bay. It was the kind of outing the children loved. Tanya said in advance that she did not want to go, but her sons begged and begged and the ideal family agreed to take them and be responsible for them. Their son, the same age as Tanya's boys, was very put out to think his best friends might not be coming. Tanya was tired of having people around her all the time and wanted a day on her own, away from the ceaseless hullabaloo. She had no prior arrangement with Andrey, and indeed genuinely did not know that he too had decided against joining the excursion.

After she had seen the children off early in the morning, Tanya spent the day lounging around, reading Thomas Mann in her muggy room, dozing off, waking up, and dozing off again. It was evening before she got out of her chair, took a shower (the water had warmed up during the day), shaved her armpits, made herself a facial from the owner's shot cucumbers, brewed herself some coffee, and took it out to the garden table. This was the moment Andrey appeared.

"Hello, Tanya. What are you up to?"

"Having my morning coffee. Fancy a cup?" She answered him unfazed but aware that this was the moment she had been waiting for all month.

"I don't drink coffee. It makes my ears go all buzzy." It was a phrase they had used in the old days. "Let's imbibe some of the local beverages."

They strolled down to the promenade where Crimean wines were sold directly from the barrel. Tanya was relaxed and feeling on top of the world, the unbuttoned cuffs of her man's white shirt flapping. They drank the white Aligoté, then the local port, then the sticky-sweet red Kokur, constantly putting off a moment that was already behind them.

Everybody else was renting rooms in landladies' houses. Only Andrey was living like a general in a small separate cottage in the grounds of a military sanatorium. Its medical director had ceded his official accommodation in consideration of a large sum of money.

They walked along the embankment a fine hairsbreadth from each other, talking inconsequentially about the weather, and the thin crust above the abyss was still bearing their weight but sagging markedly. They had done the rounds of the wine barrels and were walking back to the sanatorium, rather than to Tanya's accommodation. They went in the service entrance and across the crunching gravel straight to the little cottage set among rosebushes. The door was unlocked and they didn't turn on the light.

"Only, please, don't say a word. . . ."

*Oooh, what a lot I've forgotten: the metal brace behind his front teeth where he had them knocked out . . . no, I haven't forgotten; my tongue in here, under the brace. . . .*

My poor dear home, abandoned, given over to a stranger. Your porch, your steps, your front door . . . your walls, your hearth! What have you done, Tanya? Andrey, what have you done? Instead of those three children, there might have been someone quite different. Perhaps not one. . . . What have we done?

These are not two foolish cells rushing toward each other for a mindless continuation of the species. Every cell, every filament, a whole being is thirsting for them to enter each other and be still, to be one. One flesh laments, crying out to become.

Wordlessly the flesh lamented until morning. Then it came to its senses. They still had a whole day before evening. They had something to eat and crawled back under the crumpled sheet. Tanya ran her finger from the top of his head to his chin.

Andrey saw very clearly how it was going to be: Everyone would come back from the cove, get their things together, and return to Moscow. He would take his family home, and then he would take Tanya and her boys to the dacha. It would be cold in the winter. His car would get stuck in snowdrifts. He would clear a path to the gate with a wooden shovel and drive the boys to school. Olga and his daughter . . . well, he had no idea what they would do. Perhaps he would have to take Vera to kindergarten as well.

Tanya supposed Vitya would just shrug it off. He would probably even be pleased and run off to some Regina. Difficult to imagine Andrey in our house. He must have worn out his red terry-cloth dressing gown by now. He doesn't drink coffee in the morning, only tea. And then, the crystals. Of course, there were the crystals to think about. Actually that might be the biggest worry. What was to be done about the crystals?

Tanya wanted it more than anything in the world, he could tell, and that was why he said nothing. Neither did she, until again it was she who gave in.

"Well, then?" This could be understood in many different ways. It could just mean it was time to split.

The flesh had groaned its last groans. What a fantastic figure Olga had, though. Those breasts, that waist, those legs. No, this wasn't going to work.

He ran his finger over Tanya's face. "*Amour perdu.* Time to get up."

She jumped up lightly, laughed, and shook her head. Short hair had suited her better.

"No, you can't fool me. Not *perdu.*"

"It's not on, Tanya."

She put on the white shirt, raised herself on her improbably high heels, and left.

NEXT MORNING Olga was sweeping the cottage. With the besom, she brushed a triangle of cotton wool out of a corner.

"Yuk! What's this?"

Andrey gave it a glance. She really must have been born yesterday. Well, in 1939. How could she know what it was for? "I feel I've had about enough of this holiday. Why don't we go back a bit early? Maybe tomorrow?"

Olga was amenable. "Anything you say, Andryusha."

# Dauntless Women of the Russian Steppe

$T$HE TABLE was laden with the improvidence of the poor, the food untouched by human hand, having been bought at Zabar's, an upmarket delicatessen on 81st Street, and lugged by Vera the whole length of New York to Queens before being dished up in haste in rather basic Chinese bowls. There was twice as much food as necessary for three women who were trying to lose weight, and enough drink for five hard-drinking men, of whom, as luck would have it, there were none.

The overprovision of spirits was unplanned. Vera, the hostess, had put up ordinary bog-standard vodka and had a bottle in reserve in the cupboard. Both her guests had brought a bottle each, Margot contributing Dutch cherry brandy and Emma, a Muscovite on a business trip, producing counterfeit Napoleon brandy, acquired at the food hall on Smolensk Square for a special occasion. The special occasion had now arrived, since she had landed this fantastic expense-paid trip that was almost more than she could have hoped for.

Margot and Emma now sat before the feast provided by Vera, but their hostess had gone to take Sharik for a walk; because of his advanced age, he couldn't contain himself for long. His good breeding meant he couldn't bring himself to

excrete at home, with the result that he was riven by inner conflict. They sat in silence by the lavish spread and awaited the
return of Vera, with whom Margot had become very friendly
in America. Vera and Emma had not met before but knew a lot
about each other, because Margot was a chatterbox. Since
yesterday evening some long-forgotten cat had run between
Margot and Emma, and Emma was now trying to remember
why she had sometimes distanced herself from Margot long
ago in Moscow, before returning to her as if to an ex-lover.

EMMA WAS staying not at a hotel but with Margot, whom she
had not seen for a full ten years. They had been born in the
same month, lived on the same block in Moscow, studied in
the same class, and until they were thirty had never been apart
for more than a few days. When they met up again they had
been sure to pour out to each other every detail of their
adventures during the intervening period. They both had
babies in the same year, and their children brought them even
closer together. Having put them to bed, they would meet up
in Emma's kitchen, smoke a pack of Java cigarettes each, con-
fess to each other as a matter of course all their thoughts and
deeds, their sins of omission and commission, and would part
absolved, replete with conversation, after two in the morning,
with less than five hours left for sleeping.

Now, after a separation of ten years, they had clasped themselves to each other's bosoms and known a joy of mutual com-
prehension such as is usually experienced only by musicians in
a good jam session, when every twist and turn of the theme can
be anticipated through the agency of a special organ not present in other human beings. They knew all the events of the
other's life, since they corresponded not often but regularly.
There were many things, however, that you couldn't put in a
letter, that could be communicated only by a tone of voice, a
smile, an intonation. Margot had divorced her alcoholic hus-

band, Venik Goven, three years previously—Shitty Bogbrush, as she called him—and was now passing through the phase of her exodus from the darkness of Egypt. The wilderness in which she was wandering afforded her limitless freedom, but she was not happy. There was a void that had previously been occupied by Venik, with the empty vodka bottles in his briefcase, in the wardrobe, among the children's toys; with the ignominy of his drunken sex; with his stealing of family money, the children's, the rent, whatever. There now sprouted in this empty space dreadful quarrels with her elder son, sixteen-year-old Grisha, and complete alienation from nine-year-old David. All this she now explained to Emma, and Emma could only tut-tut, shake her head, sigh, and, without actually coming up with any practical advice, empathize so passionately that Margot felt a whole lot better. Emma saluted her successes in émigré life, her truly heroic achievement in getting her university degree recognized and landing a modest goldfish in the shape of a job as nursing assistant in a private cancer clinic, with good prospects of herself becoming licensed in due course, and so on. It was a long story.

The first three days in Margot's apartment—or, rather, nights, since during the day the friends had to rush off to their work—had been spent mainly discussing the extravagant behavior of Bogbrush. Emma could only marvel that the absence of a husband seemed to preoccupy Margot every bit as much as had his presence. It might have been expected that someone who had endured so many years with a bad person, an alcoholic in the bargain, and reluctant because of her Oriental origins to separate, should now be feeling very pleased with herself for having finally plucked up the courage to get divorced. Alas, no. Now she was agonizing over why she had put up with it for so long and was reliving the saga in great detail and at great length.

The evening did, however, eventually arrive when Margot

got around to asking Emma, "So how are you getting on? What's the score with your hero?" That might even have been genuine interest in her voice.

"It's all over." Emma sighed. "We've split up, at last. I'm beginning a new life."

"When?" Margot was suddenly interested, having also finished her old life but being quite unable to find a new one to start.

"The day before I came here. On the eighteenth."

She went over her last meeting with Gosha. She had gone to his studio, which was crammed with people made of twisted metal. She thought they looked tragic, as if they had accidentally come to life not in a body of flesh and blood but in unyielding metal and were now tormented by feelings of rusty inadequacy.

"Do you know what I mean?"

"Well, yes, I think so. What then? You met—"

"We were going nowhere. It was a dead end. There was no way out. His wretched wife is completely useless. One daughter is ill, and the other is a downright psychopath. He can't get away from them, and I was only making things worse. Our relationship wasn't helping anyone, and he was drinking because it was all so hopeless."

Margot gave Emma her Armeno-Azerbaijani look. Disquiet was replaced by distaste, which broke through as an improper question. "Emma, do you sleep with him when he's pissed?"

"Margot, in the past eight years I have seen him sober perhaps twice. He is simply never *not* pissed."

"Poor girl." Margot screwed up her overlarge eyes. "I do understand."

"You don't, you don't." Emma shook her head. "He's fantastic, and it doesn't matter if he's drunk or sober. He is just what every woman needs. He is all man. It's just he's in this dreadful situation, and he dragged me into it. He owes me nothing, it's just life, but I have finally decided to break up with him. I'm getting out. I mustn't stand in his way. He is creative, he is special. He is quite different from all those engineering plodders. The whole world is different for him. Of course, I will never meet anyone remotely like him again, but he belonged to me. That is part of my life, a whole eight years, and nobody can take it away. It is mine."

"What makes you think this is your final breakup? You have already written to me three times to say you have broken with him, and every time you go back again. I keep all your letters," Margot reminded her, rather unnecessarily.

"You know, before I only thought about what was best for him, but now I have looked at things from the other side. I am thinking about myself now, what's best for my own life. I am past forty—"

"I know all about that. Me too," Margot remarked.

"Well, there you are. It's just the right moment to start a new life. We have split up on my terms, do you see? I was the one who chose the time and place. We spent our last night . . . I will never forget it, because it went beyond the bounds of what usually happens in sex. This was something else, in the presence of heaven. Those metal people he welds were there like witnesses. You can't imagine what it's like, living with an artist."

"No, I can't. Venik is a software engineer, admittedly a very good one. He is not at all heavenly, as you know. He is the ultimate egoist, and he really doesn't need anything other than his computer and his vodka. You were always extraordinary, though, Emma, and so were your lovers. That Hungarian hunk you had! What was his name?"

"Isztvan."

"And your husband, Sanek, was such a decent man. You will find another and get married again, but I?" Margot pushed her thumbs under her brassiere and raised her still flowering but slightly wilting tackle. "In spite of all this"—she stood up and turned around, swaying her hips to show off the wonderful receptacle she was, with her breasts, her slender waist, the convincing firm roundedness of her rump—"damn little good it does me. In my entire life, since I was eighteen, I have slept with no one other than Shitty Bogbrush. Explain to me, Emma, if you will, how things have worked out this way. You have no figure, your tits aren't even a size two, and, forgive me for saying it, you are bowlegged. So why do you always have shoals of lovers?"

Emma laughed good-naturedly, not offended in the least. "What I love about you, Margot, is your directness. I can tell you why, though, and anyway I have been saying this for a long time. It's the Armeno-Azerbaijani conflict. You have to resolve it in yourself. Are you an Oriental woman or a Western woman? If you are Oriental, don't divorce your husband; if you are Western, get yourself a lover and don't see it as a problem."

Margot was unexpectedly upset. "But I know your whole family, your mother and your grandmother. What way are your Jewesses better than my Armenian mum? What makes you so Western?"

"Western woman respects herself. Do you remember my grandmother?"

Margot certainly did. Cecilia Solomonovna was a grand old woman, a czarina, but actually she was bowlegged too. Was she really a Westerner?

On that note of bathos Margot had cleared the dishes from the table the night before, looked at her watch, and sighed because, as in their days in Moscow, it was already past two o'clock and she had to get up at seven. They had gone off to their rooms to sleep, Margot to the bedroom and Emma to the sitting room where there was a new convertible divan. It had been bought after the departure of Venik, when there was suddenly a lot of money in the house again, as if she had had a big win in the lottery.

NOW VERA returned, her wrinkled but still youthful face flushed and her hair badly dyed. Behind her, Sharik waddled like an old man and sat down to the left of her chair, feigning indifference to the food on the table.

There's a couple who don't disguise their age, Emma thought admiringly.

Vera flopped down in her wicker chair, which gave a thin screech. She reached for a bottle. "The date's an odd number, but I count in lunar months. It is seventeen months today since Misha died."

She poured out the vodka without asking, and Emma noted that the glasses came from Moscow, crystal from the Stalin era.

"May the Kingdom of Heaven be yours, Misha," Vera exclaimed joyously, and drained the glass. Then she sighed. "A year and a half. It seems like yesterday."

She took a piece of smoked turkey from one of the plates and threw it to the dog.

"Pig yourself, Sharik. This is pure poison for you."

The dog appreciated his mistress's gesture. He was again torn between two powerful urges. One was to immediately lick her hand in gratitude, and the other was to no less immediately swallow the piece of meat with its golden tan and heavenly taste. He froze in consternation. Sharik had a complex personality.

"Now for a blowout," the hostess murmured hazily. "Dig in, girls! Since Misha passed away I don't think I've cooked a meal once. It's been all fast-food outlets. Margot! How about it?"

Either because they were all really starving or because the dog was growling in ecstasy over his turkey, they fell upon the food, forgetting about forks, the proprieties, and pausing for breath. They were suddenly ravenous. They didn't even say how good the food was, just chomped in silence, helping each other to more, passing around the vodka. Sharik became quite animated under the table as they threw him some as well. Everything was so delicious, the skate and the salads, the pie and the pâté, and just the sheer un-American taste of the food, which Margot mentioned.

Vera laughed. "Un-American: Of course it is! The food tastes Jewish. The store where I bought it, Zabar's, is Jewish. Misha and I took a fancy to it as soon as we arrived. It was really expensive, and we had no money then. We bought four-ounce portions at a time: potato and herring *forshmak,* pâté; there was no black bread to be had in America at that time, except in Zabar's. Here in America, Jews from Russia are called Russians, and people like me who actually are Russians become incredibly judaized."

Vera laughed, addressing herself to Emma, who was ignorant of these local nuances.

"My poor grandmother died on the eve of our wedding, I suspect from grief that her beloved granddaughter was marrying a Jew. But Mother just kept saying, 'Who cares if he's a Jew? At least we'll have one son-in-law who isn't a drunkard.'"

Vera chortled with mirth; her wrinkles gathered in bouquets on either cheek and, paradoxically, made her look even younger.

"Was he a heavy drinker?" Emma asked. It was a question in which she had a personal interest.

"Of course he was!" Margot frowned.

"God, yes. Wasn't he just!" Vera turned her smiling face to the large portrait of her departed husband. The quality wasn't too good. The portrait had been blown up from an old photograph taken just after the war: a young soldier with an unruly shock of curly hair springing out from beneath his cheese-cutter hat and a cigarette in the corner of his mouth. "A bit of all right, eh? Everything about him was all right, including his drinking. He died of cyrrhosis of the liver, Emma."

Margot put her head with its luxuriant tresses on the veined marble of her arm. She was a goddess, a natural goddess, with a Roman nose that grew out of her forehead, improbably large eyes, and lush lips shaped like Cupid's bow.

"Vera, your Misha was, of course, a lovely man, charming and altogether outstanding, but let's face it; he put you through hell with his drinking. I know all about it. What good can come from drinking? It's tantamount to surrendering your humanity! You don't deny that, do you?"

Vera pushed aside the empty vodka bottle. They had some-how got through it without noticing. She produced the second and said, still with the same smile, "Stuff and nonsense! Get-ting drunk liberates you. If someone is a good person, he gets even better when he is drunk, and if he is shit, he gets shittier. You can take my word for it, I know what I'm talking about. Wait a minute, though, something's missing."

She jumped up, poked about on a shelf, produced a cas-sette, and put it on to play. The gravelly, compelling voice of Alexander Galich half sang, half spoke: *A bottle of samogon, halvah, two bottles of Riga beer, and herring from Kerch. . . .*

"Misha loved him. They were drinking partners, friends."

Nobody listened to the poor guitar, and the voice from the past went unheeded as they drank and talked about matters nearer home. Vera drank vodka, Emma her suspect brandy, and Margot took a bit of everything.

Strangely enough, as they went on drinking they gradually changed but in different directions. Vera became more cheer-ful and her spirits rose, Margot became glum and tetchy and seemed cross because she couldn't see why Vera was enjoying herself so much, while Emma watched both of them and had a sense that she was about to learn something vital that would help her begin her new life. She sat listening closely but saying little, all the more since the alcohol seemed not to be having much effect on her today.

"I don't care what you say." Vera made a sweeping Russian gesture with her arm as if about to launch into a folk dance. "In Russia all the best, most talented people since ever was have been drunks. Peter the Great! Pushkin! Dostoyevsky! Mussorgsky! Andrey Platonov! Venedikt Yerofeev! Yury Gagarin! My Misha!"

Margot goggled. "What's your Misha doing in that list, Vera? Gagarin if you must, damn him, but Misha? Misha, for heaven's sake!"

Vera suddenly went quiet and became serious. She said softly, "Well, he was one of Russia's best . . . so honest. . . ."

Margot had got the bit between her teeth, however, and there was no stopping her. "And what's Peter the Great doing there? The man was mad! He was a syphilitic! Okay, he was at least an emperor, but your Misha was a complete Jew! What was so honest about him, eh? The amount of shit he made you eat! Honest, indeed!"

By now Margot was addressing herself not to Vera but to Emma.

"Honest! Him? I can't bear to hear it! How many abortions did he put her through, her Mr. Honesty? How many women did he put himself around to while you were going through hell with all those abortionists? There wasn't one of your friends he didn't poke. It was disgusting!"

"Well, he didn't try it on with you, did he!" Vera snorted.

"What do you mean? You think he tried it on with everyone *except* me? He just didn't get lucky with me!"

Margot proudly cut her short. "Well you're stupid! If

you'd slept with Misha, things might have gone better with Bogbrush!"

"That's enough! My Bogbrush may be shitty, but your Misha didn't come to much either. Randy old man!"

Sharik got up laboriously, ambled over to Margot, and barked listlessly. Vera chortled.

"Girls! Margot! Emma! You mustn't speak ill of Misha in the presence of Sharik. He'll tear you to pieces."

Sharik, aware that he had been praised, waddled over to his mistress and opened his black jaw with its raspberry-red lining in anticipation of a reward. Vera tossed him a piece of French cheese.

Margot, her blood now off the boil, downed a glass of brandy. "I didn't like it, Vera, the way he just did as he pleased. He was unfaithful to you right, left, and center, and you went on loving him and forgave everything. I would have killed him. If I have a husband I love him, but if he cheats on me I cut his throat, I swear to God!"

COULD IT really be that in America, a world away, in the city of New York in 1990, this completely zany conversation was taking place, bitchy, more at home in a Moscow kitchen, and before you know it likely to boil over into a fight?

Emma listened in wonderment and observed her old friend, who had hardly changed at all. As Margot had been, so Margot remained, an Armenian woman with an Azerbaijani surname that had her Armenian relatives looking askance at her throughout her life. Her father, Zarik Husseinov, had died in a climbing accident when Margot was only six months old. There was no getting away from it, her passport might be American but her mentality was resolutely that of a woman from the Caucasus. She would feed everyone, give away all she possessed, but if you forgot her birthday she would kick up such a fuss you would hear about nothing else for the next year. "I'll cut your throat!"

"MARGOT, you don't understand at all!" Vera said. "The problem is inside yourself! You are simply incapable of loving. If you love someone, you *do* forgive them everything. Anything and everything."

"But not to that extent!" Margot shrieked, shaking her symmetrical curls. "Not to that extent you don't!"

Vera poured herself a drinking tumbler of vodka, not a full one, just half. She held it pensively and looked at the portrait diagonally across from her. It was as if the young Misha with his postwar shock of hair was gazing straight at her, although she had never known him when he looked like that. They had met later, when she enticed him away from his postwar second wife for her own—as it then seemed—private enjoyment. She had been wrong. Oh, how wrong she had been! He had run back even to his wartime wife, Zinka, which she had known about, and to his postwar wife, Shurochka, and there had even been another one. She looked unflinchingly at the portrait and at Margot.

"You are a fool. Listen, I loved Misha with all my strength, with my body and soul, and he loved me. You have no idea how much we loved each other. We made love drunk and sober, especially drunk. He was a great lover. He was not unfaithful to me, he just slept with other women. I wasn't a bit jealous. Well, perhaps just a bit," she corrected herself. "But only when I was young, before I understood. He had a talent for loving, and when the cyrrhosis caught up with him, we really loved each other with passion, because time was running out. We both knew it. . . .

"He had a girl in the hospital, a nurse, who fell in love with him one last time. I knew all about her; he didn't hide it. He slept with her. Then he said, 'No, I don't want anyone else.

There is not much time. Get them to discharge me. I want to die at home, with you.' We screwed until we cried. He kept saying, 'How lucky I've been. I was seventeen when I went to the front in 1943, and I survived. I fought right through the war without killing anyone, I was in the maintenance section, repairing tanks. Women always loved me. I was sent off to the prison camps in 1949—they arrested me at college—but I lived to tell the tale. And again, women loved me. And you, my joy'— that's what he said, *my joy*—'and you, my joy, fell in love with me. You were just a young girl and you went for an old goat. You saw what you wanted. Clever girl. Let me feel those folds, and what knees, what shoulders. I don't know what to go for first.' Two days before he died that's what he said, with me already past my half century! What shoulders, what knees . . .

"They're nothing of the sort. You're a fool, Margot, a fool. You've let everything slip through your fingers, you haven't seen anything. You are incapable of loving, that's your problem. Your Bogbrush is nothing to do with it. He was out of luck, your Bogbrush. Perhaps another woman could have loved him and taught him to love, but what sort of a woman are you? All leafy top and nothing down below!"

Margot started to cry, stricken by this drunken truth. Perhaps that was right? Perhaps she was the problem? Perhaps Venik would not have drunk if she had loved him as much as Vera loved her Misha? Or perhaps he would still have drunk but would have loved her terribly. Then there would not have been the shame and embarrassment of drunken copulation, when you lay there filled with loathing while two hundred pounds of meat jerked up and down on you, braising your dryness, making you feel you were being impaled, and your breasts ended up covered in bruises as if you had been beaten and the brown marks took a year afterward to fade. The stench of the vodka he'd drunk and the smell from down below made waves of nausea roll over you, and you felt as seasick as if you were down in the hold of a ship, and you just hoped you could make it to the toilet to spew everything out into its gleaming white depths. *What? Wasn't that enough? You want more? Get away from me with your insatiable prong! What are you doing? What do you want now?*

Emma too began to cry. What had she done? Gosha, I love you as I have never loved anyone, as nobody has ever loved anybody. No, no, I don't want a new life. Let me just have this one back, with eternally drunk Gosha, with the despair every day, the worry, the trips hither and thither in the night in the ambulance, the redemptive third of a bottle of vodka in the mornings, the warm pie wrapped in newspaper. And all of it under the contemptuous gaze of her daughter: *Has he had you flapping about in a panic again?* All without the hope of any halfway normal life, without anything in return, without acknowledgment, without gratitude, without compensation. You just give and give, and that's it.

"You just give, and that's it! You don't ask what you're going to get in return!" Vera declaimed, ablaze with a drunken radiance and her visceral feminine wisdom. She poured out more vodka—in tumblers this time, not in the crystal liqueur glasses. She was chain-smoking and stuffing the cigarettes before she had finished them into a huge ashtray more appropriate to a public smoking area than to the private needs of a widow living on her own. She stubbed out a cigarette, rose to her full height, rocked forward, and clutched the edge of the table. The table also rocked but did not fall over. She kept her feet and shuffled across the floor as if it were an ice rink, chuckling and supporting herself against the wall, to the toilet.

"Vera really is drunk," Margot commented, and immediately a crash was heard from the bathroom followed by a loud expletive. Several items had fallen, one of them heavy. Margot and Emma jumped up to run to her aid, but somehow couldn't. They bumped into each other, which stopped their unwise attempts at running, and walked uncertainly toward the bathroom. Vera was floundering there on the floor, rubbing one of her celebrated knees and muttering to herself,

"People are always leaving their clothes on the floor and tripping you up. . . . Margot, why are you standing there like a cow? God knows, I've broken all my perfume bottles."

The floor was indeed covered with wet glinting pieces of glass, and the smell of perfume hit you like an antitank shell.

They picked Vera up off the floor. She was a bit riotous, but in a cheery way, and kept demanding just a little bit more. Alas, all the bottles were empty: both the vodkas, the brandy, the liqueur, and a bottle of French wine, which had appeared from nowhere and which they had drunk without remarking its premium label.

"The premises are to be searched! Misha always had something hidden away. . . . In Moscow before we left, the KGB conducted a search. They found more hidden bottles than hidden books." Vera opened all the drawers in the writing desk. "I have admittedly searched everywhere here on more than one occasion, but there must be something somewhere. Mishenka! Hello!"

She supplicated her husband's portrait, raising to heaven her long arms, which were sagging slightly at the shoulders. Then she got down on her knees, not before the portrait but before the bookcase, pushed back the glass, and started hauling books out of the bottom shelf in slithering piles. She emptied the lower shelf: There was nothing there.

Emma and Margot were standing propped up like two trees leaning against each other, one thick and one thin. Margot was assailed by hiccups.

"You need something to drink," Emma counseled.

"I'm looking, aren't I? It's got to be somewhere."

Vera lay down on the floor on her back and kicked the books out with her foot, by now from the second shelf, on to the floor. One book split open and clinked. It was a pretend book with only a cover, within which there nestled a partly drunk bottle of vodka. Vera seized it and pressed it to her breast.

"Misha! My faithful friend! You thought you could hide it from me. Why did you even try? Found it!"

They poured out this final vodka, a present from Misha, and at last could drink no more. They were full to their ears with alcohol, to the upper limit of a woman's capacity. Vera, before crashing out, told them to carry her to Misha's study, and while they were en route completed her last drunken confessions, which might not have been confessions at all but only fantasies.

"Put me on the couch in the study, with Misha. I've got myself a gentleman visitor, a Puerto Rican boy, very handsome. I always make sure to put him down on this couch. It smells of Misha. Misha can watch him. He's young, only thirty-five; Misha can watch him f-fucking my brains out. Misha enjoys it. 'Enjoy yourself, my joy,' he says, 'enjoy, enjoy.' That's what he tells me."

Margot tried for ages afterward to remember whether Vera had told her she had a Puerto Rican lover, or whether she had just imagined it because she was so drunk.

They deposited Vera on the couch. Sharik was already snoring there and didn't take kindly to having to move. Margot and Emma headed for the bedroom, where a double bed, as wide as Vera's Russian soul and just as soft, had been made up for them before the festivities began.

Margot, the last respectable woman on the continent, who still wore lace-edged bloomers, chastely extracted her brassiere from beneath them and collapsed onto the nostalgia-inducing feather bed. It had emigrated together with Vera from Tomilin on the outskirts of Moscow where, to this day, Vera's mother and two elder sisters slept on similar mattresses.

Emma took off everything and slipped under the sheet in

the nude, but everything immediately began to sway and rock, first in one direction, then in the other. "Oh, I feel bad," she groaned.

"For whom is life in Russia good?" Margot responded brightly, remembering her Nekrasov from school. "The main thing is, don't go to sleep before you feel better. Poor Bogbrush, can he really have felt as bad as this every day?"

"Even worse," Emma whispered. "In the morning it's always even worse than in the evening. Poor Gosha."

An inexplicable feeling of tenderness welled up in Margot, and she couldn't even tell toward whom it was directed. It might almost have been for Shitty Bogbrush. She sniffed, because her tears were ready to trickle, and put her arms around Emma's skinny back. She was as thin as a fish and just as smooth, only not wet but as dry as toast, and slippery under her hands. Margot began to stroke her, at first her back, then her shoulders a little, and a warm powerful wave swept over her, carrying her out into uncharted waters. Emma just kept groaning, but she lay there completely still and motionless, and Margot raised herself a little. She stroked Emma's insignificant breasts and was amazed at how delightful it was to touch them, as if the whole of her adolescent body had only been made to be stroked. She pressed her lips to her neck, and Emma's skin smelled not of Vera's explosive perfumes, which still had the entire apartment reeking as if someone had burned the milk. It smelled of something that caught you and entered the very center of your being, the very center. Margot felt as if a flower were opening up inside her belly and reaching out toward Emma, and she melted with pleasure. She touched Emma's breasts, first with her lips and then with her fingers, lovingly, around the button of the nipple. . . .

Emma groaned. She was floating who knows where, but her stomach was lurching quite separately and she very much wanted to be sick. In order to do so, however, she needed to stay still, she needed to make an effort, but the swaying was so strong she couldn't stop it. That anyone's hands were stroking her was something of which she was quite unaware. Her feelings were concentrated in her stomach, and a bit in her throat.

Margot's flower, however, was swelling up and about at any moment to burst open. She pressed her belly to Emma's side, and her fingers rejoiced in the feel of Emma's firm breasts, such a solid gland, she was palpating the inferior part, following a cord upward to the nipple, and farther left, a second one. A lump, another one. A textbook case. Cancer! No need for a biopsy! She must be operated on immediately!

Margot sat up with a jolt. "Emma!" she yelled. "Emma, get up! Get up at once!"

The intoxication vanished as if it had never been. Everything fell away. She stood there in her yellow lace-trimmed combinations with her sagging but perfectly healthy breasts; she had a mammogram twice a year, as any civilized woman does. She caught Emma under the armpits, set her on her ragdoll legs, shook her, and continued yelling.

"Stand up, will you, you silly bitch? Stand straight. Put your arms out, like this. It's your armpits I need, not your elbows. Hold my shoulders!"

And with searching fingers she pressed into the soft hollow of Emma's armpits, probing the depths. The lymph gland on the left was hardened and swollen, but not very much. The gland on the right was problem-free. She squeezed the left nipple.

"Ouch!" Emma responded.

"Did that hurt?"

"What do you think?!" Emma snapped and flopped back onto the bed.

Margot's fingers were damp. "Emma, have you had a discharge from your nipple for long?"

"Give over, I'm already feeling sick enough. Give me something to drink."

Margot dragged her to the bathroom. Emma was sick, then had a pee. After that, Margot pushed her under a cold shower. Morton was on duty at the clinic today, the best of their doctors. He was an old man who really knew his job and was very accommodating. They were in luck.

Margot pulled Emma out of the shower. By now she was looking entirely together. "Get ready quickly. We're going to my clinic."

"Margot, are you mad? I'm not going anywhere. I've got today off."

"Me too. Get ready quickly. You've got God knows what going on in your mammary gland. It needs to be checked right away."

Emma saw the situation at once. She pulled a towel off the rack and dried herself. She prodded her left breast. "Here?"

Margot nodded.

"Put the kettle on, Margot, and calm down. Do you think it would be very expensive for me to phone Moscow?"

"Go ahead. Do you know how to dial through?"

Margot brought the telephone. Emma dialed the code, then the Moscow number. Gosha didn't answer for a long time.

"What time is it there now?" Emma suddenly wondered.

"It's half past five here, plus eight. Half past one in the afternoon," Margot calculated.

"Gosha! Goshenka!" Emma shouted. "It's me, Emma. Yes, from New York. It's all off. No split-up. I was being stupid. Forgive me! I love you! What's up, are you drunk? Me too! I'll be back soon. Only, you've got to love me, Gosha. And don't drink. I mean, don't drink so much."

"I need half an hour to get my things together. No,

forty-five minutes. I'll order a taxi for six-fifteen," Margot announced, taking the telephone out of Emma's hands.

"Hey, what's the hurry? Is it really that urgent?"

"It couldn't be more urgent."

At the door stood Sharik, old age making his needs, too, very pressing. He stood there waiting and smiling, with his tongue stuck out engagingly. They would have to take the old codger out for a walk before the taxi arrived.

## ABOUT THE AUTHOR

Ludmila Ulitskaya is the author of *The Funeral Party* and *Medea and Her Children*. Her novels and short stories have been published in more than twenty-five languages. She has received many awards for her writing, including the Russian Booker Prize. Born in Bashkiria, in Russia's Urals region, she was trained as a geneticist. She currently lives in Moscow.

## A NOTE ON THE TYPE

This book was set in Mrs. Eaves, a typeface designed in 1996 by Zuzanna Licko and modeled after the work of John Baskerville but named for Sarah Eaves, who became Baskerville's wife after the death of her first husband.

Zuzanna Licko (b. 1961) is a type designer with more than thirty typeface families to her credit. She is a cofounder of Emigre, a pioneer digital type foundry.

*Composed by Creative Graphics, Allentown, Pennsylvania*

*Printed and bound by R. R. Donnelly & Sons, Harrisonburg, Virginia*

*Designed by Robert C. Olsson*

9\1